She reached across the table, as though she wanted to touch him as they spoke. He couldn't bring himself to suffer the contact, knowing that her hand had so recently been touching and stroking another man. Desdemona allowed the hand to linger between them, as though she was prepared to wait for him to respond.

'I get satisfaction from other men,' she continued. 'And I've always known you were aroused by the thought of me being unfaithful. If we can combine these two complimentary attitudes, I think this will be the right way forward for us and our marriage.'

By the same author:

WIFE SWAP

Other titles available in the Nexus Enthusiast series:

CUCKOLD

Amber Leigh

The LAST
WORD *in*
FETISH

enthusiast

This book is a work of fiction.
In real life, make sure you practise safe, sane and consensual sex.

First published in 2007 by
Nexus Enthusiast
Nexus
Thames Wharf Studios
Rainville Rd
London W6 9HA

A catalogue record for this book is available from the British Library.

www.nexus-books.com

Typeset by TW Typesetting, Plymouth, Devon
Printed in the UK by CPI Bookmarque, Croydon, CR0 4TD

The Random House Group Limited supports The Forest Stewardship Council (FSC), the leading international forest certification organisation. All our titles that are printed on Greenpeace approved FSC certified paper carry the FSC logo. Our paper procurement policy can be found at www.rbooks.co.uk/environment

ISBN 978 0 352 34140 2

Distributed in the USA by Holtzbrinck Publishers, LLC, 175 Fifth Avenue,
New York, NY 10010, USA

Foreword

Cuckolds Lights is a genuine lighthouse in Boothbay Harbour, Southport, Maine. It was named for the similar shape of the coastline to Nelson Dock (which was then known as Cuckold's Point) the largest bend on the Thames, London. Histories relate that King John gave concessions and land around the area on the Thames to compensate a miller whose wife he had seduced after a hunting trip. Horns, the traditional sign of a cuckolded husband, once marked the spot to commemorate this incident.

However, all other characters, locations and creations within this novel are purely fictitious.

Honest.

Amber Leigh 2007

Symbols key

 Corporal Punishment

 Female Domination

 Institution

 Medical

 Period Setting

 Restraint/Bondage

 Rubber/Leather

 Spanking

 Transvestism

 Underwear

 Uniforms

One

The brass keyring said WORKAHOLIC but it wasn't true. Edwin Miller did work hard but only because it was a convenient alternative to thinking. He had developed the habit on the day he got married. He watched Bartholomew Jacob Mathers (Jake, as he preferred) study the brass fob. Edwin said nothing as he tried to guess where this impromptu meeting was headed. Because Jake was the latest fresh-faced graduate to be recruited to the director's board under their nepotism programme, Edwin knew the visit to his office was not just a friendly assignation.

'You do work hard,' Jake said, as though agreeing with the keyring. He toyed with it a moment longer before tossing it back onto the minimalist clutter of Edwin's desk. The fob and keys landed with a heavy clatter. 'I think you work a little too hard.'

Edwin raised a sardonic eyebrow. 'I'll try not to do it again.'

Jake circled his desk. Edwin thought the habit was both annoying and disconcerting. He wondered if this was one of the management techniques they now taught in university. It was easy to imagine some sadistic sociology professor lecturing on the positive benefits of invading an employee's personal space: reminding workers who was really in charge by penetrating their comfort zone. Not bothering to rise to the challenge of this particular mind game, Edwin sat back in his chair and tried not to act defensive. He had already made the decision that he didn't care for Jake.

'Who's this pretty lady?'

Jake held the obligatory framed family photo that belonged on Edwin's desk. It was a three-year-old snapshot dating from their honeymoon. Jake stroked the glass as though caressing her cheek. To Edwin's eye, the frozen smile on the picture seemed to widen for the graduate. He didn't know if it was the light in the office or a trick of his imagination but he could have sworn his wife's eyes sparkled as Jake held her photograph. He inwardly glowered at her treachery.

'That's my wife.'

'Does she have a name?'

'She has two. Three if you count her maiden name.'

Jake's sharktooth grin faltered. 'And her name is?' he prompted.

'First, last or maiden?'

'First.'

'Desdemona.'

Jake laughed. Because his hands shook, Desdemona's photograph appeared to share his amusement.

Edwin scowled.

'Desdemona is Othello's wife,' Jake began enthusiastically. He spoke as though this was a subject he had been forced to study. He spoke with the enthusiasm of a man who has finally found an outlet for his arduously acquired knowledge. And he spoke with the fatuous assuredness of one arrogant enough to believe he was the only person to ever have read *Othello*. 'Desdemona is the true victim of Iago's diabolical machinations to avenge himself on Shakespeare's tragic hero. Her story is the . . .'

'This is a different Desdemona.'

Jake put the picture back where it had been. Desdemona's gaze followed him as he walked away. As soon as he was out of the range of her picture's vision Edwin watched the perfidious smile return to the same static pose she had assumed for the past three years.

2

Jake glanced at the framed painting on Edwin's office wall, a picture of Cuckolds Lights, Southport, Maine. He pointed a casual finger in the direction of the painting, looked set to ask about it, and then folded his hands back together. As though he was trying a different tactic, he asked, 'Does Desdemona work?'

'She's an artist. She works from home.'

'Fascinating. Children?'

'No.'

'I'm interrupting your work, aren't I?'

Edwin thought of saying: *only the important stuff*. He decided he had already been too confrontational and simply nodded.

'Then I'll make this quick and let you get back to what you do best.'

Edwin waited.

'HR tell me you haven't taken a holiday in the past three years.'

'I've been busy.'

'Too busy to take a holiday?'

'It would seem so.'

Jake sighed. 'I want you to take a holiday.'

'That's very thoughtful of you. I'll consider your advice.'

'It's not advice. It's an instruction. My business degree concentrated on health and safety legislature. In my dissertation I argued that leave should be compulsory. Mandatory. I don't believe anyone is capable of working five days a week, every week of the year, and still remain effective. The board agreed with my arguments when I presented them at last month's AGM. Mr Wise concurred that it was only fair. Mr Mathers thought the humanitarian aspect of the idea worked alongside the ethos of caring for . . .'

'You're *forcing* me to take time off work?' Edwin had to make an effort to keep the hostility from his voice. 'You're *forcing* me to take a holiday?'

Jake appeared uncertain. His boyish smile faltered and he flexed it warily. 'You make that sound like it's a

3

bad thing.' He paused, looked as if he was waiting for Edwin to assure him forced leave wasn't being viewed as some innovative punishment, and then pressed on as the silence between them stretched. 'I discussed your case with the HR director. You've worked for Mathers & Wise for more than eleven years. For the past three you've done ten-hour days, five days a week and then come in for an extra eight hours each Saturday. You come into the office during every bank holiday except Christmas and Easter.' He laughed bitterly and said, 'There are chairs that spend less time in this office than you.'

Edwin maintained a poker face. 'Very well. I'll book a day off.'

Jake shook his head. 'A fortnight.'

'A fortnight!' Edwin couldn't dull the sharp edge of his outrage.

'I'll give you a month to make arrangements.'

'And if I haven't booked a holiday by then?'

Jake considered him coolly. 'Mathers & Wise don't have the legislation to force you to take a holiday if you don't want one. But I've come here to tell you the board are anxious to be seen as caring employers. Annual performance reviews take place next month and your willingness to cooperate with this innovation will be considered during that process.'

Edwin closed his mouth. Inwardly he translated the veiled threat: *take time off or your annual pay rise will suffer*. He glanced at his right hand, surprised that it was aching. His fingers had curled into a fist that was tight and bloodless. The impotence of his position reminded him of sex but he couldn't understand where that association came from. It was only when he returned to that single, hateful word – *impotence* – that he understood.

'A fortnight.'

Jake flashed a smile that Edwin could have punched. 'You never know, Eddie. You might enjoy it. I've told

4

HR to give you priority authorisation on any holiday time you requisition. In the event of any problems I insist you call me straight away.'

He plucked a business card from his pocket and placed it firmly on Edwin's desk. It was a vellum cream, the details written in an italicised script that looked pretentiously understated. Passing the card made him leer over Desdemona's photograph. His smile broadened as he admired the three-year-old snapshot. Glancing at the picture, Edwin could have sworn Desdemona returned the same lascivious glint.

'That lady must be desperate for a break,' Jake observed. 'Take her somewhere nice. Enjoy yourselves. Live your lives. Even if it's only for a fortnight.'

Edwin said nothing.

Afterwards he thought of a dozen arguments he could have used against Jake. He could have asked if the quality of his work had become an issue; if the board were unhappy with his loyalty; if it was now a Mathers & Wise policy to penalise industry. The weakness of those thirteenth-hour objections left him frustrated and drained and ready to vent his spleen.

He picked up the phone and called Desdemona.

'Hello.'

She sounded breathless. Her greeting was laboured and released on an exhausted sigh. It would be the way she spoke if she had answered the phone while in the middle of sex.

He quietly cursed the anonymity of telephones. In those ridiculous science fiction movies, the ones that Desdemona liked to watch, technology had improved so that telephone calls were replaced by video communications. Rather than having to rely on the pitifully ambiguous sense of hearing, those futuristic communications allowed callers to see each other and get a fuller picture of what was happening on the other end of the line. If Edwin had been able to see his wife he would have a better idea of whether or not she was panting

5

from having hurried to answer the telephone, or if she was naked, plastered with sweat and semen, and breathless from the exertion of her most recent climax.

'Hi, Des. It's me.'

'Eddie!' She sounded delighted.

He wondered if the emotion was genuine or if she was just a good actress. Desdemona was an artist by profession and he knew she had harboured dreams of an acting career while at school. Surely any decent actress could fake pleasure at receiving a call from her husband, even when it interrupted something more appealing and sexually fulfilling. Before his internal censor could stop the words from coming out he asked, 'What are you doing?'

'Aerobics.' Two heavy sighs. As though she was waiting to see if he had accepted the lie. 'I've just finished the third disc on those exercise DVDs you gave me for Christmas. I ache in places where I didn't even know I had places.'

He processed what she had said. If she had been doing physical exercise it would certainly account for her breathlessness. Similarly, if she'd spent an arduous hour naked and on all-fours, with a well-hung stud pounding between her legs, the explanation that she had been doing aerobics would excuse the exhaustion in her voice. Either scenario could be true. The only person who knew for sure was Desdemona.

'I was just about to climb in the shower,' she added.

Edwin wondered why she said that. Was she scared he might be able to hear from her voice that she was naked? Had she told him about the shower so he didn't suspect anything when he returned home and found the laundry basket contained more soiled clothes than should be expected? Or was she simply sharing a part of her day with him: the way a faithful and loving wife would? He blocked the relentless questions from his mind.

'Are you going into town today?'

'I can do.'

6

'Anywhere near the travel agents?'

'If you want. Why?'

'Could you pick up a couple of brochures?'

'*Holiday* brochures?'

'Yes. Holiday brochures.'

'Eddie! What's this for?'

'For booking a holiday.'

'Really? Oh-mi-God! *Really?* Which destination? Where should we go, Eddie? Where do *you* want us to go? Which brochures should I get?'

The excitement in her voice was a soothing balm to his blackest fears. Her enthusiasm was childlike and genuine. It was hard to imagine she had really spent her day in the arms of another man; stripping herself naked for him; allowing him to use his tongue on her; taking his erection in her mouth; sliding her small, dovelike hands over his body; parting her thighs and opening her sex for him; groaning as he plunged into her pussy; moaning as he pressed his length into her anus.

'Get a selection of brochures,' he said. 'Pick places that you fancy.'

'I will. I'll do more than that. I'll get a bottle of red and some steak so we can have a special meal when you get home tonight.'

He grunted. 'I might be late this evening.'

Her sigh was suddenly stiff with impatience. In the silence beneath the sound he could hear an undercurrent of antagonism. 'That's nothing new,' she whispered.

She expected him to be late? Did she make plans around his routine? Her husband was out of the house from six-thirty in the morning and didn't usually return home until seven-thirty or later. Aside from her painting, what did she do during those hours? Who called on her? Was she visited by friends? Men? Women? Lovers? Casual fucks?

Desdemona said, 'I'll let you get off now.'

He wondered if she had said those words too quickly. Was there an unseen person in the background at

Desdemona's end of the conversation? Had she been interrupted by the caresses of another man urging her back to the bedroom? Was someone fingering her while she spoke on the telephone? As Eddie asked his wife to collect a selection of holiday brochures, had Desdemona been enjoying another man's mouth against the slippery lips of her sex? His stomach hurt as though it had been punched. The erection in his pants was a witless traitor: hard now it was unneeded. Aroused by thoughts of the most despicable flavour.

'You too,' he croaked stiffly, assuming she had said, 'I love you.'

He slammed the phone into its cradle. His chest was tight with anxiety. His head throbbed from the ache of trying to decide whether his wife was as faithful as her outward appearance would suggest or as shameless as the harlot who dwelt in his darkest suspicions. Glancing at the obligatory framed photo on his desk, Edwin studied the innocent smile she had worn for their honeymoon. The sight might have appeased him, if not for the memory of how her picture had responded to Jake. Vowing not to think about it, adamant he wouldn't spend another moment of the day locked in a black fugue of brooding, he turned to the computer on his desk and opened up a pair of spreadsheets.

Some of his afternoon was spent discreetly finding out more about Jake. His full name was Bartholomew Jacob Mathers, son of Bartholomew Isaac Mathers, CEO of Mathers & Wise. With his BA from combined business studies and business management, it was generally believed he deserved his place on the company's board. It was said by one source that he would have been there regardless of his relationship with Bartholomew Isaac Mathers. Edwin treated that sycophantic remark with the contempt it deserved. No one ever reached the board of Mathers & Wise because of their BA or MA. It was only ever because of their DNA. After one short month with the company, Bartholomew Jacob Mathers, Jake as he preferred, was already proving himself a major source of gossip to the girls on the Mathers & Wise switchboards. Rumour said he'd bedded three secretaries in the first month, one of them married and two of them at the same time. His lechery was scandalous but never reported as though it was offensive. Contrarily, Edwin got the impression that those women who gossiped about Jake's sexploits privately wished they were an active part of the budding legend.

In business matters Jake was alleged to follow the same liberal ethic with which his father ruled Mathers & Wise. A few of Edwin's sources suggested the junior Mathers possessed a determined streak his father lacked. But so few of Edwin's sources had spoken with Jake personally that he could only conclude he was hearing guesstimates and hearsay. Edwin didn't know what he had expected to discover when he started trying to learn more about Jake, and he wasn't sure what to make of the information he had gathered. He supposed he had been worried the forced holiday was a ploy to usurp him from his secure position with the company. But that idea, like so many others that plagued him throughout the day, now seemed fatuous and paranoid.

He delayed the drive home until seven-thirty, completing a pair of projects that had been too complicated for anyone else in the department. Making sure his logout time was properly recorded, and belligerently hoping Bartholomew Jacob Mathers would notice the extra hour he had worked after being advised to do less, Edwin climbed into his car and began the dreaded journey home.

Fluctuating traffic meant the drive to work took an hour or longer on a morning. The homeward journey rarely took half that time but Edwin still preferred the first journey of the day. In the morning there was too much happening on the roads for his thoughts to return, compass-like, to Desdemona. Crawling learners, truculent truck-drivers, and a gamut of speeding Escorts and

Fiestas all combined to keep his concentration on the traffic conditions.

But it was never like that on an evening.

There was too much time for thinking.

For the three years since his wedding he had tried various tricks and ruses to distract himself while driving. But none of them worked. Pop radio played songs about love, sex and funking. Those few lyrics he could understand screamed about promiscuity, sexual satisfaction and tangled relationships. The serenity of the classical music station just allowed his thoughts to drift down their own dark avenues. He had briefly tried listening to snatches of audio books, hoping to lose himself in the narration of an entertaining story. And the first three he had purchased turned out to be tales of betrayal, deception and infidelity.

He snapped her name into his bluetooth headset. When she picked up the phone he said, 'Hi, Des. It's me.'

'You're on your way home?'

He could detect an inflection of anxiety in her voice. Was it going to be a struggle for her to eject the lover currently servicing her needs? Or did she need more time for this one to satisfy the urges he had awoken? Would she crassly ask Edwin to drive around the block before parking in the driveway? Desdemona had never done such a thing before but it wouldn't surprise him if she did make that request. Was he going to see fresh tyre marks on the drive? Would he catch the scent of another man's sweat as he walked inside his home? Would the house reek of her musk and a stranger's ejaculate?

'I'll be back in half an hour.'

'I'll see you then.'

She sounded ready to sever the connection. His heart lurched heavily in his chest. Between his legs his erection throbbed so hard it was momentary agony. Was she really that eager to get rid of him from the phone? And why? Was there genuinely another man there? Did she want another swift ride on her lover's massive length before her inadequate husband returned and spoilt the evening for her? Or did she simply want to get on with preparing their evening meal for them? If they were going to eat together, he supposed she could be hungry, and anxious to make a start on dinner.

The line went dead before he thought to say anything else.

The remainder of the journey was a torment as he pictured Desdemona frantically rushing around the house, ejecting the muscular stud who had just been fucking her, then hurrying around their home with the vacuum cleaner, an air freshener and a sharp eye for any detail that might have been overlooked. Sweat lay slick on his brow. The erection in his pants remained as hard as the gearstick. His stomach was leaden and his bowels overfull. The urge to find a convenient lay-by, stop the car, climb outside and vomit was overwhelming. Instead, he pressed the accelerator harder, determined to catch her *in flagrante delicto*.

But, when he returned home, the house only smelled of the incense she used to disguise the odour of paint thinners that crept from her studio. And Desdemona was calm and simply pleased to see him. Their meal was delicious: lightly grilled steak, onion rings and a side salad. The bottle of red complemented the dinner perfectly. Desdemona showed him the holiday brochures she had collected, an eclectic selection that covered most parts of the world with the exception of Iraq and the Gobi Desert. Together they decided the language barrier of America would probably present the least number of problems for their holiday. They retired to bed discussing the advantages of one package deal over another, and promising to resolve the final detail of their holiday destination the following evening.

Half an hour later, and unable to sleep, Edwin climbed quietly out of bed and poured himself a scotch from the bottle he kept in a cupboard beside the fridge. He still felt unwell and anxious after a day tortured by

11

thoughts of his wife with other men. As he settled on a high stool at the breakfast bar he cautioned himself to curb the paranoid fantasies before he either spoilt what he and Desdemona had or became seriously ill from the groundless fears of her promiscuity. There was no reason to suspect Desdemona might be untrue. She had never given him any reason to believe she was less than one hundred per cent faithful and he tried to understand where his suspicions came from. He supposed the scotch wasn't going to help coherence in his introspection but, sipping its bittersweet taste, he decided he needed the drink to help him sleep.

They had been married more than three years. Their fourth anniversary would be with them in October. She was twelve years his junior and had been twenty-six on their wedding day. They had met at a Mathers & Wise charity function where she was attending as the friend of a friend. Desdemona had approached him and together they had found each other's company agreeable. A week later they had shared their first date and, two months after, they were seeing each other regularly. It had been an inauspicious beginning but they were comfortable with that. When the subject of marriage was eventually raised, they both agreed it was a good idea.

On Edwin's insistence they saved sex until their wedding night.

There was no more scotch in his glass. He hesitated before pouring another and then did it anyway. The bottle was almost empty.

That first night of making love with Desdemona still remained in his thoughts. Her naked body, so youthful and responsive, had been his to explore. Her breasts were pale, full and tipped with nipples that stood hard in anticipation. Her sex, concealed beneath a whisper of blonde curls, was virgin territory to him. He kissed her, delighted when she touched his hardness.

And then they explored each other.

Her mouth brushed against his shoulders, chest and stomach. He kissed her face, breasts and thighs. When the intimacy became bolder – her lips on his length and his tongue between her labia – Edwin had thought his arousal would never be more poignant. But when they finally joined their bodies he had realised that thought was pitifully wrong.

The lovemaking had been a revelation.

Instead of recalling the event as a beautiful experience, Edwin remembered it had been fraught with worries. Desdemona was twelve years his junior and, he assumed, expecting him to be competent and worldly. Her responsiveness frightened him and he feared he would not be man enough to meet her ferocious needs. She lay beneath him and was clearly nervous at first. But, after he had thrust inside her, she became an enthusiastic and demanding participant. Wrapping her legs around his back and urging her sex to meet him, she gave herself to the passion with a hunger he hadn't expected. Goading him to climax, she raked her nails against his back and pressed lascivious kisses against his face and chest. Her needs were spat in guttural snatches; hissing for him to fill her; begging for him to use her; urging him to ride faster and harder. She used words he had never expected to come from such sweet and innocent lips. *'Fuck my cunt, you bastard! Fill me with your cock. Fuck me hard, Eddie. Fuck me deep. Make me come!'* When she wasn't growling obscenities, Desdemona used her mouth to bite and suck at his shoulders and chest. He had thought her needs were more than he would ever be able to meet. And, on top of that thought, he wondered how long it would be before she took a lover to provide the physical satisfaction her body required.

As that question came into his mind, Edwin ejaculated.

The memory of that humiliation made him painfully hard.

13

He pressed a hand against the fresh discomfort in his pyjama bottoms and drained the last dregs of his second scotch. Deciding to finish the bottle, he poured himself a third glass and tried to work out where his thoughts were going and why he was torturing himself with this excursion to a seamy avenue off memory lane.

Admittedly, on those occasions when he and Desdemona made love, she still displayed a voracious sexual appetite. It was easy to assume that, because she had always been so responsive for him, she would be that way for any other man. He knew it was wrong to decide she would be unfaithful simply because she had a healthy appreciation of sex. But he couldn't accept that she would remain true to him when he wasn't able to leave her spent and truly sated.

His arm slipped from the breakfast bar. The base of his whisky glass slammed loudly against the counter. 'Crazy,' he muttered. The word echoed hollowly from the kitchen tiles. It was slurred by the remainder of the third scotch. Forcing himself not to talk out loud, sure the verdict of craziness could only be confirmed if he compounded his current problems with a solitary conversation, he sighed and decided it was now long past the time to put the obsession behind him. Desdemona had never given him any reason to believe she was unhappy with their marital situation. Admittedly, she became impatient after their Friday night lovemaking. Her conversation became clipped. He had even heard her being cynical. Sarcastic. Callous. But that was understandable. He was leaving her frustrated. All the ideas of her faithlessness had sprung from his suspicions and imagination. It was time to cast aside his paranoia or spoil what they had.

Rinsing his glass before placing it in the dishwasher, then taking the empty scotch bottle to the rubbish bin, he told himself that, if his thoughts continued to accuse his wife of groundless infidelities, he would do the only sensible thing and seek professional help. It was a bold decision but he was ready to acknowledge that his obsession bordered on neurosis. Confident that he might now be able to lift the dark veil of gloom from his day-to-day routine, he opened the lid of the pedal bin and started to place the empty scotch bottle inside. He stayed his hand, remembering the bottle didn't belong with the non-recyclable waste.

The glint of something shiny made him glance at the contents of the pedal bin. He was briefly worried something valuable had been inadvertently thrown away. A momentary relief touched him when he recognised the shine came from a torn wrapper: a foil interior to keep the contents fresh. That relief was banished when he saw it was the wrapper from a condom.

Two

There would be an explanation. Not the obvious explanation. Not the hateful explanation that he couldn't bring himself to contemplate and couldn't scourge from his mind. But there would be *an* explanation that innocently clarified why he had found an empty condom wrapper at the top of their pedal bin.

Edwin sat in silence, trying to think of one explanation that didn't involve Desdemona tearing the foil wrapper open with her teeth; plucking the oily ring of rubber from inside; and then rolling it down the thick erection of a man he didn't know. The image was agonisingly vivid. He could see her fingernails: short but well-cared for, save for the smear of Hooker's Green acrylic that she always managed to pick up when working on landscapes. Her small, delicate fingers were dwarfed by the size of the thick shaft they sheathed. He could see the erection: fat, beefy and veined with dusky blue lines. The mahogany mushroom-head was reddened at the fraenum, as though arousal had already irritated and excited the penis's owner. The shaft's base was hidden in a thatch of thick, dark, manly curls. Desdemona's tiny hand could barely encircle the broad base as she tugged the condom downward. Keeping her hand tight around the girth, holding the sheath in place, she straddled the monstrous length and rolled the end against her labia. The teat-shaped end of the condom slipped easily against the flushed split of her pussy. And then it disappeared as the vast mushroom-head of the cock pushed inside.

Edwin clutched his stomach and slapped a hand over his mouth. He forced his throat closed and held his breath, trying to quell the rising flow of nausea. His erection refused to subside. His scrotum was taut and throbbed. Every thought seared like a scorch-mark inside his skull.

Patiently, he took a deep breath.

Sitting back in his chair, he glanced around and assessed the room. The polarised glass in the windows told him he was in his office. The sun was low, either dusk or dawn, but the angle of his window wouldn't allow him to tell which. His view of the car park showed three vehicles other than his own, which could have meant it was either very early or very late. It wasn't until he had checked his computer that he saw the day was finished and the time was fast approaching nine o'clock at night.

The realisation slapped him with a mild dose of shock. Since making that appalling discovery the previous night, his mind was a blank. He didn't remember if he had returned to bed. He couldn't recall the morning drive to work. And he didn't remember what he had been doing in the office throughout the day. Calling up files on the PC's screen, scanning quickly through the logs of his completed projects, he saw a list of documents that indicated he had been working busily.

But he didn't remember anything since finding the condom wrapper.

He dragged a deep breath into his lungs and told himself it was time to get the advice of a doctor. His hands had started to shake. The worry of what damage he could have caused while driving in a haze of fury and imagination; the lesser fear of the errors he might have made in his work; all convinced him he needed medical assistance. His hand paused over the telephone. At this time of night, his regular GP wouldn't be in the office.

17

He didn't think his condition merited an ambulance or emergency treatment. And, when he thought about what a doctor might say to him, he eventually dragged his fingers away from the handset.

'*What caused this episode, Edwin?*'

'*It started when I found an empty condom wrapper in the dustbin of my wife's kitchen.*'

'*Is your wife having an affair?*'

'*I don't know. I mean . . . the condom wrapper certainly suggests she . . . but I don't think . . . I mean . . . she would never . . . but . . .*'

'*Have you asked your wife if she's having an affair? Or why there was an empty condom wrapper there?*'

He stopped the imagined conversation from progressing any further. It was one thing to speculate about Desdemona's fidelity; it was even more disconcerting to lose an entire day to the shock and worry of *why* there was a discarded condom wrapper in the waste bin; but he wouldn't bring himself to think about asking Desdemona outright if she was untrue. The prospect was too daunting. The question suggested he lacked faith. And, while that might be true, he didn't want his wife to know that he feared she was making him a cuckold.

'Eddie?'

He glanced up to see Jake enter his office.

'Are you still here, Eddie?'

'It would appear so.'

'It's nine o'clock at night.'

The university education hadn't been wasted. Clearly Jake Mathers could tell the time. 'So it is,' Edwin muttered.

'You really do work too hard.' Jake stepped into the office and settled himself in the seat facing Edwin's. The tie at his throat had been loosened. His hair, ordinarily smoothed into a stylish helmet of sleek black grooming now looked casually untidy. He reclined in the seat and glanced wearily around the grey little room. 'Is it your birthday?'

18

'No.' Edwin wondered where that question had come from. He saw Jake staring at a brightly wrapped package on the edge of his desk and blinked as though it had only just appeared there. Hazy recollections of the day were starting to come back to him. If he concentrated hard enough he could recall a furious drive to the office that morning. He remembered most of his day had been spent in an angry rush to complete work. The driving force that powered his urgent actions was hidden behind a mental wall erected as a barricade against thinking. Work stopped him dwelling on those things that were too painful to contemplate.

At some point, late in the afternoon he guessed, one of the girls from the switchboard had brought the gift in for him and placed it by the side of his keyboard. He had grunted to acknowledge her. But this was the first time he had allowed himself to notice the present. Considering the gaudy wrapping paper, red and yellow stripes with red print on the yellow, and yellow print on the red, he could understand Jake's assumption that it was a birthday gift.

'It's not my birthday for another six months.'

He toyed with the ribbon on the package and then noticed the tag. The glimpse of Desdemona's signature was enough to make him snatch his fingers away as though they had been scalded. He glanced at Jake, expecting the man to ask why he had responded so peculiarly to the box.

Instead, Jake asked, 'Did you get a chance to consider our conversation yesterday?'

'Holidays? I looked at some brochures last night.' Edwin stopped the sentence abruptly. The less he thought about the previous evening the better chance he would have of following this conversation. His right hand had begun to tremble. He placed it on the arm of his chair and gripped tight to disguise the involuntary shiver.

Oblivious, Jake smiled. 'That's good. Where are you looking at?'

'Lots of places.'

'I spent my gap year drifting through Europe,' Jake reflected. 'That was an experience.'

'It might be more than I can manage in a fortnight,' Edwin said quietly. His gaze kept flitting towards the box and he wondered why it was there. Their wedding anniversary wasn't for another eight months. It wasn't his birthday. It wasn't her birthday. Christmas had long since passed and he could think of no other occasion when people were likely to exchange gifts. There was no reason Desdemona should have sent him a present. Yet the gift – the size of a small shoebox – remained on his desk. The red and yellow wrapping paper, interspersed with the italicised words *Just For You Just For You Just For You*, silently begged him to discover its contents. Did she know he suspected? Was this gift her way of apologising for an indiscreet tryst? If that was the case, did she truly believe he was so shallow his crushed emotions could be bought with a mere bauble?

'. . . Baltic very pretty.'

Edwin glanced up and realised he had not heard whatever it was Jake had been saying. A glance at the clock on his computer told him Jake had been talking for fifteen minutes. He realised he must have lost his grip on the surrounding world for a moment. This time embarrassment was more prevalent than shock. He marvelled it was so easy to accept something as horrific as vast lapses in concentration. 'I'm sorry,' he mumbled. 'It's been a long day and I guess my thoughts had started running off.'

Jake's benign smile showed no offence. 'It's been *too* long a day,' he emphasised. 'You look totally wasted.'

'I suppose I should get off soon.' He had meant to say 'I should get *home* soon,' but he couldn't voice those words, much less contemplate facing Desdemona. Entertaining the thought made his cheeks blush and washed him with sweat. There was someone he wanted to talk with before he considered going back to the house. Someone who might be able to give him the advice he so desperately needed.

'There's no suppose about it.' Jake grinned. 'Although I'm glad I caught you. I wanted to chat about something you mentioned yesterday.'

Edwin raised an eyebrow. His gaze was repeatedly drawn to the red and yellow wrapping paper on the present. Curiosity nagged incessantly. He forced himself to look away from the box and concentrate on Jake Mathers.

'Being honest, it's more about your wife than you.'

Edwin lifted his face and studied Jake quizzically. He struggled to remain calm but could feel his anger showing through the tight smile he had reflexively assumed. Did Jake know something or have some suspicions? How could Mathers possibly know anything about Desdemona?

'My wife? What about her?'

'You said she was an artist.'

'Yes.'

'Is she any good?'

Edwin nodded towards the painting on his wall. Aquamarine waters beneath a summer-pale sky; the horizon broken by a sandstone promontory, picked out in burnt umber and sienna from the base of yellow ochre; a shielded white building, with a squat lighthouse tower protruding from its red-slate roof. 'That's one of hers.'

'Really?'

His enthusiasm was enough to make Edwin's head pound. Jake climbed from his chair and went to study the painting more closely. His long fingers, with their fussily neat nails, smoothed the edge of the gilded frame that housed Desdemona's oil painting. His eyes and smile showed genuine appreciation. 'Is this a real location, or something she made up?'

Edwin blushed. 'Before we met she went through a phase of painting lighthouses. This is one of those.'

'Where is it?'

He couldn't say its real name. That word could not have been wrenched from his throat without causing blisters and drawing blood. 'It's a lighthouse near Southport, Maine. Somewhere near Boothbay Harbour, I think.'

Jake turned from the picture and grinned apologetically. 'You mentioned her name yesterday but, I'm sorry, I've forgotten it.'

'Desdemona.'

'Of course.' Devilish merriment sparkled in his dark-brown eyes as he added, 'But not the same one who married Othello? Right? Is she busy?'

Edwin held his breath. He could picture his wife being very busy at the moment, tearing another condom wrapper between her teeth, plucking the oily ring from inside and then rolling it over the . . .

'Why do you ask?'

'I've been wanting to brighten up this entire building since I landed on the board,' Jake explained. He returned to the chair facing Edwin. His smile glowed like a leer. 'I know other guys have come in, slapped a coat of emulsion on the reception area, and then considered their work done. But I'd like to have a series of original landscapes giving the place some class. I'm hoping to encourage foreign trade through our doors and I'd love to give the impression that Mathers & Wise has a little more style than our current dowdy surroundings. Do you think Desdemona would be able to work on a series of landscapes for us?'

'I'll mention it to her.'

Jake plucked a business card from his pocket and passed it to Edwin. It was identical to the one he had handed over the day before. 'She's good. If she thinks she can do it, tell her to call me so we can meet.'

Edwin stared numbly at the card. There had been a moment earlier this evening when he had worried he was suffering from Alzheimer's disease. Or one of the many other syndromes associated with blighted memory.

Losing an entire day from his consciousness; not remembering a gift had been brought into his office; having to concentrate to remember birthdays, anniversaries, Christmas dates and other reasons for the exchange of presents. Each of those incidents had given him cause to fear his mind might be failing. But, after talking with Jake Mathers – eighteen years his junior; unable to remember an unusual name from twenty-four hours earlier; or recall he had already presented the same business card – Edwin decided his worries of senility were not as serious as he had feared.

He took the card. 'I'll mention it to her.'

'Be sure you do,' Jake said. He glanced at his watch, frowned, and said, 'And please don't stay here much longer, Eddie.' He grinned as though they had become firm friends. 'You make the directors look like a bunch of slackers.'

Edwin thought the directors *were* a bunch of slackers. He often opined that a hard day's work would be tantamount to the death penalty for them. He didn't share either of those thoughts with Jake. 'I'll be leaving shortly,' he promised.

As soon as Jake left the room he dropped the business card into his waste bin and then threw the switch on the office lights. In the gloom, he warily considered the gift. Why would Desdemona send him a present? He supposed the simplest way to get an answer would be to open the wrapping paper and look inside. But he kept backing away from that idea. Opening the present would mean he accepted the gift. And could he really accept a gift from a wife who was potentially unfaithful? If he took a gift from her, wouldn't that be the same as accepting her infidelity? The link between those ideas would have ordinarily struck him as spurious. But this evening, as he sat in the shadows of an unlit office, staring out at a car park where only his vehicle now remained, it seemed like a perfectly reasonable supposition.

Accept the gift: accept Desdemona's adultery.

His stomach folded. The throb of his erection was an agony. His neck ached from tension and he glanced wildly around the room for something that would take his thoughts from his treacherous wife. Desdemona's picture smiled back at him from the desk. The framed oil painting of Cuckolds Lights leered down at him from the wall. The WORKAHOLIC keyring on his desk had been a gift from Desdemona. Everything kept dragging his thoughts back to her. On a mad impulse, he snatched at the present, pushed his nails into the wrapping paper and tore it angrily from the box.

A mobile phone.

He blinked, startled by the discovery. He could not have imagined anything more surreal or unexpected if he had unwrapped the present to discover a talking fish. Edwin grinned to himself and accepted that a talking fish probably would have been slightly more surreal. But still, it was an unusual present and it was enough to make his anger and jealousy abate as he tried to fathom a reason for the gift. He rummaged through the discarded wrapping paper, trying to find the tag that had labelled it a present from Desdemona. The card was torn into two pieces and he had to hold them together with trembling hands to read her words.

'Since you've said you fancied seeing me face-to-face when we speak, I saw this and thought of you, Des. xxx.'

Three

He stopped at The Horn on his way home. The pub was close to the town centre, but not so close that it catered for the overspill of rowdiness from the nightclub crowds. A solitary building, standing alone by the side of the road. Bright lights over the doorway and at the windows suggested a lively and fun world away from the night's cold and loneliness. Pulling into the car park at the unlit rear of the pub, trembling slightly as he tried to understand what was happening in his life, the beam from Edwin's headlights illuminated a burly figure in the back door of The Horn. He was relieved to have arrived at the right moment to catch his brother outside, having a cigarette in the kitchen doorway.

'Ed?' Robin waved, recognising the car.

Edwin wound his window down and waved back. Finding Robin outside the pub meant he wouldn't have to elbow his way through the drunken crowd that usually occupied The Horn on a Friday night. He didn't mind the atmosphere of his brother's pub but he didn't relish the idea of returning to Desdemona with the smell of tobacco and beer entrenched in his clothes.

Robin trudged to the side of Edwin's car and stood by the open driver's window. He dropped his cigarette to the floor and crushed it into the gravel. 'Problem?' Robin asked cautiously. His features were grave and Edwin realised with reproof he didn't visit his brother often enough. Unexpectedly calling on him at this time of night he was viewed as a harbinger of doom. Robin's broad and manly features were etched with concern. 'Something wrong?'

'Have you got five minutes to sit in the car?'

'Shit? It's that bad?'

'No.' Impatient, Edwin shook his head. 'I just wanted to ask your advice. It's for a friend of mine. From the office.'

Robin went to the rear door and climbed inside.

Edwin had expected him to move to the passenger side of the car and climb into the shotgun seat. But, he reflected, with Robin sitting behind him, it might be easier to talk more openly. Admittedly he had already made the decision to disguise his cry for help behind the problems of a fictitious work colleague. But this seating arrangement meant he didn't have to study his brother's face and see any symptom of pity, scorn, understanding or amusement.

'Go on,' Robin said, slamming the door closed. He brought a smell of cigarettes and the cold night into the car. Edwin caught those scents before the familiar tang of clean sweat and beer. As landlord of The Horn, Robin wore the blend of those latter two fragrances like a permanent cologne. 'What's the what then, bruv?'

'Cheryl cheated on you, didn't she?'

'Insert knife,' Robin chuckled. 'Open old wound. Are you going to offer me a little salt to go with this?'

Edwin blushed. 'I'm sorry. I didn't mean to be so blunt. I was just . . .'

Robin clapped him on the shoulder. The gesture was enough to explain that no real offence had been taken. 'Don't sweat it. You're right. Cheryl was a cock-happy bitch who couldn't keep her fucking legs together. She didn't have elastic in her knickers: she had a fucking yoyo string. Don't tell me Des is fucking around? That's not why you're here, is it?'

'NO!'

26

He knew he had said the word too loud. Too quick. But he didn't care. 'No. Not Des. Not Des at all. Like I said before, it's a problem that *my friend* at work has.'

'Poor fucker,' Robin murmured. 'What's he gonna do?'

'That's what he's been asking me. But I don't have a clue what to say. I've never been in this situation before. His situation I mean. I came to you for advice because I know you've been through it two or three times.'

'Ouch! You didn't just want to open *one* wound this evening? You fancied plucking the scabs from a couple of others?'

Edwin apologised while Robin laughed and brushed over the matter.

'Cheryl and I split up because she had a cock-addiction,' he said easily. He spoke without malice, his tone flowing smoothly from the back seat of the car. It sounded like a narration he had made many times before and one that he probably altered depending on the sympathy of his audience. 'Then there was Katy, and we never suited each other. We decided to go our separate ways when I started looking at The Horn. She said she wasn't bringing up her kids over a fucking pub.' He sniffed to punctuate the sentence. 'I'll be honest and admit that I did cheat once or twice behind Becca's back. But we split up when I caught her pissed out of her brains and gobbling one of the pot-washers in the kitchen.' He shook his head, grinned and added, 'Things are going OK with Alice at the moment. That's partly 'cos we've got a mechanical pot-washer. But mainly 'cos she spends weekday afternoons visiting her mother, so I have a little free time to play.' He chuckled quietly, as though he had said something clever.

It was only as an afterthought that Edwin realised his brother was surreptitiously bragging about infidelities. Not wanting to follow that line of questions, he asked, 'How did you find out about Cheryl?'

There was a moment's silence from the back of the car. The quietness was so intense they could hear the tinkle of faraway music from inside The Horn. Edwin thought it sounded like Bon Jovi, 'Livin' on a Prayer'. 'Everyone 'cept me knew about her,' Robin said finally. 'Cheryl wasn't exactly discreet. I got back from work one night. Not suspecting a thing. I sat down in front of the TV with a tin of beer and a curry. When I was playing a game of hunt-the-fucking-remote, I found a sock stuffed under one of the cushions on the settee.'

In the stillness that followed, Edwin realised his original thought had been correct: it was Bon Jovi. He felt awkward for upsetting his brother's mood and quietly cursed himself for being so thoughtless. Nevertheless, now he had come this far with his questions, he couldn't go back. 'Could it have been one of Cheryl's socks?'

'For a size eleven foot? With a MAN UTD logo on the side?'

Edwin flinched from his brother's bitterness. He couldn't decide if Robin was angrier at the memory of her deceit, or the fact that she had taken a lover who supported Manchester United. People often remarked that Edwin and Robin were more different than was usually expected of siblings. They were physically dissimilar: Robin broad and stocky, Edwin lean and rangy. Robin followed whatever career prospects were available to him at the time while Edwin had remained monogamously faithful to Mathers & Wise for eleven years. But, despite their differences, Edwin suspected they shared similar attitudes towards the prospect of being cheated. Because Robin had firsthand experience of the situation, Edwin was anxious to gather all he could from his brother's learned wisdom.

He glanced through the windscreen and watched a couple stagger from the pub's doorway. The girl wore a short skirt and stumbled hurriedly across the gravel as though she had drunk too much. Her heels were not designed for the treacherous surface of The Horn's rear car park. The young man pursuing her weaved with a similar gait but his trainers kept him stable. When they met, by the side of the kitchen door, they clung to each other as though needing support. As their arms wrapped around each other Edwin began to realise the pair weren't holding each other for balance.

The man's hands touched the woman's breasts.

Their mouths were locked in a suction-like kiss.

Edwin couldn't tear his gaze from the developing scene.

'What did you do when you discovered the sock?'

'I told Cheryl to pack her bags and fuck off.' There was no longer any trace of Robin's usual amusement in the voice that came from the back seat.

Edwin felt guilty for making his brother touch on these unpleasant memories. Because Robin always presented a façade of cheery optimism Edwin had not expected his brother to turn morose with the questioning. Robin usually lived his life with the brazen philosophy that women were like vacuum cleaners: *once they stop sucking, it's time to change the bag.* His solemn response to Edwin's curiosity indicated he wasn't totally indifferent to the upset caused by his failed relationships.

'How did you discover Becca was being unfaithful?'

Robin's laughter was caustic. 'When I saw the pot-washer's cock sticking in her mouth, that gave me my first clue.'

Edwin blushed and mumbled another apology.

His gaze never left the couple by the side of the kitchen doorway. Despite the cool weather and their exposed location they were clearly intent on enjoying each other as fully as possible. She had unzipped his pants and removed his erection. He had pulled up her skirt and pulled her panties down to her ankles. The couple were a good distance away; only lit by moonlight and an overspill of rays from the kitchen door. They were far enough from Edwin's car so he could only see the general suggestion of their movements without

29

noting any details. The sight did not excite Edwin. He watched with the same detachment he would have used to observe a pair of squirrels foraging. 'Did you give Becca the same message you gave to Cheryl? Pack your bags and fuck off?'

'I packed them for her,' Robin said gruffly. He cleared his throat and mentioned something about the smoky atmosphere of the pub to excuse the sound of tears in his tone. 'So, what's the problem with your friend?' It didn't sound as though his upset was completely behind him. But it sounded as if he was trying to force it away. 'His wife's fucking around, is she?'

'He found a condom wrapper in their waste bin.'

'Shit. That's pretty conclusive, isn't it?'

'I don't know,' Edwin said quickly. Driving to the car park he had come up with a potential scenario where Desdemona might have had an innocent use for a condom. If she had needed to keep one of her many paintbrushes either dry, or in airtight conditions, it was feasible that she might fasten a condom around the end. It was a lame thought and in his mind's eye the condom looked pathetic and ridiculous dangling from the insubstantial girth of Desdemona's paintbrush. He steadfastly refused to consider whether the greasy chemicals inside a condom might react adversely with any of the paints she would want to keep airtight, aware that such thinking would destroy this last hope for a reasonable explanation. 'There could be any number of reasons she had an empty condom wrapper in the waste bin.'

'Sure.' Robin sneered. 'I can think of three reasons straight off the top of my head: oral, anal, or straight in her cunt. Sort of retard is this friend of yours? Can't he see an obvious sign when it's staring him in the fucking face?'

Edwin didn't bother mentioning paintbrushes. Robin knew that Desdemona was a painter and Edwin didn't want to make his brother suspect there was no imaginary friend behind this conversation. Also, the more he continued to dwell on the idea of Desdemona draping condoms over her paintbrushes, the more it struck him as being a ludicrous scenario.

'You think he should tell his wife he saw it there?'

Robin gasped. 'He hasn't said nothing?'

The incredulity in his voice made Edwin blush. He was thankful that the car's interior remained unlit and the moonlight outside was not bright enough to show his embarrassment. His hands gripped the steering wheel with frenzied force. His cheeks were seared by the heat of impotent shame.

Impotent shame.

'Sounds to me like this guy doesn't wanna see something that's plainly fucking obvious.' Robin leant forward and pointed through the windscreen. The wavering tip of his finger, coloured and scented with nicotine, indicated the couple having sex by the kitchen door. 'Those two are dating other people, you know?'

Edwin said nothing. He wasn't sure if he should be shocked, appalled or indifferent. Everyone was fucking someone else. He only knew of one person who wasn't committing adultery. He watched the woman spread herself against the wall beside the kitchen door. She assumed the same stance as captured villains in American cop movies. It looked as though she was about to be frisked for weapons or contraband. The man stood behind her, pushing his erection towards her buttocks. Because Edwin's window was open, the faraway cries of her pleasure whispered into the car.

'They're in The Horn most nights with their regular dates,' Robin explained. 'They pretend they don't know each other in the pub. Every week night at around ten-thirty, earlier if it's a quiz night, they rush out here and fuck like bunny-rabbits by the side of my kitchen door.' He shook his head sullenly. 'It scared the shit out of me when I first found them. They never take any longer than five minutes. Dunno if that's 'cos she's an easily pleased slut,

31

or he's got a dodgy trigger mechanism. I guess they're anxious not to let their regular partners find out what they're up to.' His sigh was world-weary. His voice was as free from colour as the monochrome world outside the car. 'Just goes to show: everyone's fucking someone they shouldn't. I suppose, as long as no one finds out, everyone's happy.'

Edwin stayed silent for a moment. 'You really don't think there could be any other explanation for this condom wrapper my friend found?'

Robin snorted. 'What would you think if Des shoved a johnny wrapper in your rubbish bin?'

'I don't know what I'd think,' Edwin replied evenly. It took an effort to keep his voice from breaking into a hysterical giggle. 'That's why I came for your advice.'

They fell silent as the couple by the kitchen door disengaged. He pushed his spent length back into his pants. Then he reached for her face, held her cheeks, and kissed her. The romance of the moment was spoilt when they parted. The solitary woman looked ungainly as she wriggled her knickers back up her hips and then pulled down her skirt. Edwin wondered if it was coincidence that his brother had taken to having a smoke by the kitchen door when this nightly ritual occurred. He discarded the notion as unjust. But he allowed that it was possibly not inaccurate.

'What should I tell my friend?'

'Tell him . . .' Robin fell momentarily silent. Thoughtful.

Eventually he asked, 'Does the guy love his wife?'

This wasn't a question Edwin had expected. Robin loved beer and he loved Everton. But Edwin had never thought of his brother *loving* women. Robin married women; Robin had live-in partners and stay-over girlfriends. But the word *love* in this context wasn't something he had expected from his gruff and brusque brother. 'I don't know. I mean: I assume he does. But I've never asked. Does that make a difference?'

Robin shrugged. His hand was on the interior handle of the car. 'Dunno,' he admitted. The conversation had clearly drained him. 'After the way I got rid of Cheryl and Becca, I'm probably the wrong person to give advice on this subject. My philosophy has always been: if it don't make your dick hard, don't do it.'

'In its own way that's quite Zen,' Edwin growled. Inwardly, he thought it was another puzzling statement that would keep him awake and brooding through the darkest hours of each night. *If it don't make your dick hard, don't do it.* What the hell did that mean?

Robin climbed out of the car and went to the open driver's window. 'Personally I'd tell the slut to pack her bags and fuck off,' he reiterated. 'But if the guy loves her, and doesn't mind his wife banging all and sundry, he should just learn to live with it. From what you've said about him, I think he'd be happier with that option in the long run.'

Edwin hadn't realised he had said much, if anything, about his fictitious friend. 'Is that really your advice?' Edwin asked. 'Or are you just winding me up?'

Robin laughed. 'Don't go losing sleep over this guy's problems,' he warned. 'Sounds to me like he's one of those blokes who enjoys the thought of his wife getting her card stamped. A condom in the rubbish bin? And he doesn't have the balls to say anything to her?' Robin shook his head. 'The chances are this guy is tugging himself silly at the thought of other men poking his wife.'

Edwin turned crimson.

'The next time you see this friend, just say: *either tell the bitch to fuck off, or learn to live with it.*' He slapped his hand on the roof of the car to punctuate the end of the conversation.

Edwin mumbled his thanks and drove away. His brother's words of wisdom resounded through his thoughts. *Either tell the bitch to fuck off, or learn to live with it.* And, qualifying that sentiment: *if it don't make your dick hard, don't do it.* He had gone to Robin for help and advice. In return he had received trite and vulgar truisms that got him no closer to a solution.

Four

Friday night was their night for intimacy.

After speaking with Robin, the confusing rage of the day clouded his thoughts like a dense and threatening fog. But, when he returned home, Edwin wouldn't let himself think about the black ideas that had plagued him since the previous night. Desdemona had been generous enough to buy him a present of a mobile phone and, considering the way it so perfectly met his needs, she had clearly thought about the gift. He didn't recall mentioning a desire to see her when they spoke on the telephone, although that lapse meant nothing. He didn't recall most of the last twenty-four hours so his description of the mobile phone upgrade he desired would almost certainly have slipped through the net of his failing memory.

He handed her a bouquet of flowers when she greeted him at the door. Nothing special. One of the over-priced bunches of dying weeds sold by petrol stations to guilty husbands and thoughtless sons on Mothers' Day. The purchase had been made late on an evening when nothing else was available. Buying them he had certified himself insane. His wife had still given him no reason to believe she was faithful; the issue of the empty condom wrapper in their waste bin was completely unaddressed; and yet he was buying her flowers.

'*Either tell the bitch to fuck off, or learn to live with it.*'

She kissed him gratefully. Her arms were around him. Her breasts crushed against his chest. She murmured thanks in a sultry whisper as her pelvis rubbed at his loins. And then she pulled away from him, hurrying to get the bunch of weeds in a jar before the last of them expired. 'I take it you received the mobile?' she called from the kitchen.

He followed her into the room. 'That was unexpected. And appreciated. Thank you, Des.'

'They were doing a demonstration in the town centre,' she gushed enthusiastically. With the flowers in a vase she turned her attention to preparing food. 'When I saw they had video-messaging I remembered you saying how much you wanted to see me when we spoke on the phone.'

It was more than Edwin remembered saying. He grinned. Kept the thought unspoken. Glanced at the copy of that morning's paper on the kitchen table. Half the crossword was completed and he considered trying to finish it. 'What were you doing in town?' he asked, patting his jacket for a pen.

'Errr . . .'

She hesitated.

He glanced up sharply. He had vowed he wouldn't let his thoughts take him on any treacherous diversions this evening. But there was something about her vacillation and blushes that instinctively made him suspicious. She was hesitating. As though she was hiding something.

'I went back to the travel agents to get a couple of prices,' she said quickly. Too quickly. He could hear her sigh, as though she was relieved by the ingenuity of that reply. 'Since we'd all but settled on America, I thought we could make a more informed choice if we had an idea of the prices.'

'That makes sense,' he agreed. He relaxed and picked up the newspaper. Relieved by her explanation he asked, 'Which one seems most reasonable?'

'Errr . . .'

Edwin's chest tightened.

'They're all about the same. No real difference in any of them.'

'What's the average price? How much are we looking at?'

'I've got it written down somewhere. I'll find it out for you later.' She spoke too quickly. Her tone was evasive. 'What's with all the damned questions, Eddie? You finally come back from your bloody office and it's like I'm facing the Spanish Inquisition.' The flare of potential hostility in her voice made him quickly retreat. Her gaze was on a hundred different things. Everywhere but Edwin. She glanced at the newspaper in his hands and her eyes grew momentarily wider. He could see an inflection of horror on her face and looked down to see what might be causing the problem.

The eleven-letter word across the centre of the crossword had been completed in blue-ink block capitals. The answer was scrawled neatly but firmly. The letters had been written hard enough to blur into each other and stretch into the black spaces that shaped the crossword. For one mad instant he thought the word across the centre was: SUCKMEBITCH.

Desdemona snatched the paper from his hands.

He was sufficiently surprised to let her take it.

'I can use that for the peelings.' She spread the paper out on one of the kitchen's worktops. Covered it with the remnants of carrot shavings and onion skins. She moved with frenetic speed, snatching fat trimmed from the gammon and including that among the mix of rubbish she wrapped in the newspaper. After the addition of a couple of used tea bags, and the sullied oil from a frying pan, Edwin realised that whatever had been written there would no longer be legible.

He held his breath, too stunned to know what he should say.

'*Either tell the bitch to fuck off, or learn to live with it.*'

'Have you had a chance to look at your mobile?'

The potential for confrontation had passed. The knife of an argument had pressed between them but it hadn't

37

cut. At least, it hadn't drawn blood. Edwin heaved a silent sigh of relief. 'I've unpacked it and glanced at some of the features. It's lovely. How come you had it sent to the office?'

'They included gift-wrapping and delivery in the sale. Because they said they could get it to you this afternoon – they had one of those courier lads on a bike. You know the ones? They wear those peanut helmets and have those painfully tight shorts? I thought it would brighten your day to receive an unexpected gift. I got myself the same model so we matched. Like those sad couples you see wearing identical anoraks in the park.'

'How romantic.'

Her laughter was a semitone too high. As though she was still trying to conceal something. And while a part of him was desperate to know what she was keeping from him, a greater part insisted he should just let her keep whatever secrets she needed.

'*Either tell the bitch to fuck off, or learn to live with it.*'

'One of my new bosses was admiring your artwork today.'

'I didn't know you had a new boss.'

'The directors keep dragging their prodigal children onto the board. I think it's a way for them to write off private education as a tax-deductible expense. I call it the nepotism programme. This latest dropout was admiring the lighthouse you gave me as a wedding present.'

'Cuckolds Lights?'

He winced at the name, grateful she had her back to him as she prepared the food. He was proud that she had given him one of her paintings but he despised the name of that particular location. That first word stung like sweat in a paper cut. Struggling to keep his tone even, Edwin said, 'He wondered if you'd be able to supply them with landscapes for the reception, main thorough-fares, and a couple of the hierarchy's boardrooms.'

'Eddie! Oh-mi-God! Are you serious?'

He was mildly startled by the pleasure and surprise in her voice.

'What did you tell him?'

'He asked if you could give him a call and arrange a meeting to discuss his requirements.' Remembering he had dropped Jake's second card in the office waste bin, but still had the original in his jacket's breast pocket, he plucked it out and passed it to her. 'Bartholomew Jacob Mathers,' he said. 'But everyone calls him Jake.'

Desdemona wiped her hands on a dishcloth before taking the card from him. Her eyes shone with eagerness. Her hands shook with excitement. The smile on her face was wide enough for him to easily forgive any imagined transgression.

'What's he paying?'

Edwin shrugged. 'Discuss it with *Jake* when you call him.'

She put the business card in the back pocket of her jeans and then knelt in front of his chair. The kitchen lights were kind to her, turning her face into something not too dissimilar from the honeymoon bride she had been three years earlier. An identical image of the face that smiled from his desk photo each day. The ultra-fine laughter lines around her mouth and eyes were concealed by her smile. Her blonde hair shone as though it was caught in summer sunshine. 'I'm too tired to eat and can't be bothered to cook. Why don't we go to bed now? If we're still awake and hungry in an hour or so, one of us can order a takeaway, yes?'

He agreed.

They walked to the bedroom together.

Edwin watched her constantly, expecting her to do something else that might suggest infidelity. When he found the bedspread smooth and the bedroom meticulous he wondered if that was because she had only recently finished covering up her day's misdemeanours. The worry struck him as groundless but, while he was still fretting over the condom wrapper, the crossword

39

puzzle and her secrecy for being in town, it was difficult to stop being suspicious.

'*Either tell the bitch to fuck off, or learn to live with it.*'

Naked she was divine.

The golden hair fell to her shoulders and down her back. The glistening tresses spilt onto her perfectly round breasts. Her nipples were already hardening for him, the crinkled areolae slowly turning plump. Her narrow waist and flat stomach went down to a neatly trimmed cleft of rose-gold curls and long, slender legs.

'You've bruised your thigh.'

She glanced down at herself. In the muted light of the bedroom she might have been blushing. He couldn't tell. 'That damned desk in my studio,' she said casually. 'I'm forever banging into it.'

He nodded. It was at the right height for such an injury. It was only his imagination that made him think the bruise looked like it had been caused by a thumb. Fingers holding her legs apart weren't responsible for the smaller marks at the other side of her thigh. That would be the damned desk too.

'You must like bruises,' she ventured.

He glanced down and saw his erection stood hard and proud. Embarrassed, and not sure how to explain the swelling, he lowered his gaze and said, 'In case you hadn't noticed over the past three years, you have that effect on me.'

Desdemona coaxed him onto the bed. She laid back, eyes closed, legs parted and body available. For a moment he was too confused to know where to begin. It was a familiar feeling that had struck him on nearly every Friday night for the past three years. Her beauty was intimidating. Daunting. Her sexuality was too great a gift for his inept abilities. Drawing kisses against her thighs, chest and stomach, he wondered if she was excited by the intimacy, or unmoved by his dry lips against her bare flesh. Her nipples had been hard when

40

they began their foreplay but he noticed that stiffness subsided as he licked and lapped at them.

'Do me, Eddie.'

He caught his breath. Did she want him to hurry because he had ignited her desire and she urgently needed satisfaction? Or was she anxious to end this unfulfilling episode of embarrassment? He lowered his mouth to her sex, inhaling the sweet perfume of her cleft and marvelling at the beauty of those golden curls and the flushed pink lips. His erection raged for her. But he wanted to drink her flavour and hear her eager sighs before enjoying the indulgence of penetration.

'No,' she complained. One hand held his hair, tugging his face and mouth away from her sex. 'No kisses there, Eddie. Not tonight. I just want to feel you inside me.'

He did as she asked. His mind was an empty canvas deliberately wiped clean of images such as half-completed crosswords and empty condom wrappers. He stared past her, focusing on the pillow by her side as his length slipped through her velvet muscles. She sighed and then released the breath with a shiver. Desdemona made no objection as his fingers reached for her breasts and squeezed and kneaded. She rocked her hips lightly forward to meet each thrust he urged inside. The muscles of her sex sucked on him with a languid frenzy. The need to climax came quickly to him and he struggled back the urge to release.

But it was a futile battle.

Regardless of how passionately he fought ejaculation, other imperatives were always stronger. He was in the arms of the woman he loved. The sensation of her sex around his length was the most potent feeling he had ever experienced. She had a way of gripping him that made the pleasure unbearably intense. Desdemona possessed a beauty that he knew was too great to be trusted in the hands of someone as unworthy as himself. Even though he was deliberately not thinking about her possible infidelity – thoughts which he knew would drive

41

him beyond the brink of containing the explosion – Edwin still teetered on the verge of losing control.

He closed his eyes. And remembered the condom wrapper. Desdemona drew a sigh. The sound reminded him of how she had hesitated when talking about her excursion uptown. He screwed his eyes more tightly closed. The crossword puzzle swam into focus. Eleven letters scrawled in blue. SUCKMEBITCH.

He climaxed.

She lay still as his erection pulsed uselessly inside her. Her arms embraced him and she allowed his shaft to spill from between her legs along with the slick movement of his semen. Not unkindly, she coaxed him to lie next to her. Some nights she would simply turn away from him after sex. Cold. Disappointed. Untouchable. But this evening she seemed content to suffer his embrace. With one hand she touched the bedside lamp and plunged them into darkness.

'You really do need to take a lover,' Edwin whispered. He knew he had said the words before but, as was always his way after they made love, he felt they needed saying again. 'You need a man who can properly satisfy your needs.'

She laughed as she cuddled against him. He braced himself to hear her dismiss the suggestion with her usual assurance of love and devotion.

Instead, she said, *'Perhaps I already have taken a lover?'*

42

Five

He stole out of bed early the following morning, leaving Desdemona alone and asleep. As the kettle boiled for his morning mug of coffee, Edwin rummaged through the rubbish in search of the newspaper. As he had expected, it was near the top. Wrapped in a tight parcel. As though it was clinging to protect a secret. The edges of the paper were wet with grease. He grimaced as the unpleasant sensation registered on his fingers. Wilfully, he tried to think past the stink of the waste bin. Unravelling the parcel of remnants and peelings he started looking for the crossword.

The kettle turned off with a snap.

He flinched from the sound and jerked as though he had been caught doing something furtive. A handful of peelings fell to the lino and scattered. The black bin bag slipped from his fingers and he suddenly found himself standing in a pile of foul-smelling garbage.

Edwin studied the empty kitchen, his heart racing as he tried to work out whether or not he had been discovered. There was nothing wrong with a man looking through his own rubbish, was there? But even as that defensive argument sprang to the forefront of his thoughts, he recognised it as a shallow excuse to cover suspicion, mistrust and other improper behaviour. The real truth of the situation was more obvious.

He was rummaging through their waste and looking for further signs of Desdemona's infidelity. Aside from unwrapping a parcel of peelings, in the hope of seeing a vulgarity written in a foreign hand, he was soon searching through the remainder of the waste as he prospected for condom wrappers. The only one he found was the one he had seen before. Ordinarily he would have balked at the idea of being able to identify a used condom wrapper on sight. But as he stared at the torn-open packet, he realised the memory of this one had spent a lot of time embedded in his thoughts. He screwed the wrapper into a tight ball and despised himself for getting an erection as he handled the hateful packet. Bitterly, he tossed it back into the bottom of the nearly empty bin bag.

Wrappers from dishwasher tablets, shredded junk mail, teabags, the remains of meals they had shared and not completed. His fingers brushed through them all as he examined the bin's contents. Two empty McDonald's cartons were nestled like lovers inside each other. He blinked at the paper boxes, trying to think of the last time he and Desdemona had eaten burgers. They occasionally opted for fast food when Des didn't have the time or the enthusiasm to cook. But he thought it had been a couple of weeks or more since they last ate a Big Mac together. Too long for these to be those cartons. From what she said about her daily routine, Des occasionally took a break for a burger while she was painting. But there were two packets in the bin and they were fastened together as though they had been eaten on the same day and at the same time.

'Perhaps I already have taken a lover?'

He stared at them for an age, trying to work out if his wife would have ordered two burgers for herself, if it were likely she had a platonic friend over to share a fast food lunch, or if the empty packets suggested she had been unfaithful. He vaguely remembered an advert, either on the TV, radio or in a newspaper, promoting a 'two-for-one' promotion at McDonald's. She could have bought a burger and received a second to eat or

44

discard. Was the explanation as innocent as that? Or had he inadvertently found evidence equivalent to the MAN UTD sock that Robin had discovered?

'Perhaps I already have taken a lover?'

He drew a deep breath.

The air was rank with the decaying stench that rose from the waste bin's contents. It was almost enough to make him gag. He was still dressed in his pyjamas, his body crusted with night-sweat and his eyes sticky from sleep. His mouth was parched, the kettle would need boiling again before he could have his first drink of the day, and he continued to kneel in a pile of garbage. 'Is this what she's done to you?' he whispered. 'Is this what she's reduced you to?'

But the question was unfair. Admittedly he was scavenging through the rubbish. A thousand clichéd similes sprang to his mind comparing him to rats, roaches and associated vermin. All of them confirmed he had sunk to new depths. But Desdemona had done nothing to reduce him to this: he was there because of his own lack of trust and his paranoid imagination.

'Perhaps I already have taken a lover?'

'Call a doctor,' he growled. 'Call the men in white coats.'

The words echoed hollowly around the kitchen. The sound of his own voice added conviction to the fear that he was going insane. But because it was Saturday morning the idea had to be put aside. The only doctor likely to work on a Saturday morning would be one scared of spending too much time with a beautiful wife. A doctor fearful of discovering something that shattered the fragile balance of his life. Edwin knew the psychological profile of that type intimately well. They shared the same motive for going to work this Saturday morning.

'Put it all back in the bin and put it out of your mind,' he told himself.

The words sounded like sage counsel, even if they did come from a lunatic who talked to himself while he rummaged through refuse. He couldn't build an accusation on two empty McDonald's cartons and a condom wrapper. Perhaps, if he went through the rubbish bin in Desdemona's studio he might find something more incriminating. But he stopped that thought before it could be properly completed. It was bad enough he had prospected through the crap from the kitchen waste bin. It would be a true sign that he had gone out of his mind if he started filching through the other bins in the house looking for more fuel for his imagination. Pushing everything back into the black bin bag, hurrying as he tried to put the chore behind him so he could pretend he hadn't sunk to such depths, Edwin hesitated over the newspaper parcel.

SUCKMEBITCH.

Had he really seen that word? Could those three words have been a genuine answer in the puzzle? He almost laughed aloud at that thought. *The Times* crossword for sexually suggestive vulgarians: One Across: ASSFUCKING; One Down: ANAL; Two Down: FISTING; Three Down: COCKSUCKING. Hysterical giggles choked at the back of his throat. It was only when his mind reached Thirteen Across: SUCKMEBITCH, that he regained his composure.

And unwrapped the newspaper.

Wiping fistfuls of wet carrot shavings and grease aside, he sneered with disgust and tried not to breathe. The newspaper had turned transparent in splodges. The black print had thickened to unreadable obesity. The crossword wasn't on the page immediately against the rubbish. He quickly tried to separate the damp sheets of paper. They tore as he pulled at them, remaining tightly glued together and refusing to give up their secrets. Edwin forced himself to peel them apart more gently. Still they clung to each other as though conspiring to keep the truth from him. He could feel his anger and frustration mounting as his endeavours turned the newspaper into a pile of wet and useless pulp.

The telephone rang.

Its shrill bell made his heart leap.

Edwin didn't know if he cried out in surprise but he felt sure he came close. He glared angrily at the handset, his mind working at furious speed. If the phone rang again the noise might wake Desdemona. If Desdemona awoke now she would find him in the kitchen rummaging through the rubbish. In that situation he could think of no sane reason to excuse his search through their waste. She would ask him what he was looking for; he would tell her about his suspicions; and she would despise him for doubting her. Their marriage, already sullied by his inept abilities as a husband, would be destroyed. He threw himself at the telephone and picked it up before it could ring a second time.

'Hello?'

There was silence on the line. His heartbeat thumped. He could taste adrenaline and the stench of the rubbish at the back of his throat. Edwin was sickeningly aware he had placed a smear of gooey brown filth on the handset. He made a mental note to clean it off before leaving the house that morning.

'Hello?' he repeated. 'Is anyone there?'

'Sorry, mate. Must've phoned the wrong number.'

Then he was listening to the dial tone of a severed connection.

He put all the rubbish back in the bin bag, placed the bag outside with the non-recyclable waste, mopped the kitchen floor, wiped the telephone handset clean and finally sprayed around the room with an air freshener. The antiseptic smell was pungent, and almost as unpleasant as the stench of filth and waste, but it covered the last traces of his investigation. Not bothering with coffee, simply showering, dressing and driving off to work, he detoured past McDonald's and tried to see if there was a promotional banner suggesting they were still running a 'two-for-one' offer.

A pair of large trucks, inconveniently overtaking each other, prevented him from seeing any displays outside the restaurant. And, while he knew it was always an option that he could circle back and go there for breakfast, he considered that choice would be tantamount to spying. If he tried to check up on his wife in such an underhand way, Edwin felt sure he would be starting on the slippery slope towards private investigators, hidden cameras around the house and microphones inside the telephone.

In the office his gaze fell briefly on the painting of Cuckolds Lights. Remembering the title stabbed him with its usual gut-wrenching impact. And then he had his PC switched on and booting up while he started to go through his mail for the morning. The minutiae of his workload was sufficient distraction to stop him thinking about Desdemona, condom wrappers, crosswords, McDonald's boxes and the 'wrong number' he had answered that morning. It was almost enough to stop him thinking about the remark she had made as they had drifted to sleep.

'*Perhaps I already have taken a lover?*'

He should have asked her what she meant. It was almost as though she was making a confession. He should have found the courage to discover if she was joking or trying to broach an awkward and embarrassing truth. Her response could have answered so many of the relentless questions continually bouncing around inside his head that he marvelled at his own stupidity for missing the opportunity. Had she been trying to tell him something? Or was she simply exploiting the arousal that always touched him whenever he thought about her being with another man? Was there any way he could pick up that conversation when he saw her this evening? It wasn't an exchange they could have over the phone, not even over the new video messaging phones they now shared. But wasn't it possible he could say, '*Last night, when you said . . .*'

'Eddie?'

He glanced up and saw Jake standing in the doorway of his office. It took a physical effort not to grimace.

'Tell me you went home last night, Eddie.'

'I went home last night,' Edwin replied dutifully.

Jake's grin was mildly sour. He entered, uninvited, and fell easily into the chair facing Edwin's desk. Rather than wearing a suit, and probably because he believed the weekend allowed such leniency in the office dress code, Jake wore jeans, trainers and a university sweatshirt. He looked despicably young, handsome and successful. Edwin's loathing became a cold, black hatred.

'That was an unusual night,' Jake laughed. He leant over Edwin's desk, his smile twisted into a conspirator's leer. 'I was boinking Sally from the switchboard when my girlfriend, Maisy from Uni, turned up.' He shook his head, grinning like a naughty child admitting an enjoyable sin. His eyes sparkled and his features were unblemished by contrition. 'It turned into a really hot night.' His voice was a confidential whisper.

Edwin stared at him, wondering why Jake was entrusting him with such an intimate confession. He didn't like the young man and couldn't care less about the bastard's sexual conquests. Struggling not to let those thoughts show on his face, reminding himself Jake was the son of the CEO and a director in his own right, he tried to keep his expression blank.

'I was riding Sally doggie-style,' Jake went on. 'When Maisy just walked in and stared at us. She's a super-cool bitch. She took one look at me and said, "That looks like fun. Do either of you mind if I join in?"'

Jake cackled, as though he had delivered a punchline for the most hilarious *bon mot*. He seemed oblivious to the loathing in Edwin's expression.

'I really wasn't expecting that. I almost shot my wad up Sally's snatch. Sally said she was cool with it. And less than half an hour later I had my cock inside Maisy while she drank the come from Sally's snatch.' He shook his head, pleasantly bewildered. 'It was a shame to leave them alone in bed this morning. I'd swear the dirty bitches are licking each other out as we speak.'

49

Edwin thought of shy and reserved Sally. She was the girl who usually managed a weak smile and a polite 'Good morning, Mr Miller,' before dutifully going on with her mundane work in the office. He tried to think of her naked and on all-fours as Jake boinked her doggie-style. The image refused to form inside his mind. The idea of her in bed with another woman, her face buried against the open split of musky labia, was more than he could summon. He swallowed down a bilious taste at the back of his throat and said, 'It does sound like a most unusual night.'

'It's left me knackered,' Jake admitted. 'And I'm sure Sally left teeth marks in my foreskin.'

Edwin tried to process the statement: sweet Sally from the switchboard leaving teeth marks in Bartholomew Jacob Mathers's foreskin. Each time he brought the image into his mind Sally's face evaporated and was replaced by Desdemona's. It was improper to think of either woman performing oral sex on Jake and he eventually gave up trying to create the mental picture. Sitting back in his seat, realising something more was expected from him, he said, 'If you're still tired you should go back home and rest.'

'I might do later,' Jake agreed. 'But not until I'm fairly confident those two have left the building. Morning-after conversations are the pits when you've boinked both girls. They're constantly wanting to know which of them was the best fuck. How do you tactfully rank one over the other? Even if Maisy is a better lay than Sally?'

Unable to stop himself, Edwin drew an exasperated sigh. If his personal problems were as shallow as Jake's, he would have fallen to his knees and thanked God for granting such bright blessings and felicitous favours. Having to listen to the puerile little bastard whine about the social dilemma that followed a threesome ranked as being a somewhat petty and pathetic problem in Edwin's opinion.

'I stopped by to tell you that Des just called,' Jake explained.

Edwin stiffened. He didn't like the way Jake used his wife's name with such familiar intimacy. Jake referred to Desdemona with the same casual inflection he used when talking about Sally or Maisy. It was all too easy to think of him saying 'I boinked Des,' in his hatefully garrulous manner.

'Des suggested I pop over to her studio this lunchtime and glance at some of her artwork.'

Edwin kept his features blank.

'I was wondering if you'd be there?' Jake asked.

'I've got a lot to do here,' Edwin said quickly. He wondered why Jake should care whether or not he was at Desdemona's studio. Was the immoral little bastard hoping to have a chance at boinking Des? He'd seen her picture in the desk photograph: had that been enough to make him want her? Had Des suggested something illicit in their telephone call? Or had she simply told him to make sure he called on her when her husband was safely ensconced in his office? 'I'm going to be working until three or four at the earliest.'

Jake shook his head. He was frowning. 'That's no way to spend a Saturday. Isn't there a match on?'

Edwin shrugged. 'I don't know. I don't follow football.'

'Rugby?'

'No.'

'Golf? Boxing? Bowls? Synchronised swimming?'

Edwin shook his head. 'Competitive sports don't appeal to me. I'm happier working.'

Jake released a heavy sigh. His gaze flitted towards the painting of Cuckolds Lights and his smile momentarily resurfaced. 'I hope you're going to ease off a little from the overtime once you've had your holiday.'

Edwin was able to get rid of Jake by reminding him that it was already close to noon and then mentioning that Desdemona usually took her lunch early. He watched the cocky upstart saunter from the room and

51

then trembled with relief once the man had gone. It wasn't true that Desdemona took her lunches early. Because she rose late in the day, and their evening meal was close to being a supper, he knew she often had her lunch around two or three o'clock. But because it worked as a viable reason to get rid of Jake, Edwin thought the lie wouldn't cause any great hardship. He reached for his desk phone, intending to call Des and let her know that Jake might be arriving earlier than she'd anticipated. Fifteen rings later, and with no reply, he assumed she was either locked in her studio or out shopping. Tapping the number of her new mobile into his phone, handling the unfamiliar handset awkwardly, he was relieved that she picked up on the fourth ring.

'Hi, Des. It's me.'

'Eddie?'

He blinked. There was surprise in her tone but he could also detect genuine affection in the way she spoke his name. Beneath her voice he could hear the clatter of glasses and mechanically swirling water. 'How come you didn't call me with video messaging?'

The honest answer was that he hadn't had a chance to figure out how to select that feature. And he supposed the modicum of urgency that had inspired this call had made him simply dial her number rather than trying to take advantage of the new feature. 'Jake Mathers is coming to see you this lunchtime.'

'I know. I'm quite excited. I've organised for him to call at the studio so he can see some of the stuff I've already done. I'm hoping he wants to commission something new. I've got a hunger for painting some landscapes that I haven't tried before.'

'I called to say you should expect him early.'

'I'll get back home now. Thanks for letting me know.'

He stopped himself from asking where she was. The question would come out sounding like an accusation and he couldn't trust himself to deliver the enquiry in an innocent tone. 'Talk later.'

'Later, Eddie.'

He kept the telephone in his hand and dialled his brother's number. When a woman answered he said, 'Alice? It's Edwin.'

'I'm not Alice. Is it Alice you want? Robbie's here. But Alice is round at her sister's.'

Edwin assumed the woman was either a barmaid or one of Robin's perpetually changing girlfriends. Robin's barmaids and girlfriends were often one and the same person but Edwin was tactful enough to be discreet about this peculiarity. 'I'd like to speak to Robin, please. If he's there.'

'I thought I saw him skulking towards the kitchen. Hold on a minute.'

He patiently waited, listening to the sound of the telephone being left uncradled and hearing the noises from The Horn with its early Saturday trade. A slot machine whirred and pinged from somewhere faraway. He could hear the distant mumble of faraway conversations and almost smell the cigarette smoke and alcohol. As a background to the noise he thought he could hear the clatter of glasses and mechanically swirling water.

Edwin frowned.

'Eddie?' Robin was panting. 'What's wrong, bruv? That mate of yours again?'

'What's the noise I can hear behind you?'

'Fruit machine.'

'No. Not that.'

'Can't hear nothing else, Eddie. Interference on the phone? What you want?'

He wanted a full explanation for that noise, which sounded so similar to the one that had accompanied his call to Desdemona. Faced with his brother's question he couldn't remember the original reason for his call. He hesitated for a moment before falling back on a convenient excuse. 'I just called to thank you for last night,' he said quickly. 'I haven't seen my friend here yet but, when I do, I'm going to tell him exactly what you said. I'm sure he'll appreciate it.'

Robin sounded less convinced. 'If you say so, Eddie. But there are lots of guys out there who get off on the thought of their wives screwing someone else.'

'You mentioned that last night,' Edwin remembered. He didn't want to pursue the conversation but felt compelled to ask. 'What happens to those guys if their wife really is screwing around? Do they demand a divorce? Or can they really get off on it in some way?'

Robin chuckled and then lowered his voice. 'I'm screwing a married woman right now. Should I ask her husband?'

'You're a laugh a minute,' Edwin said drily. 'I just thought, since you have all the answers . . .'

'If I had all the answers I'd clean up on quiz night,' Robin said quickly. His voice was loud and gave the impression the conversation was reaching ears he didn't want hearing the exchange. 'Speaking of which: might I see you here for Sunday's quiz night?'

'It's unlikely,' Edwin admitted. 'Des and I don't often do the pub thing.'

'Your loss.'

Edwin could hear Robin shrugging in the background. He could also hear that maddening sound so similar to the one that had accompanied his phone call to Desdemona. If he concentrated hard enough Edwin knew he would be able to recognise what it was. Not wanting to draw out the conversation, and aware Robin was anxious to get back to something more important, Edwin thanked his brother and hung up.

The day dragged slowly. Even though there was sufficient work to keep him occupied, he couldn't stop his thoughts from returning to Desdemona.

The used condom wrapper.

'Either tell the bitch to fuck off, or learn to live with it.'
SUCKMEBITCH.

Her evasiveness when he had asked about her being up town.

Two McDonald's cartons in the bin.

'Perhaps I already have taken a lover?'

He closed his eyes and rubbed at the ache in his forehead. His suspicions were based on intimations and rubbish. There was no way he could consider confronting her with such flimsy evidence to support his case. He hated closing his eyes because images of a naked Desdemona always came to the forefront of his mind. It wouldn't have been such a curse if she had only been naked. But in his mind's eye she was invariably with other men and enjoying their attention. This time she had her mouth wrapped around an erection. It was clear she was revelling in the experience. Her eyes were wide and enthusiastic as she sucked on the length. Other hands clawed her breasts while fingers plundered her vagina.

He opened his eyes quickly.

The clock in the right-hand corner of his PC's screen told him it was close to five o'clock. 'Shit!' he muttered. 'Where did that day go?'

He shook his head, aware that the lapses in concentration were growing more frequent. The easy way he accepted them as a natural part of his life was unnerving. He vowed, first thing on Monday morning, he would call his doctor and make an appointment to discuss all the things that had been troubling him. Edwin had no idea what a doctor might be able to do. Counselling. Medication. A lobotomy. Any of those options had to be better than the hell he was currently enduring. He added an entry to his PC calendar for Monday, reminding himself to make the appointment. It was the last thing he did before deciding it was time to head back home and spend the remainder of the weekend with Desdemona. Now that he had done something as decisive as remind himself to make the doctor's appointment he felt sure he would find the courage to ask Desdemona what she had meant when she asked, *'Perhaps I already have taken a lover?'*

Six

The TVR in the driveway put Edwin on his guard. Curious to know who their visitor might be, forcing himself not to be stirred by the usual suspicions, he stretched a cheerful smile on his lips as he entered their home. Edwin knew Jake had planned to call on Desdemona; but that had been a lunchtime appointment and their meeting should have been long since concluded. Surely, the cowardly bastard hadn't spent the entire day with Desdemona as he hid from the unwanted guests at his own home?

Desdemona giggled in the kitchen. Her laughter was throaty and filled with coarse amusement. It was the same mischievous sound she released when she heard a bawdy story or the rudest of rude jokes. His brow furrowed as he tried to work out what might have caused such merriment. Walking faster, anxious to solve the mystery before paranoia could accuse his wife of more inappropriate behaviour, Edwin hurried to the kitchen.

'Eddie!'

'Eddie!'

'Des,' he nodded in his wife's direction. Glancing at Jake he nodded again and added, 'Jake.' He was surprised to see Jake was still there. He had thought a glance at Desdemona's paintings, and a cursory discussion of his needs and the cost, would take less than thirty minutes. To discover that Jake had spent five or six hours with his wife stirred familiar prickles inside Edwin's gut. It was a struggle not to glower at the man.

They stood in a loose embrace, Jake holding Desdemona across the back at her waist, Desdemona touching his shoulder from behind. They each held a tin of lager and, because it was a brand Edwin didn't recall purchasing, he assumed Jake had brought the beers. Arousal and anger fought for control of his reaction. What the hell had been going on?

'You didn't tell me your boss was such a great laugh!' Desdemona exclaimed. She eased herself from Jake's embrace, stepped to Edwin's side, and placed a perfunctory kiss on his cheek. A perfume of beer radiated from her. Her lips were full and wet.

'There was a reason I didn't tell you that.'

Jake exploded into a hearty guffaw. Slapping his hand against the kitchen worktop he shook his head. His cheeks were rouged and his eyes had the bloodshot tinge of someone who has drunk too much. 'Christ, Dezzie,' he laughed. 'Your Eddie is such a droll bastard!'

Dezzie? Edwin wondered. *Who the hell is Dezzie?*

'Jay's staying for dinner,' Desdemona said flatly.

Jay?

It was a statement. Not a question for him. Nor an invitation to Jake. She said the words with the authority of a woman speaking fact.

'If you're both sure,' Jake said quickly. He glanced at Edwin. His expression lay somewhere between beseeching and doubt. But it was Desdemona who responded.

'We are sure,' she told him. Turning to Edwin she said, 'Can you rustle up something to eat while Jay and I go back to my studio for half an hour?'

Jay? Edwin's mind swirled. Jay and Dezzie were going to the studio while he cooked a meal for them. Why did everyone have different names? Was he still Edwin? What the hell was wrong with Bartholomew Jacob Mathers? How many names did one man need? Why couldn't he stick to using the same one all the time?

Aloud, he asked, 'Will steaks do?'

'Perfect.' Desdemona smiled. She beckoned for Jake to follow her, summoning him with one curled finger. They walked out of the kitchen to the garden entrance of Desdemona's studio. Edwin followed them with his gaze, still bewildered by this turn of events. He had come home from a long day at the office and was now expected to cook for his wife and his boss. He didn't mind cooking for Desdemona (*Dezzie?*) because he knew she could often put long hours in at her studio, and he didn't expect her to play the role of the dutiful wife. But he had to cook a meal for that snotty little upstart Bartholomew Jacob (*Jake – Jay???*) Mathers! The idea of spitting on Jake's steak made him grin maliciously. He labelled the thought as petty but didn't put it aside completely. Grudgingly, he conceded it was better to think about the food and the cooking rather than dwell on what the pair might be doing in her studio.

There was a couch in the studio where models occasionally posed. More frequently Desdemona would lie there when wrestling with her inspiration. The room was spacious. The lighting could range from painfully bright to cosily dim. It had a couch and a lock on the door.

Grabbing a triptych of frozen steaks from the freezer, slamming them heavily under the grill, Edwin threw three generous fistfuls of chips onto a tray in the oven and then opened a couple of tins of veg. He could hear nothing from Desdemona's studio but he couldn't decide if that was because the pair were only talking and their voices hadn't travelled to reach him, or if they were forcing themselves to be quiet. Rather than brood on the silence he busied himself by laying a clean cloth on the kitchen table and setting out crockery, cutlery and crystal. Once he'd uncorked a bottle of Merlot he was left in a torturous silence of sizzling steaks and bubbling vegetables. Alone in the kitchen, with the preparations complete, his suspicions began to simmer.

Jake and Desdemona tumbled happily from the studio thirty minutes later. Edwin had just been about to shout that their meal was ready. They sat down at the table, Jake pouring glasses of wine and Desdemona wiping tears of mirth from her face. A trace of Hooker's Green acrylic daubed the nails of her right hand.

The pair looked as though they had genuinely enjoyed each other's company throughout the day. That thought fuelled a conflicting gamut of responses that Edwin was able to hide as he served their meals. He was happy his wife had been entertained but why had she chosen to find amusement with Jake? And how had they been enjoying themselves? Jake was a self-confessed womaniser who took his pleasure from married secretaries, switchboard operators and threesomes. Could he really have had so much innocent fun staring at a collection of oil paintings and acrylics in an artist's studio?

'Your wife is incredible,' Jake told Edwin.

'I like to think so.'

'Jay's just trying to make me feel better because he screwed me for such a bargain,' Desdemona demurred.

Edwin's head pounded. '. . . *he screwed me* . . .' The words made his stomach uncomfortable. His erection swelled invisibly beneath the table. He dropped his fork with an embarrassingly loud clatter and then apologised gruffly.

Jake and Desdemona (*Jay and Dezzie*) talked animatedly about universities. Not having been educated at a university, Edwin was outside the conversation. He listened as they chattered about faculties, degrees, refectories and other things that meant little to him. Cynically, he didn't think it would be long before the former students moved the topic to their favourite drinking games. In his experience that was the inevitable path of conversations between alumni. When Jake excitedly exclaimed 'Pub Golf!' Edwin had to place a hand over his mouth to conceal a triumphant sneer.

Bored, he listened as Jake explained the facile rules for a pub-crawl where each pint had to be drunk in the fewest number of sips. Edwin's lack of interest in the subject was the mirror opposite to Desdemona's enthusiasm.

'We used to play Keg Stand,' she giggled.

Her meal was almost finished. She had eaten without commenting on the food or thanking Edwin for his efforts. Her attention was devoted entirely to Jake and Edwin realised his presence in the kitchen was unimportant and unnoticed.

'You have to do a headstand in front of a keg,' Desdemona giggled. Her cheeks were flushed. The fullness of her lips had never looked more ripe or kissable. As she spoke she constantly wafted a hand in Jake's direction, touching his shoulder, his arm or his chest. 'The winner is the one who can drink from the keg for the longest. I used to be a champion at that game.'

'You have to drink while you're upside down and doing a headstand?' Jake shook his head, clearly impressed by this route to cirrhosis of the liver. Clearing his plate, he spoke through a mouthful of food and said, 'It must be hard swallowing in that position.'

'I can swallow in most positions,' she giggled.

Edwin blushed. The embarrassment was so severe his ears burnt. Standing quickly, making an excuse that he was going to retrieve a bottle of cognac he kept in the dark space beneath the stairs, Edwin rushed to escape the room.

'You really are a dark horse,' Jake marvelled.

Edwin could hear their exchange as he fled from the kitchen.

'A dark horse in need of a rider?' Desdemona responded. Her voice was a sultry purr. 'Are you volunteering for the role of jockey?'

Edwin slapped his hand over his mouth to stifle a groan. His erection hurt so badly it was impossible to walk upright. Bent double, stumbling to the door beneath the stairs, he was torn between the options of listening to their conversation and not wanting to hear any more. Standing silent, straining to catch any sound that came from the kitchen, he could only make out noises that could have been the innocent chomp of them chewing the remainder of their steak.

The idea that they were touching, kissing and caressing wouldn't leave his thoughts. Desdemona's flirting was outrageous. It was something he'd never encountered before. He wondered where this change in her personality had come from. A part of him was willing to blame it on the booze – clearly she and Jake had been drinking throughout the day – but he didn't think alcohol was entirely responsible.

'*Perhaps I already have taken a lover?*'

He swallowed down the acidic taste of bile. His erection continued to ache. His balls were so tight they throbbed in a scream of agony. Snatching hold of the cognac he stormed back to the kitchen. This time he was determined to make his presence felt.

Desdemona and Jake pulled apart as he entered the room. She blushed. Jake mused idly. It sounded like the tail end of a contrived conversation. The atmosphere was electric and so intense Edwin could feel the waves radiating from them. He was an intruder in his own kitchen and wondered if he should simply leave the cognac for Jake and Desdemona, then make himself scarce. The idea seemed so correct it was frightening. He presented the bottle to Jake like a sycophantic wine waiter trying to impress a generous customer.

'Brandy!' Jake cried jubilantly. He took the bottle from Edwin as though cradling an infant. Lurching into a passable Scot's accent he cried, 'Claret is the liquor for boys; port for men; but he who aspires to be a hero must drink brandy.'

'Johnson,' Desdemona laughed. She clapped her hands together, surprised, pleased and clearly besotted with Jake's intellectual wit.

Edwin wished he had smashed the bottle against Jake's skull. The only faults he could see with that plan were that it would be a waste of cognac and might hamper his rating at the forthcoming performance reviews. Nevertheless, they were minor drawbacks compared to the pleasure he would have gleaned from stoving the cognac against Jake's empty head.

Jake held the bottle so that Desdemona could read the label. Speaking to her; speaking as though they were alone in the kitchen; speaking as though they were nowhere near the nuisance of Dezzie's ineffectual husband, he said, 'Now we've got a bottle of liquor, do you fancy playing Pennies?'

'Pennies?'

Jake peeled the protective cap from the bottle of cognac and then held out his hand to Edwin. Realising he wanted a corkscrew, Edwin hurried to a kitchen drawer to fetch the item. He was nothing more than a convenient servant to the pair of them. The idea made him feel angry and, paradoxically, grateful they were allowing him to be included in their fun.

'Pennies is the game where one of us tosses a coin and the other guesses heads or tails.' Jake's words were slurred as he tried to reiterate the rules. He stared only at Desdemona. 'If you guess right, you get to toss the coin and I have to guess heads or tails. If you guess wrong, you have to drink a shot of brandy and then guess again.'

'Did you take your BA in drinking games?' she snickered.

'You're telling me you never played Pennies?'

Desdemona snorted more laughter and clapped her hands over her cheeks before they turned red. 'Oh! Christ!' she exclaimed. 'I've just remembered a variation on that game we used to play.' Her eyes were wide with horrified glee as she added, 'And there's no way I'm going to tell you about it.'

Jake raised an eyebrow. 'Don't tell me you played Strip Pennies?'

Desdemona's blushes deepened. She curled her upper teeth over her lower lip and glanced for a horrified moment in Edwin's direction. 'I never said that, Jay,' she hissed. 'I never said that.'

He stared at her, shaking his head in wonder. 'You dark horse.'

'Riderless horse,' she murmured. She dropped her voice to a whisper.

All Edwin caught was the word: *jockey*. His chest tightened. The air was too thick for him to breathe and, because he stood while they sat, he felt sure one of them was soon bound to notice that he was an awkward presence in the room. He passed the corkscrew to Jake and then mumbled an apology for not having brought the brandy balloons.

'Forget balloons,' Jake snapped. Now he spoke to Edwin as though addressing a servant. Clicking his fingers arrogantly, he said, 'We need shot glasses for this game.'

Edwin found three shot glasses and then realised he hadn't been invited to the game. Aware that they didn't need him – this was clearly a two-player game for alumni only – he placed two shot glasses on the table and quietly excused himself. Not letting himself think about his actions, he climbed the stairs, showered and then went to bed.

Neither Jake nor Desdemona acknowledged his departure.

And, although he was no longer in the same room as the pair, Edwin couldn't stop thinking about what they might be doing. Desdemona was being hatefully familiar with Jake. The pair had been obscenely close since he arrived home. He hated to think how close they might have been before he returned.

His bed sheets tent-poled as his erection hardened.

In the space of one evening Jake had learnt more about Desdemona's days at university than Edwin had managed to discover in three years of marriage. The easy way she confided intimate secrets to the young man, and her lewd use of the metaphor about being a riderless horse, made him ill from the thought that she might be untrue.

He caught himself on the verge of rubbing his aching erection. With a determined effort he stopped his hand from creeping down to his loins. It was sickening enough that the idea of Desdemona's infidelity caused excitement. There was no way he was going to compound that involuntary reaction by wanking and using her unfaithfulness as the source of his masturbatory fantasy. He gripped his hands into fists and clenched them against his chest.

A shriek of laughter carried up from the kitchen below.

A wave of nausea washed over him.

His erection throbbed.

Desdemona had played Strip Pennies at university. Edwin had never heard of the game before this evening but it didn't take a great stretch of the imagination to work out the rules. If the rules of the drinking game were any indication, one person tossed a coin and the other called heads or tails. A right guess gained control of the coin. A wrong guess meant you forfeited an item of clothing. Was it possible Desdemona had really played such a game? Who the hell would she play that with? What happened after the last item of clothing had been removed? Was Dezzie playing that game right now? With Jay?

His scrotum twinged in an agony.

Again he stopped his hand from reaching down to the sore length of his erection. Drawing breath in rapid gasps, he closed his eyes and prayed that he might fall asleep. Anything to escape the torment of the images that his mind kept producing.

Jay and Dezzie were both drunk. With a few swigs of brandy inside them (mixing pleasantly with the lager and the wine) he guessed their inhibitions would have long since emigrated. How long would it be before their

game of Pennies became Strip Pennies? How long before
Dezzie had shown Jay her bra? Her panties? Her breasts?
More? How long before Jay was removing his boxers
and revealing an erection that put her husband's meagre
offering to shame? And what would they do then?

That question was all too easy to answer.

The breath he released was a whispered groan.

He could picture Desdemona placing her mouth over
Jake's swollen length. '*I can swallow in most positions.*'
Her ripe lips encircled him. Her tongue teased the shape
of his purple glans. She drew the tip against the eye of
his cock. Tasting him as her eyes shone with fresh
excitement. '*I can swallow in most positions.*'

Or would she do more?

In his mind's eye her lips were now around the foil
wrapper of a condom. He watched her tear the paper
between her teeth to remove the oily ring of rubber.
With her left hand, her wedding ring glaring at Edwin
like a stark reminder of her treachery, Desdemona
rolled the sheath down Jake's shaft. She moved her
mouth back to the teat at the end. Kissed him through
the thin veneer of latex.

Edwin shivered.

Positioning herself over Jake, still holding his
sheathed shaft and stroking his end against her sex, she
whispered, 'I'm a dark horse in need of a rider. Be my
jockey, Jay. Be my jockey and ride me good and hard.'

Edwin's ejaculation inspired a groan. He hadn't
thought he was so aroused. The pulse of his climax was
both a torturous relief and a sickening surprise. His
shaft thickened and twitched, spurting an embarrassing
flood of hot semen into the crotch of his pyjamas. He
trembled, still unable to shake the image of Desdemona
with Jake, and then hurried to the bathroom. Shedding
the pyjama bottoms, showering again and then donning
fresh nightwear, he skulked back to the bedroom and
strained his ears to hear any sound from downstairs.

Sleep stole over him as he lay alone in bed.

Seven

On Sunday morning he climbed out of bed, grabbed his
jogging suit and trainers and fled from the house before
properly waking up. The exercise was part of his weekly
routine and he never dared question its benefits. An
extra minute in bed and he knew he would find an
excuse to demur. Any time spent thinking in those first
few seconds would be long enough for his mind to find
a plausible reason not to jog.

He took a familiar route, away from the urban utopia
of neatly groomed semis, towards the local park. Two
circuits around the tree-lined paths, and an annoying
encounter with a lump of dogshit, all accumulated to
leave him sweated, shaking and vowing to avoid the
exercise in future. He staggered back home, taking the
circuitous route past the newsagent's so that he could
pick up a handful of Sundays with which to while away
the day.

Jake's TVR was still parked in the driveway.

Edwin scowled. He hadn't noticed it on the way out.
He hadn't noticed anything much from leaving the
house until he slid on the vast clump of dogshit. He
contemplated scratching the TVR with one of the few
coins left in his tracksuit pants, and then decided that
would be unjustified. He also thought it might be more
physically rewarding if he simply kicked one of the
lights out or landed his foot hard enough against a door
panel so that it bent inwards. But, after the exertion of

the jog, he didn't really believe he had the strength to inflict much damage on the motor. He walked past the vehicle, aware his thoughts of vandalism were as impotent as so many other aspects of his life.

Did the TVR mean that Jake had stayed the night? Or had he been too drunk to drive and sensibly called a taxi to take him home? Edwin could picture Desdemona offering Jake the use of their spare bedroom. Too easily, he could picture her offering him more than that. Racking his brains, suddenly sickened by a thought, he couldn't remember if Desdemona had been by his side when he crawled out of bed. Always considerate, and anxious not to disturb her, he had dressed in his tracksuit without turning the lights on. But he had been so sleepy he couldn't recall if she'd been in their marital bed. He strained with the effort of trying to remember but the detail remained elusive. Letting himself back into the house, keeping his footsteps quiet for fear of waking Desdemona, his heart hammered more ferociously than it had while he was running his fastest lap around the park.

'Eddie! You're an early riser, aren't you? I never had you down for a jogger.' Jake sat in the kitchen, a mug of coffee in both hands as he blew at the scalding contents.

Edwin stared at him, realising the bathrobe Jake wore was one of his own. On the table, resting on its side, lay the empty bottle of cognac. *'You've had my food, my brandy and my bathrobe,'* Edwin reflected. *'What else have you had, Jake?'*

'You stayed the night,' he said numbly. Without waiting for a reply he went to the kettle to make himself a drink. Ordinarily he had either orange juice or mineral water after jogging but right now he felt in dire need of a caffeine fix.

'It was late. I was pissed. Dezzie insisted.'

Dezzie.

Edwin glanced at him. Jake looked weary but not suffering too greatly after a night of too much brandy.

His hair was dishevelled. There was a red mark against his neck just beneath the jaw line. Edwin wondered if it might be lipstick. He crushed the thought. Assessing Jake, noticing the front of the bathrobe was open; he saw the mat of dark curls that covered the man's chest. Equally thick hairs were apparent on his bare arms and legs.

'Is there an *Indie* in there?' Jake asked, pointing to the pile of newspapers Edwin had placed on the table.

'Probably,' Edwin said, mildly peeved that Jake had chosen his favourite of the Sunday papers. He said nothing more, listening to the rustle of Jake opening a newspaper until the sound was drowned out by the boiling of the kettle. Once he had poured himself a coffee he sat at the opposite side of the table and contemplated saying something polite.

'*Did you fuck my wife last night?*'

The words almost came out before he could choke them back. Trying to distance himself from making such a horrendous accusation, not wanting to take the conversation down the plummeting incline of that particular cul-de-sac, Edwin retrieved the new mobile phone from his pocket and began to examine its features.

The silence in the kitchen was oppressive. Edwin's phone beeped and chirruped occasionally as he pressed unfamiliar buttons and discovered how to make a video call, how to take photographs and how to use a variety of other features and functions. He immersed himself in the study of the phone, ignoring Jake and not allowing his thoughts to sidetrack him with queries about where Desdemona had spent the night and what she might have done with their houseguest. He was still thirsty when he finished his coffee so he put the phone aside and went to make himself another drink.

'I wouldn't say no to another cuppa,' Jake said. He spoke from behind the *Independent on Sunday*. His dark gaze studied the interior pages. 'And either some cereal or toast if you've got some.'

Edwin bristled. Without giving a response he snatched Jake's empty mug from the table. Because the man had looked like he was enjoying the coffee, Edwin poured him a cup of tea. Finding a bowl, and one of Desdemona's packets of muesli, he dashed a generous helping of the dusty cereal into a bowl and then slammed it in front of Jake. Without waiting for a response he found a spoon and a carton of milk and placed them by the side of the bowl.

'Perfect,' Jake said. He folded the paper and put it by the side of his breakfast. 'Dezzie and I didn't disturb you last night, did we?'

Edwin shrugged. 'I slept like a log.' Sensing Jake was now in the mood to converse while he ate, Edwin left his coffee to cool by the sink and took Jake's used teabag to the bin. He could see empty beer cans inside and rolled his eyes with exasperation. Cans and bottles were meant to go directly into the blue recycle bin: not be lumped in with the regular unrecyclable waste. He began to fish out the six empty cans and then found himself studying the rubbish in a surreptitious hunt for empty condom packets.

It was a foolish way to spend his time, he thought. But, as much as he didn't want to be looking at the contents of the rubbish bin, he couldn't drag his gaze from the melange of packets, peelings and general crap that lay beneath the empty cans. There were no condom wrappers visible but that non-discovery did nothing to put his mind at ease. The absence of condom wrappers either meant nothing had happened, or Jay and Dezzie had found somewhere else to hide the evidence, or they had fucked and not used condoms. From out of nowhere he recalled that the word 'bareback' was the common term for sex without condoms. It made him think of horses and riders and Desdemona's deliberate attempts at flirtation with Jake the previous evening. '*A dark horse in need of a rider?*' He clenched his jaw closed, sure a groan would escape if he didn't make every effort to keep the sound contained.

'You OK there, Eddie?'

'Recycle bins,' he grumbled, heading out to the bins and dropping the empty tins noisily inside. He returned to the kitchen, found the brandy bottle and then took that out to the same bin. For once the nuisance of having to categorise and file his rubbish was a blessing. It kept him away from Jake's unwanted conversational gambits. He remained by the side of the bins in the back garden, reluctant to go back into the house, but knowing it had to be done. Taking a deep breath and steeling himself for the chore, Edwin returned to the kitchen and almost screamed.

Desdemona stood in the kitchen next to the kettle.

She wore a pale satin robe that hugged her body like a second skin. Her long bare legs were visible, almost up to the cheeks of her backside. The satin cord around her waist was cinched tight. When she turned to face Edwin, he could see that it was open enough to expose a vast amount of cleavage. She looked groggy, as though she had not coped with the cognac as effortlessly as Jake. But otherwise she was his beautiful young wife. Nearly naked in the kitchen with his boss.

Jake grinned at her. His smile was an appreciative leer.

'How you feeling this morning, Dezzie?'

'Like shit. Are you always this chipper on a morning?'

'Usually I'm more chipper,' he laughed. 'But since you screwed me up to twenty-four grand for those paintings, I'm a little muted compared to my usual chipper morning personality.'

'. . . *you screwed me* . . .'

The words resounded through Edwin's mind again and again.

'. . . *you screwed me* . . . *you screwed me* . . . *you screwed me* . . .'

He knew they were discussing money and the payment for the landscapes. It sounded as if the price had changed from their original agreement of the previous day. He knew he should have been pleased Desdemona had negotiated a decent price for her artwork. But the logic of those thoughts was pushed aside by the hatefully repeated refrain.

'. . . *you screwed me . . . you screwed me . . . you screwed me . . .*'

She turned away from the kettle with a teaspoon and a mug in her hand. The movement was so swift that her skimpy robe came close to opening. Edwin bit back a startled cry when he thought one of her breasts was about to expose itself to Jake.

'Do you want a drink, Jay?'

'Eddie's sorted out my drinks, breakfast and morning paper,' Jake declared. 'One day he's going to make someone a lovely little wife.'

They both laughed at Jake's wit.

Edwin enjoyed a brief mental image of clubbing the fucker to death.

'You've been for your run?' Desdemona asked, finally glancing at him. She looked tired. Her sapphire eyes were dulled by the pink tinge that darkened the whites. He could also see she was studying him with brief concern, as though trying to assess if something was troubling him.

'I've done my run. I was thinking of getting in the shower.'

She shrugged as though the matter was of no importance. As though his presence was of no importance. Moving across the kitchen with a lithe grace that made him feel ill with need for her, Desdemona slid easily into the chair facing Jake's. Her legs were boldly displayed when she sat down. Although the edge of the table covered her lap, Edwin wouldn't have been surprised to discover she was not wearing panties. The satin had certainly clung to her buttocks as though it was hugging bare flesh. He wondered if Jake had noticed her state of undress. On top of that thought, he wondered if Jake was unaffected by the experience because he had already witnessed so much more of Desdemona's nudity.

'Have you got half an hour to confirm the landscape locations, Jay?' Desdemona asked. 'If we do that now I can build up an itinerary and give you a rough idea how long it will take to complete the project.'

'Good idea,' Jake agreed. 'Eddie? Will you get me a pen and paper before you grab that shower? This is going to be easier if Dezzie and I can take notes.'

Edwin shivered. His thoughts were blackened by hate and anger. He didn't know what to make of the way Desdemona was dressed other than drawing the most obvious conclusion. His breathing was ragged as he forced himself to stay calm and consider every option before he vented his anger.

One day he's going to make someone a lovely little wife.

Realising Jake now expected a pen and some paper, Edwin found his briefcase in the coat-cupboard and retrieved a notepad and a Parker fountain pen. He placed them firmly on the table and was ignored by both Desdemona and Jake. His throat was parched and he longed for another coffee but it was intolerable to remain unwanted and unacknowledged in the same room as his wife and their houseguest.

'I like your idea of doing landscapes local to our regional offices,' Jake told Desdemona. 'That will give the theme of the paintings some relevance.'

'And you can use that conversational lead to sell your company more subtly to visitors and customers,' Desdemona added. They both leant over the table, their heads almost touching. They sat so close it was easy to imagine their feet beneath the table were involved in a sly game of footsie. Jake was doodling something on the pad when Desdemona plucked the fountain pen from between his fingers to write something beneath the title he had put on the page. Her fingers curled easily around the length and slipped it from his fingers. His smile inched wider and he studied her with an expression that was virtually a leer. Edwin watched Jake's gaze flicker towards the indecent amount of décolletage that Desdemona displayed.

'I'm having a full refurbishment beginning on Monday,' Jake went on. 'The whole thing's going to take the best part of a month. Maybe two. Your paintings will be the cherry on the top of that particular cake. How soon can you have them ready?'

'Seven months.'

'You're kidding?'

'That's if I can get all twelve completed within a month. I'll want to varnish the surfaces once they're dry, so you've got artwork your company can treasure forever.'

'But seven months?' He sounded incredulous. 'Can't you reduce that? For me?'

Desdemona shrugged. 'I could use a couple of the faster drying linseed mixes. But they don't always produce the colours I expect.'

Unnoticed, Edwin slipped from the room.

He went to the shower after snatching jeans and a sweatshirt for the day and stood beneath a frigid rain as he tried to get his thoughts in order. Had Desdemona and Jake done more than spend a night drinking together? Was he seeing proof of her unfaithfulness where there wasn't any? Was he being obtuse and overlooking obvious signs because he couldn't face the truth? The questions bombarded him harder than the cold water.

He took his time in the bathroom, shampooing, shaving and doing every possible thing he could to avoid having to go downstairs again. When he felt as though he had spent an embarrassingly long time away from the pair he finally unlocked the door and dared to face them.

Desdemona sat alone at the kitchen table flicking through a copy of the *Observer*. She had a mug of coffee in one hand and offered to make him a drink when he appeared.

'Where's our guest?'

'Gone home.'

'I thought he'd taken up residence.'

'He was fun. I didn't think he overstayed his welcome.'

Edwin said nothing and made his own drink. Desdemona's words rang hollowly in his ears. It suddenly crossed his mind that she might have extended an invitation for Jake to return again that evening. The idea was too horrible to contemplate and he spoke without glancing at her. 'Are we going to The Horn tonight?'

'The Horn? What on earth for?'

'Robin called me at the office yesterday and asked if we were going to the quiz night. I thought it might be something fun and different for us to do. I meant to tell you last night but what with . . .'

His voice trailed off. He didn't know how to finish the sentence. It was difficult to say Jake's name without grimacing in disgust. He could see that Desdemona liked the bastard, which made it more awkward to refer to him in a politic manner.

'The Horn might be fun,' Desdemona allowed. 'Although I can't see I'll be any good at a quiz night. You know how hopeless I am at giving answers.'

Yes, he thought quietly. Desdemona only seemed able to evoke an endless supply of questions: never any answers.

Eight

The A-Frame blackboard outside The Horn said 'THE FUN' would begin at 8.00 p.m. However, by 8.32 according to Edwin's watch, the bustling pub showed few signs of bursting into life with the advertised quiz night. The fun had never seemed further away. The air was rich with the flavour of beer and tobacco. Laughter, music and the growl of conversation bubbled around the table he shared with Desdemona. But it never quite touched them. The silence they shared seemed perverse against a backdrop of such friendly noise and he wondered why they weren't conversing. Admittedly Desdemona had never shown a great interest in pubs but he couldn't recall ever sitting in such a stilted awkwardness with his wife.

Yet Edwin couldn't bring himself to say anything to start a conversation. Every time an idea came into his mind he saw it was either an attempt to ask her what she had done with Jake Mathers or a shallow excuse to avoid that unpleasant topic. In his heart, he didn't want to indulge in either type of exchange. He glanced down at his barely touched pint and tried to remind himself why he had bothered coming to the damned pub. Remembering the reason, he realised it had been a direct ploy to avoid Jake Mathers. After taking a reluctant sip at the drink, he stared around the room and saw a woman near the dartboard who seemed vaguely familiar.

75

Trying to put a name to the face, he struggled to recall who she was.

He visited his brother's pub so rarely he felt sure he must know her either from the office or somewhere else related to his work. It was only when he caught a glimpse of her short skirt that he saw she was the woman who had been illicitly fucking another man in The Horn's car park on Friday night. The memory of that sight made him look away quickly as he blushed. She had stood with her hands against the wall while taking her boyfriend from behind. Had he just been entering her vagina from that position? Or had he been plundering her anus? Edwin shied from those questions, not sure why they had occurred to him. Appalled his thoughts could be so coarse and vulgar. However, it was a relief to think about something other than the worries that had plagued his mind throughout the day. He slyly studied the woman as he pretended to inspect the quiz's potential competition.

A couple entered the pub: a tall man and a portly young woman. He had his arm around her shoulder. She fumbled through the contents of a pathetically childish purse. They were dressed like the uniformed majority in The Horn: jeans, wash-weary sweatshirts, trainers and jackets similar to the rag of a shell Edwin wore for jogging. Edwin recognised the tall man as the other half of the illicit couple he had watched on Friday night. The tall man walked casually past the tables towards the bar. Still embracing his plump girlfriend, he nodded a cordial greeting to his covert lover.

She smiled coolly but said nothing.

Edwin marvelled that the pair could be so indifferent to each other inside the pub and so eager and passionate outside. The innocence of the woman's deceptively cool smile was an impressive feat of clandestine greeting. The eyes were bright but defied all trace of pleasure: only acknowledgement. The lips were held perfectly still and it was only with concentration that Edwin could discern the strict muscle control involved in creating that seemingly innocent and innocuous greeting.

'You're not thinking of playing darts, are you, Eddie?'

He glanced at the dartboard behind the object of his interest and then turned to grin at Desdemona. 'Not the way I throw darts. It wouldn't surprise me if Robin had written my name in the Health and Safety guidelines when it mentions the dartboard.'

She laughed. The sound made him forget so many of his worries and fears. As long as they were able to laugh together he figured their relationship would be able to weather any other storm regardless of how dark it became. Desdemona was his wife. She loved him as much as he loved her. Her infidelities were almost certainly the product of his overactive imagination and he was going to spoil the beautiful thing they had unless he got a grip of his paranoia. Remembering he had left a reminder on his desk – a memo that would prompt him to book a doctor's appointment – he decided that spending some time with his GP would probably be the most sensible course of action. It could prove the thing that saved both his marriage and his sanity. When he took another sip of his pint it was almost as though he was drinking to celebrate the change in his outlook.

'Ed?'

He looked up sharply as Robin approached.

Desdemona flashed Robin a cool smile. Her dark-blue eyes were bright but showed no pleasure at the greeting: only acknowledgement. Her crimson lips were held perfectly still in a seemingly innocent and innocuous greeting.

Edwin's stomach churned. The smile was an exact replica of the deceptive one he had witnessed moments earlier. Was Desdemona having an affair with Robin? Was that who she had been screwing? Had his fears about Jake been nothing more than a misdirection for the day? He slapped himself hard on the thigh, pounding the heel of his palm into the muscle. The pain made him flinch. The jolt was supposed to shift his thoughts away from their licentious route. Instead it only brought puzzled and enquiring looks from Desdemona and Robin.

'Ed? You OK?'

'Is everything all right, Eddie?'

He pretended he had suffered a cramp. Explained he wasn't used to such low seats. Robin told him he was getting old. Desdemona regarded him suspiciously. Her expression was almost enough to have him giggling with hysterical mirth. *Desdemona with the used condom wrappers, crudely completed crosswords and her adulterer's smile was regarding him suspiciously*. He wouldn't let his thoughts return to the subject for fear that he might start braying lunatic guffaws into her face. Hurriedly, he gulped down another mouthful of beer.

'Did I give you the number for my new mobile?' Robin asked. He flipped open a shiny new handset. 'Can't remember if I told you.'

'Popular model,' Edwin marvelled. 'That's the same type Des got for me and her.'

Robin nodded. 'Yeah. We picked them up at the same time. A couple of Scousers came in here last Friday and . . .' His voice trailed off and Edwin realised his brother was staring uncomfortably at Desdemona. From the corner of his eye Edwin realised his wife had been shaking her head. Forming her lips into a shushing gesture. The stilted silence between the three of them was momentarily so intense it bordered on being painful.

'Is Alice working behind the bar tonight?' Desdemona asked.

'Just making herself pretty to host the quiz night.' He glanced at his watch, as though looking for an excuse to flee. 'Probably why we're half an hour late before we've begun.'

Desdemona sniffed. 'You're a sexist pig, Rob.'

He laughed. 'You wouldn't want me any other way.'

An agonising feedback whine interrupted the uncomfortable conversation and Alice's soft-spoken voice bellowed shrilly around the pub. 'GOOD EVENING EVERYONE AND WELCOME TO THE HORN'S SUNDAY NIGHT QUIZ NIGHT.' The noise was so high-pitched and intense Edwin feared glasses were about to shatter. The echo thundered through his skull at a volume that drowned out every other sound. It was loud enough to be inescapable.

'. . . the fucking PA down!' Robin exclaimed. His words became audible as the volume subsided. Sighing heavily, apologising that he was needed elsewhere, he hurried off to join the barmaid twiddling with the control knobs for the sound system. Watching him go, Edwin got the impression his brother was thankful for the excuse to leave their table and return to his sanctuary on the other side of the bar.

Alice was a short but stocky woman. Pretty in a way that made Edwin think she was trying too hard. Too much makeup and a dress that might have suited either a woman two sizes smaller or one a few years younger. Edwin listened as she reintroduced the quiz night at a more acceptable volume. He quietly berated himself for being so unkind to Alice. Alice was always cheerful and tolerated her life alongside Robin with saintly grace. She set out the rules for the quiz night as though instructing retarded chimpanzees. Conversation in the pub fell to a muted babble.

'What was wrong before?' Desdemona hissed. 'When you smacked your leg? Why did you do that?'

'DVT,' he said quickly. 'Like on aeroplanes. Only caused by sitting on a crappy pub stool designed for an agile dwarf. My knees are up to my chin here.' The reply sounded glib but he couldn't retract it once it had been said. He flexed a smile that felt insincere and out of place. It dwindled beneath her nonplussed stare.

'We need to talk, don't we?'

Her voice was painfully serious. There was no trace of amusement in her frown. For an instant it felt as though the entire world had fallen silent. There was a nanosecond in the pub where no one spoke. All Edwin could hear was the distant swirl of the mechanical pot-washer sluicing glasses clean. The sound he had heard behind Robin's conversation on Saturday. The same sound he had heard when he spoke to Desdemona.

'Eddie? Don't you think I'm right? We need to talk? Yes?'

He shook his head to clear his thoughts. Bring himself back to the conversation. 'Why do you say that?'

'Something's troubling you. There's something on your mind. You've been out of sorts for a while now. But it's been getting worse over the past couple of weeks. You've been acting . . . You've been different. I suppose there's something I should have told you a while ago too. I think we need a heart-to-heart when we get home.'

He blushed and took a swig of beer that he didn't want to taste. She was offering him an opportunity to air his suspicions. He would have a chance to hear all her explanations for those million trivialities that had made his life unbearable. Intolerable. A living hell. He wondered what it was she should have told him a while ago.

'Yeah,' he agreed quickly. 'We should talk.'

'I love you.' She said the words suddenly. Reaching across the table she squeezed his hand. Her features were earnest and too solemn for the beery levity of the pub. 'You know that, don't you? You know I love you?' It was almost as though she wore a pained grimace. Her fingers were talons that clutched him with surprising force.

Edwin clasped the hand that held him and nodded. The intensity of her declaration was powerful and frightening. But he knew it was entirely genuine. 'I know you love me. I never doubt it.' He had the grace to blush when he said the last sentence but Desdemona's eyes were shining and he was sure she hadn't noticed. 'I know you love me. I love you.'

'That's very romantic, Eddie,' Alice called. 'But can you two do your love scene a little more quietly while we're playing the quiz?'

For the first time he noticed the pub was still. Too many eyes stared in their direction. It reminded him of the moment in so many westerns when the cowboy pushes his way into a saloon and all the locals fall quiet and glare ominously. His cheeks turned crimson. One glance at Desdemona and he saw she was also embarrassed by the attention. She pulled her hands from his and clutched her drink.

'You'll miss out on the questions.' Alice spoke with cheery condescension. 'And this is your specialist subject, Eddie. We've started off with boy bands.'

Laughter rippled through the pub. The hostile gazes drifted away from Eddie and Desdemona but that did nothing to lift the weight of his embarrassment. He tried to concentrate on the questions when Alice recommenced but it was a load of facile shit about Justin Timberlake, Take That and G4. He tried to feign interest, ultimately hoping Desdemona wouldn't think the night was dull, but his involvement quickly felt strained and pointless. And he couldn't shake the idea that something might be happening between his wife and his brother. He tried to tell himself that it was merely his paranoia returned and overactive. As usual. But there had been something in the way they spoke to each other that made him sure they were keeping a secret and he wondered if that was what had prompted her to suggest a 'heart-to-heart' when they got home.

Robin had known about Desdemona purchasing the mobiles. He had come close to saying they bought them from the same place at the same time. And he had mentioned something about Scousers in the pub, as though it was related to the subject. Yet Desdemona seldom went to The Horn, and never without Edwin. The idea she had bought the phone from some dodgy salesman at the same time Robin acquired his was unfeasible. He couldn't make it settle inside his mind. Until he recalled the sound of the mechanical pot-washer. The background noise to both conversations. As though the pair were speaking from the same location. His suspicions had been raised at the time (although he conceded his suspicions were constantly raised) but there had been something incredibly similar in both phone calls and he wondered if he had heard genuine signs that Robin and Desdemona might be . . .

'I'm going to the ladies',' she said.

Her words interrupted his thoughts before they could condemn her with another imagined treachery. Edwin nodded and raised his gaze from the notepad where he was writing his answers to Alice's irritating questions. He was tired of the bloody quiz, fed up with the atmosphere of the pub, and wished they were back home and having the heart-to-heart they so desperately needed.

'. . . *there's something I should have told you a while ago . . .*'

His thoughts were repeatedly accusing Desdemona of all manner of perfidy. His paranoia had been particularly active this evening. Watching her leave the table, he suddenly saw his fears were completely unfounded. If Desdemona had visited The Horn more frequently she would have known where the ladies' toilets were located. Watching her go to the main doors, as though she were heading outside the pub, Edwin decided his wife couldn't possibly be a regular patron of The Horn otherwise she would have known the toilets weren't in that direction.

He glanced around the wary silence of the pub, anxious to catch Robin's gaze so he could pass him a manly grin that marvelled at the idiosyncrasies of women. Her need to visit the loo while Alice was reading the quiz night's questions, and her mistake in going the wrong way, were comical enough to make him smile. When he couldn't see his brother, Edwin went back to struggling with Alice's new category of (surprise, surprise) girl bands. He was quietly relieved that another of his paranoid fantasies had been shown as an uncalled-for assassination of his wife's faultless character.

Ten minutes later, when Desdemona returned, Edwin smiled for her.

'How are we doing with the questions?' she asked.

'I don't think we're going to take home the trophy.'

'Damn,' she muttered. 'And that tacky piece of plastic crap would have looked perfect alongside the Dresden.'

He broadened his grin as he looked at her. For the first time that evening he noticed her blouse was inside out. Had it been inside out when they set off for the pub? He felt sure he would have noticed a detail like that, although he was putting less and less faith in his faculties. Wouldn't Desdemona have noticed her blouse was inside out when she got ready? Or was this some new fashion he hadn't previously observed? A cursory glance around the pub told him, if this was a new trend, Desdemona was the only one bold enough to have brought it to The Horn. He noticed his brother stepping back behind the bar, as though he had just come from the kitchens. Robin's gaze was already fixed in the direction of their table and he waved a careful greeting. With all the customers busy, concentrating on the mind-numbing quiz and not buying drinks, Edwin suspected his brother had taken advantage of the quiet and gone outside for a cigarette.

The potential truth struck him like a slap across the face.

No. It was more than a potential truth. Much more than a potential truth. It was the absolute truth punching him in the nose and he wondered how he could have been so stupid and blind not to see it before.

Her hair was untidy. Nothing like the perfect style she had worn when they left for The Horn. He glanced at Desdemona's lips. She was silently shaping the words for an answer to Alice's latest question.

'What was the real name of Spice Girl, Ginger Spice?'

Edwin glared at Desdemona's mouth. There was no trace of lipstick on her mouth, even though he remembered her applying a layer of crimson before they left. An imprint of her lower lip lingered on the side of her tequila glass. But the rest of it looked to have been kissed away.

His heartbeat quickened. In his pants his erection was sudden and swollen and unbearably hard. His stomach ached as though he was going to vomit. His bowels felt heavy and ready to burst. He shifted his hand too quickly across the table and came close to knocking his pint into Desdemona's drink. The clatter of glasses connecting brought stern glances in his direction. Then, mercifully, Alice continued to ask about an Atomic Kitten. His clumsiness was forgotten by the majority in favour of the question.

Desdemona had been fucking Robin in the car park. The thought wouldn't leave his mind.

He remembered the couple he had witnessed two nights earlier. The memory was torturously easy to recollect. It was even simpler to transpose his wife's image in the place of the young woman and Robin in the place of her lover. Edwin could picture Desdemona spread-eagled against the wall beside the kitchen. Her jeans would be round her ankles and Robin would be plunging into her from behind. It was a chilly night but, if she was determined to enjoy herself . . .

Edwin could easily see his brother tearing the blouse over Desdemona's head so that he had a chance to grope her exposed breasts. That image lingered in his mind's eye for a long time. Robin's calloused fingers, stained from too many cigarettes and not enough scrubbing, mauling and pawing at Desdemona's perfect nipples. The contrast was harsh enough to be sickening.

84

'That's all the questions for the first round,' Alice said cheerfully. 'We'll take a twenty-minute break now so you can get yourselves a fresh drink and recharge the batteries in your thinking caps.' Her words were like a command for noise. The explosion of chatter and conversation erupted around them.

'Is everything all right, Eddie?'

Instead of listening to Desdemona's concern, he turned slightly and watched a tall man head outside the pub. Wearing jeans, trainers, sweatshirt and a nondescript jacket, he looked like every other one of the pub's customers. But Edwin recognised him instantly. This was the same man he had seen fucking another man's girlfriend. As Edwin's gaze rested on the door he saw the woman in the short skirt casually saunter out. Her gait was so relaxed and unenthusiastic he didn't think anyone else in the pub would know her real intentions.

'Deceptive bitch,' he muttered.

'Excuse me?'

He glanced at Desdemona and realised she had heard his words. Shaking his head, but not truthfully able to say the words weren't directed at her, he tried to make a joke of the comment. 'I'm sorry. I think Robin's started putting alcohol in the lager.'

'We should go home,' Desdemona decided. It was another of her statements. Her lips were thin and closed. Not waiting for his approval, she snatched her purse and stood up. Edwin considered the remains of his pint and decided he couldn't face the drink. Offering his brother a short wave of farewell, noticing a frown of concern on Robin's features that he had no desire to assuage, Edwin followed Desdemona out of the pub.

They were parked at the wrong side of the building for him to be able to see the illicit couple. But their liaison was something Edwin didn't want to watch. He hurried to Desdemona's side, aware her mood was cold and strained. The journey home was made in silence. He wanted to ask if something was troubling her. Because he believed he was the injured party, he couldn't find it in himself to express concern. He punched the radio on halfway into the journey and Desdemona snapped it off immediately.

'Headache,' she said stiffly.

It was all the conversation they enjoyed until they were home. Desdemona threw off her jacket and started immediately for the stairs. Edwin stared after her as she marched up the steps, momentarily bewildered that she was leaving him alone in the hall. 'We were going to talk,' Edwin reminded her. 'In the pub we said we were going to . . .'

She had a hand over her forehead before he could say 'heart-to-heart'. When she turned to stare down at him her eyes were shaded and unreadable. Shaking her head, mixing weariness and regret in her tone, she said, 'Not tonight, Eddie. I drank too much last night and the sound of Alice's voice is still pounding in my fucking skull. Can we have this conversation another night?'

'Another night,' he repeated, and watched her climb the stairs to bed.

'Another night.'

Nine

Another day. Another Monday. The start of another week where he could torture himself with thoughts of Desdemona and her men. Edwin sat in his office, his back facing the picture of Cuckolds Lights. He stared blindly out into the car park below. He had no idea how long he'd been sitting in the same position. His telephone had rung a couple of times but, with other things on his mind, he hadn't bothered answering the calls. They probably weren't very important, he reasoned. It was only Monday. His hands rested on his lap as he stared morosely out of the window and turned his mind to more pressing matters.

What would she have said? What would he have said? Did she have a confession to make? Would she confirm his worst fears? Or was there something else? Something that might seem trivial in comparison to the idea of his wife's infidelity? Or something truly sinister that would make his worries about her fidelity laughable? Inconsequential? He squirmed in his chair, wishing he had answers for all the questions – or even just some of them. Knowing he should have learnt them last night.

A TVR convertible pulled into the car park. The paintwork gleamed silver. Its exhaust roared loud enough to shake the glass in Edwin's window. Uninterested, he glanced at the vehicle and saw three people were squeezed into the two-seater. Edwin recognised Jake. His upper lip automatically curled with disgust.

Sally sat on Jake's lap in the passenger seat of the convertible. The dark-haired girl driving the TVR (and over-gunning the engine, Edwin thought critically) was most likely the super-cool bitch Maisy.

He sighed, unable to name his mood.

Disgust? Nausea? Disdain? Envy?

Jake had clearly had a good Sunday with Maisy and Sally. Undoubtedly the three of them had all been naked and licking and sucking and fucking and writhing together in states of sweet sweaty ecstasy. Boinking one another. Edwin's thoughts were soured somewhere between revulsion and jealousy, although he would have admitted the latter emotion only on penalty of a particularly sadistic death sentence. Sally was young and reasonably attractive. From the little he had glimpsed Maisy also seemed fetching. The knowledge that the two women were happily indulging their carnal appetites with the repugnant Jake left Edwin feeling as though he had been deprived of a fantastic aspect of life. No. Not deprived: cheated.

He turned away from the window deciding resentment wasn't worth the effort. Jake might have had the pleasure of Maisy and Sally but all Edwin wanted was happiness for Desdemona and himself. His office was held in the gloom of a dreary morning but he couldn't be bothered flicking the light switch. It was more convenient to work in a semi-darkness that better suited his sombre mood.

A message on the monitor of his computer repeatedly flashed but he didn't bother glancing at it. He knew this was the reminder he had set for himself to book a doctor's appointment but he was no longer sure that was what he wanted to do. Doctors were there to treat broken bones not broken marriages. Edwin accepted he had problems but they were not something that could be fixed by a visit to his local GP. Shivering dejectedly, he glanced at the neatly stacked pile of mail that needed his attention and tried to find the enthusiasm to immerse himself in his work. The familiar equation (work = not thinking) was sufficient motivation to make him reach for the papers.

The ringtone for a mobile sounded nearby. It was a cheerful sound and hatefully jaunty. He glanced angrily at his jacket, hanging from the hook behind the door, and realised the sound was coming from there. He had remembered the ringtone as being a sharper sound – more of an alarm than a tune – and this one was far more musical. Standing up; taking the six steps necessary to reach the door; plucking the phone from his pocket: he saw he was about to accept his first video call. The prospect brought with it no excitement. It was like learning the commonplace name of a stranger. The outer screen of the phone told him Desdemona was on the other end of the line and he inwardly cringed. Normally he liked to prepare himself before he spoke to her. He loved her dearly, madly and passionately, and he didn't want to talk to her while he was feeling so dejected, low and untrusting.

But he couldn't refuse her call.

Grudgingly, he flipped the mobile open and answered. 'Hi, Des.'

'Point the camera at yourself.' Her image was pixelated and wavered in and out of focus. He looked at a head-and-shoulders portrait that showed a woman who appeared to have only recently tumbled out of bed. Blurred lips moved to pronounce words that had already fallen from the speakers. 'Point the camera at yourself, Eddie. I want to see you while we talk.'

Edwin adjusted the phone so that its tiny camera pointed at his face.

'How's that?'

Desdemona smiled. 'That's better. I can see you now.'

He blinked. He was holding a telephone in his hand that allowed him to see the woman he was talking to, and he still had less idea about her fidelity than if there had only been her voice. So much for the *Star Trek* advances in technology.

'These work pretty good, don't you think?'

'Great.'

'I'm sorry about last night.' She looked genuinely apologetic. Almost pained. He could see that much. He caught a glimpse of one shoulder and realised it was bare. Was she naked? Was she now in the habit of making telephone calls without any clothes on? That hadn't been a worry before she possessed a mobile that allowed for video messaging but now . . .

'We do need to talk,' Desdemona said quickly. 'I shouldn't have stormed off to bed like that last night.'

Had she stormed off? He wondered why he kept misreading the signs. She'd said she had a headache and he had willingly believed her. Had that been a lie? And why had she stormed off to bed? Had he done something to upset her? When he'd called the woman in the pub a deceptive bitch, had Desdemona thought he meant her? Or was she simply upset with herself? Or anxious to avoid the heart-to-heart she had suggested? The questions came with such force his head throbbed.

'Is there any chance you can get home early today?'

Out of habit he glanced at his watch. The hands stood directly at noon. He marvelled that he had been sat in his office for more than four hours and had done nothing. Slightly less impressive was the realisation that Jake was crawling into the office so late for a Monday morning. He supposed they all had their own problems. His own fears for his marriage were keeping his thoughts away from the office work. Jake's hyperactive libido and the demands of Maisy and Sally were keeping him away from his desk.

'How early would you want me home?' he asked Desdemona.

'How about now?' She followed the question with a bright, pleading smile. 'I really do think this is important.'

He shook his head. 'I can't see that happening.' When he saw her frown he added, 'I'll do what I can. But I can't promise anything.'

'We *do* need to talk, Eddie,' she told him. Again he heard the tone she had used last night in The Horn. She still loved him. He believed he could hear that much in her voice. But she was spitting the words with a furious anger that was frightening and intense. 'But it's not the sort of conversation we can have over a telephone. Not even one like this.'

'I suppose you're right,' he said quietly. He didn't agree but he couldn't argue. He wanted to talk with her. But before they had any conversation he needed to find the courage to ask a barrage of questions. He kept his features devoid of response and emotion. It crossed his mind that the video messaging was more difficult than a regular phone call because it meant lying with his face as well as his voice. Edwin wasn't sure he was particularly good at either but felt certain he wasn't capable of both. 'If I can get home earlier, I will. And we can talk.'

'I love you.' Her words came out like a desperate plea.

He clicked a button on the phone and ended the conversation. Snapping it shut, he put it back in his coat pocket and went back to his chair by the window.

What the hell did she want to talk about? Was it anything to do with his suspicions? Was she going to confess to adultery and beg forgiveness? Was she going to tell him his paranoia was making her life intolerable? It was certainly making his own unbearable. He ran his fingers through his hair, exasperated by the fact that his life was plagued by so many questions and so few answers. His gaze fluttered again around the office, searching for something that would drag his thoughts away from the constant crisis that came from brooding about his wife and marriage. The pile of mail held little interest but Edwin supposed it might prove a distraction. He was reaching for the first envelope when the phone on his desk rang.

He sighed, glanced at the computer screen and its nagging message that he should make a doctor's appointment, then plucked the phone from its cradle. His head hurt. His balls were tight with the frustration of an unspent climax. The length of his erection was an agony that perpetually throbbed. And he briefly contemplated Desdemona's suggestion that he should return home immediately. The idea of leaving the office would only have been appealing if Desdemona and her 'talk' weren't waiting for him at the other end of the journey. Before he had plucked the phone from its cradle he speculated it might be Desdemona calling him again, pressing her case that he should return. But still he lifted the telephone and waited for the caller to speak.

A male voice asked, 'Ed? That you?'

'Robin?' A call from his brother was unexpected. Unprecedented. He momentarily understood some of Robin's anxiety from Friday night. They only contacted each other in the cases of Christmas, birthdays and other dire emergencies. 'What are you calling for? Is something wrong?'

'You left early last night.'

Edwin's reply came with the smooth delivery of a well-rehearsed lie. 'Des wasn't feeling too well. She'd had a late night the night before. I guess it had taken its toll.' He waited in a moment's silence, wondering if the lie had been accepted. He was briefly thankful Robin hadn't chosen to make this call through the video messaging feature of his new phone because he felt sure his brother would be able to read more from his face.

'Des OK?'

'Yeah. Fine.' Edwin found himself listening for sounds in the background of Robin's conversation that might have been present when he spoke to Desdemona. He felt annoyed because, while looking at Desdemona's picture, he hadn't been concentrating on the background behind her. He continued trying to hear something out of the ordinary in Robin's telephone call in the hope it might trigger the memory of a memory.

'Alice thought she'd embarrassed you into leaving early.'

'No,' Edwin said quickly. *Alice just embarrassed us.* Aloud he said, 'It had nothing to do with Alice. Please tell Alice we didn't leave because of her.'

Robin chuckled without amusement. 'Much as I'd like to, I can't do that right now. Alice ain't talking to me today. She found lipstick on my cock and it's kinda hard to explain that one away.'

Whose lipstick? Edwin wondered. Movement from the corner of his eye made him glance up and he realised Jake was walking through the door of his office. He stopped himself from rolling his eyes and told Robin, 'Is there an innocent explanation?'

'There's an explanation,' Robin conceded. 'It stops being innocent as soon as I use the word blowjob.'

Jake flicked on the light in Edwin's office. The brightness was a shock and he recoiled from its brilliance. He hadn't realised the atmosphere was so dismal. Shielding his eyes with one hand, keeping the phone pressed to his ear with the other, he continued to ignore Jake as he asked, 'Why does Alice put up with you?'

'I dunno. I'd ask her if I thought it might get us talking again.'

'I've got my boss in here now, Robin,' Edwin said carefully. 'Perhaps we can talk later?'

'Just wanted to make sure you and Des were OK,' Robin assured him. 'Tell her ladyship I asked after her.'

'I will,' Edwin promised. He hung up and glanced at Jake.

Edwin didn't know how the bastard had managed it but Jake looked resplendent as usual in his ultra-sharp suit. The man had obviously spent the night (and most of the morning) with a pair of attractive and sexually adventurous young women. He had arrived late for work, holding one woman on his knee as they drove in a convertible with the top down, and Jake was still able to appear as though he was a male model from the fashion pages of *GQ* or the Freemans catalogue. His hair was styled neatly, his smile appeared even and untroubled. His complexion was perfectly unblemished.

Edwin despised him.

'I just brought this up for you to pass on to Dezzie.' Jake grinned. He presented a stiff sheet of printed paper. Edwin took a cursory glance and saw it was a list of dates and locations. 'It's a proposed itinerary for Dezzie,' Jake explained. 'I was wanting to take her round the regionals so we could find appropriate landscapes for the project she'll be working on.'

Edwin processed the information and felt ill. Jake wanted to take his wife around the country to visit their regional offices. *Jay and Dezzie, cosily ensconced in a motel faraway from Eddie.* The concept made his brow furrow. His eyes gleamed with jet-black hatred. Had they done something on Saturday night? He couldn't say for sure, although he had his suspicions. That thought made him want to laugh. He had so many suspicions. Would they do something if they were travelling around the country together? He couldn't imagine them keeping their hands off each other. The pair of them had been like hormonally charged adolescents on Saturday night. And that was when Jake was their guest and Desdemona was relaxing in her marital home with her husband nearby. If they travelled around the country together he felt certain something would happen.

A bottle of brandy each night? Games of Pennies? Strip Pennies? Or perhaps they would dispense with the juvenile excuses to get drunk and naked and simply set straight into fucking each other. Boinking each other.

'I'll see she gets it,' Edwin said dully. He put the page into his briefcase and dearly hoped Jake would piss off and leave him alone. He was in no mood to suffer the man's company and mildly anxious that he might say something offensive unless he measured every word.

Jake dropped casually into the seat facing Edwin's. His grin was filled with large over-white teeth that radiated their own light. Bloated by his own good mood, he pointed at the painting on Edwin's office wall and said, 'That's Cuckolds Lights, isn't it?'

Edwin blushed. 'I think that's what it's called.'

'Unusual name, don't you think, Eddie?'

'It's an unusual lighthouse,' Edwin countered. He could hear that his tone sounded evasive but there was little he could do about that. The message on the PC monitor continued to flash that he should book a doctor's appointment. He quickly pressed the button to cancel the silent alarm. 'I guess an unusual lighthouse would merit an unusual name.'

Jake's grin widened menacingly and he leant forward in the chair. 'I'm no expert, but I'd say it's an unusual gift from a wife. Do you think she was trying to tell you something when she gave you that painting? Do you think there's a subtle suggestion somewhere in that painting's title? Maybe the suggestion isn't even that subtle?'

'Such as?'

The silence between them lingered for an aeon. The absence of noise in the room was so intense Edwin could hear conversation from neighbouring offices. Cars on the nearby roads sighed and droned. The buzz of his office printer, resting on standby, hummed like a held breath.

Jake broke the stalemate by settling back in his chair and laughing. 'I'm sorry, Eddie,' he chuckled. 'I'm just joking with you. I had a great night on Saturday with you and Dezzie. You were a perfect host and your lady is an absolute hoot.'

'She's a hoot,' Edwin agreed. He wondered what the word meant. It was another question but this time he realised it wasn't one he would brood over. 'An absolute hoot.'

Jake didn't bother to supply an explanation. His gaze flicked back to the painting, the mischievous grin widening only briefly, and then he was leaning back across the desk. In the blink of an eye he had become a conspirator. 'I got drained again last night with Sally and Maisy,' he confided. 'Dear God, that little bitch from the switchboard really knows how to gobble cock. I've pencilled Sally in to give me a blowjob each weekday at eleven o'clock. I figure it will be healthier than a mug of coffee and a couple of custard creams. But last night, I thought she was going to suck me inside out. If Maisy hadn't fingered her to a climax I'm sure she'd have carried on until she'd taken the marrow out of my bone.'

'Thank you for sharing that image with me,' Edwin said drily.

'We had to tie her up at one point,' Jake explained. He had either missed or ignored the distaste in Edwin's voice. 'I was boinking Sally while Maisy sat on her face. It's hard to believe the things that filthy little bitch wanted us to do. She was begging Maisy to piss in her mouth and she screamed for me to shoot my wad up her . . .'

'As much as I'd love to hear all the graphic details of your weekend,' Edwin broke in quickly, 'I'm going to have to leave now.' The decision was made at the same time he said the words. Given a choice between suffering 'a talk' with Desdemona, or listening to Jake's puerile rambling about his depraved liaisons with Sally and Maisy, Edwin decided he would rather endure the more constructive embarrassment. Perhaps, he thought with rare optimism, talking with Desdemona might allay some of his fears. He brushed that consideration aside as a childish hope. But he acknowledged there was a small chance he might learn some answers to his multitude of questions.

'Leave?' Jake checked his watch and looked perplexed. 'You can't leave. It's only just turned noon.' He checked his watch again, opened his eyes wide with surprise, and added, 'Shit! It's closer to one. I didn't realise it was so late.' Glancing back at Edwin he added, 'But that's still way too early to leave, isn't it?'

'I'm not feeling well,' Eddie told him. He supposed there was a lot of truth in that statement, even if it had started as a lie. 'I'm taking the rest of the day as sick leave. You'll have to excuse me.'

'Sure thing,' Jake said easily. 'You look a little green.'

Edwin felt certain he didn't look green to any degree but he didn't bother arguing the point. He eased himself purposefully from his chair and closed down his PC.

'Do you need a lift home?'

'I should be able to manage the drive.'

'Are you sure? Maisy's borrowed the TVR today. She needed to pick up a couple of supplies from her place. But, if you need a driver, I can always take you home in your motor and have Dezzie give me a lift back here.'

Edwin considered that option for a nanosecond. He pictured Dezzie and Jay in his car, parked in a lay-by, or driving round to Jake's house to meet up with the insatiable Maisy. He clutched his stomach and put a hand over his mouth to suppress the urge to vomit. Shaking his head, and regaining a little composure, he said firmly, 'I'll manage the drive home. But thank you for your kind offer.' He walked past Jake and took his jacket from the back of the door.

'You sure you're going to be OK, Eddie? Do you think you'll be back in tomorrow?' Jake's concern seemed frustratingly genuine. Because of it, Edwin wanted to poke him in the eyes or punch him in the throat.

'I *will* be back in tomorrow,' he said quietly. 'I just need to go home and rest today.' He didn't bother saying anything else before walking out of the office and hurrying to his car.

He drove quickly but safely away from the office, anxious to get back to Desdemona and eager to have the conversation that might predicate an end to the problems that threatened their marriage and his sanity. He made a terse call to his wife, informing her he was on his way back. But he didn't allow himself the chance to listen to her response. Every time he heard Desdemona's voice he found himself listening for indications of untruths, infidelity and dishonesty. He wasn't going to torture himself with those thoughts any more, even if that meant making his phone calls short to the point of blatant rudeness. Parking in the driveway, slamming his car door shut and staggering angrily towards the house, Edwin glanced up at their open bedroom window above the front door.

The curtains were drawn. As he stood on the front step, directly beneath the bedroom window, he heard a sigh coming from inside. The sound was familiar to him as Desdemona's voice but it was made foreign by an undercurrent of sexual arousal. It was the breathy exclamation of a woman nearing the peak of orgasm.

Edwin groaned.

Slipping his key quietly into the lock, stealthily stepping inside without making a sound, he gingerly closed the door and glanced up the stairs. The sounds of Desdemona's ecstasy were louder now. He climbed the stairs quickly but silently. None of the steps creaked as he ascended and he was careful to tread only on the thickest parts of the pile. His breathing had lowered to an expectant hush. He didn't want to contemplate what he might find when he arrived at the bedroom but it was impossible not to speculate.

Desdemona's cries sounded like she was in the throes of pleasure but he supposed that interpretation could be subjective. She could simply be panting from exertion as she rearranged the room's fixtures. He remembered she had recently said the wardrobe should be on a different wall and he conceded her gasps could derive from the effort of dragging the huge piece of furniture from one side of the room to the other. A pathetic flicker of hope begged that the explanation was so mundane.

'That's it,' Desdemona cried. 'Christ! That's perfect.'

Her voice was low and lewd.

He climbed another two steps.

Although it was the middle of the afternoon the lighting in the house reminded him of twilight. He supposed that was because of the drawn curtains at the bedroom window but it made him think he had slipped into some eerie dimension where he was out of place and in the wrong time zone.

The open bedroom door loomed into sight. Even if she wasn't shifting furniture; even if there was a coarse sexuality to her tone; Edwin told himself that didn't mean she was being unfaithful. Desdemona could be masturbating. She was an attractive young woman and, sexually, he was well aware that her husband wasn't satisfying her needs. It was perfectly feasible that she spent some time each day taking care of her body's basic urges. Grandly, he conceded that anything less would be unhealthy.

The thought made him hesitate. If Desdemona were masturbating wouldn't she be embarrassed if her husband rudely stumbled in on her and intruded? He considered the idea of creeping back down the stairs and making an elaborate show of slamming the door to alert her to his arrival. He could even call up the stairs and shout, 'Des! I'm home!' as a clear warning that he had returned.

'Now tongue me deeper, you fucker.'

For an instant he thought his heart had stopped working. Her words were whispered in a sultry demand he barely recognised. If she were innocently masturbating (was it possible to innocently masturbate? wasn't masturbation always a sin?) would she talk while she was doing it? Were her eyes closed as she indulged herself in a fantasy of imagination? Was she giving instructions to the obscenely pink vibrator she kept hidden in her underwear drawer? That idea made no sense and he brushed it from his thoughts as his heart began to pound again. His lungs snatched stale and bitter air from the twilight gloom.

With two more painfully silent steps he stood on the landing.

'You're very good at that,' Desdemona giggled. Her voice wafted gently from the open door of the bedroom. 'Should I give you a reward now? Do you want me to suck it a little more?'

He pushed open the door, telling himself there would be an innocent explanation for all that he had heard. He couldn't imagine what that innocent explanation might be, but he felt sure there would be one. The memory of Robin's words clanged at the back of his mind: *'There's an explanation. But it stops being innocent as soon as I use the word blowjob.'*

Desdemona was dressed in lingerie he had never seen before. The red bra, panties, suspender belt and stockings made her look like a high-class whore. He conceded the underwear was pretty – black lace decorated the edges of the bra and panties – but it still made him think of pornographic movies and commercial allusions to paid-for-sex. Her blonde hair was tousled but only lightly out of place and he could see her face as she stared at him. She wore crimson lipstick and jet-black mascara and her cheeks were brightly rouged.

Her mouth was wrapped around an erection.

He didn't recognise the man underneath her, although all he could properly see were a pair of hairy legs and the rude pink cock that disappeared in his wife's mouth. The remainder of the man was underneath Desdemona and hidden from his view. He got the impression of a pair of large hands, holding Desdemona's buttocks apart and peeling the gusset of her panties aside so that he could get his tongue into her pussy. But at that point he supposed the man's identity was immaterial. It was sufficient for Edwin to think of him as the man with his cock in Desdemona's mouth.

Desdemona's ripe lips slipped further down the erection. The contrast of her scarlet mouth against the slick wet flesh of the cock was shocking. More startling was the way she continued to stare at Edwin as she sucked the man beneath her. The pleasure in her smile was enough to make him recoil. It took an effort not to stagger backwards. When she moved her mouth away from the swollen thickness he could see her lips were glossed with pre-come.

That's the same mouth I kiss every day, he marvelled. The thought brought him close to a premature climax. He felt his jaw work uselessly for a moment as he struggled to say something. Words refused to come and he couldn't imagine what they would be if he managed to break the speech barrier.

'Wait for me downstairs in the kitchen,' Desdemona told him.

Edwin gaped.

'Wait for me downstairs in the kitchen,' she repeated. 'I'll be finished in here soon enough.' Without waiting to see if he obeyed, she put her mouth back around the cock she had been sucking.

Obediently Edwin staggered out of the bedroom and stumbled down the stairs. It was impossible to think because he couldn't shift the image of Desdemona sucking the stranger. She was dressed like a prostitute, using their marital bed to have her pussy licked while she sucked another man's cock. It was the realisation of his every fear but he couldn't think his way through the ramifications of the discovery. All he could do was remember the image and repeatedly catch himself on the point of ejaculation.

He collapsed in one of the kitchen chairs, panting and gasping. His hands were balled into fists and he sat stupefied and alone. He heard the bed shake from above. The metal springs and hinges creaked in a vigorous and startling cacophony of action. Desdemona cried out, her screams echoing noisily down to reach him.

She wailed with satisfaction, 'Christ! Yes! Yes!'

And then.

'No! No, you bastard! Don't come in there! I want to do *this*.'

There was a moment's silence.

And then Edwin heard the grunt of a man exclaiming.

He closed his eyes and only allowed himself to see black. He wouldn't let his mind present a picture of the man thrusting into her. The erection had been thick – far thicker than his own meagre length – and he didn't want to think of that monster pushing between the slender lips of his wife's labia. He kept the vision of black at the forefront of his gaze as he listened to the mumble of a faraway conversation and then the heavy booted footsteps of a stranger ambling down the stairs. The front door opened and he heard the faraway sounds of traffic, birdsong and a midday breeze.

'See you next Monday?'

'You know you will. Thanks for that, sweetie. You brightened up my day. I think you've been practising.'

Edwin pushed the air from his lungs in a long and heavy sigh. He listened to the sound of a parting kiss and then heard the clip of Desdemona's heels as she walked briskly to join him in the kitchen. He was quietly amazed that she could walk as though the world hadn't just collapsed around them. He was even more astonished when she spoke to him and her voice was cheerful and friendly.

'You could have put the kettle on, Eddie.' Desdemona grinned as she breezed into the kitchen. 'I'm gasping for a cuppa.'

She was still dressed like a whore and wore the clothes as though they were a natural part of her ensemble. Again he noticed that they looked exceptionally good on her. Her legs were long and shapely and made enticing by the garish red stockings. The bra accentuated her breasts to maximum effect. The panties were delicate, despite their bold colours. He could see the crotch was darkened by moisture. The sight made him quiver. When she turned her back to him as she filled the kettle he saw that the full panel at the back of the panties lay uneven, exposing her left buttock and

102

concealing her right. He remembered the man beneath Desdemona had been holding the panties aside as he buried his face against her pussy. Edwin wondered if the panties had remained on while the pair of them fucked. He didn't know why he was contemplating such an insignificant detail. It just seemed there was something perverse and arousing about the notion of his wife having sex while she still wore her underwear.

'Do you want a tea or a coffee?' Desdemona asked cheerfully.

'I think I need something stronger.'

'Don't be so melodramatic,' she laughed. 'If you're in shock I'll do you a hot, sweet tea. It's far too early in the day to be hitting the bottle.'

Edwin wanted to tell her it was far too early in the day for doing lots of things, but she clearly had no qualms about breaking some rules of propriety. Inside his head the retort sounded pompous and supercilious. Aware that this was not the time to snap vicious retorts at his wife and score cheap points, he remained silent.

Moving lithely around the kitchen, looking like the embodiment of a porn star inappropriately relocated in his house, Desdemona clattered two cups onto the counter and began to make herself a coffee and a tea for Edwin. She looked as though she had stepped from the pages of some amateur pornographic production: *Sluts in Suburbia*, or *Kunts in the Kitchen*. He couldn't snatch his gaze from the sultry perfection she presented. When she sat down in the chair facing his, handing him his drink and smiling warmly, he wondered if he had finally gone mad and was now residing in a fantasy-land that was the product of his most pressing fears.

She met his gaze with a sympathetic smile. Defensively clutching the mug in both hands she confided, 'This has been the hardest year of my life.'

'What you were doing looked exhausting,' he grunted.

She put down the mug and slapped his face. Her hand moved with surprising speed and the force of the blow was sharp enough to sting. They glared at each other with defiant challenges but, even before Edwin had lowered his gaze, he knew he would be the first one to look away.

'Don't make me out like I'm the villain in this drama,' Desdemona warned. 'If you'd had a working cock in your pants I wouldn't have looked elsewhere for a little action.'

Edwin's erection hardened as she delivered the insult. Until this moment his inadequacies in the bedroom had remained an unspoken confidence. Even in their frankest and most open conversations his limited abilities were never touched upon. Their weekly appointment in the bedroom was a dull routine with boundaries that repelled the notion of discussion. Crude comments about his lack of ability and her subsequent frustration had never featured in any of their exchanges before. He didn't know how to react. And so he said nothing.

'If you hadn't kept telling me to get a lover I would never have had anyone else,' Desdemona barked. There was the suggestion of anger in her tone but he could sense she was trying to keep it on a tight rein. 'But every time we fucked you said that was what I should do. Every time you'd fulfilled all sixty seconds of your obligations, you insisted I should get a real man in the bedroom to do the job that you couldn't manage.'

'So you're telling me that you sucking that guy's cock was my fault?' He knew his voice sounded petulant but he couldn't hide the way he felt.

'If you like.' She picked up her mug of coffee and blew at its surface. It looked too hot to drink and she put it down without taking a sip. 'I'm sensing a lot of antagonism and hostility, Eddie. And I don't think you're being wholly honest with me or yourself. That's not fair because I'm being entirely honest with you.'

He contemplated her in silence. Fumes from his mug of tea wafted beneath his nose. But, even though his mouth was dry, he refused to drink. He'd just seen

Desdemona fucking and sucking another man and she had the temerity to tell him that he was the one who wasn't being honest? 'I come home to find my wife dressed like a whore and doing a sixty-nine with a stranger in our marital bed. And you're sensing antagonism and hostility? You must be psychic, Desdemona, because I never would have thought I'd be suffering either of those emotions right now.'

'Stop trying to be a man, Eddie,' she said tartly. 'It doesn't suit you.'

'What the hell does that mean?'

She held his angry glare. 'You're inadequate, Eddie. Your cock's small. It doesn't work very well. And you're never going to improve as a lover. If you can't exercise your right to fuck me properly you have no right to properly fuck me off.' Her tone rose as she spoke. It came close to cracking with the last four words.

He recoiled from the bitterness in her voice. As her anger increased his arousal heightened. The hateful length in his pants pulsed and twitched as though he was on the verge of climax. He began to perspire as a shiver of black excitement stirred in the pit of his stomach.

'You're not being honest with me or yourself,' Desdemona said again. 'Take a moment to think about what you want, Eddie. Don't say those words you think a cuckold husband should be saying. Tell me the truth as it applies to you.'

He heard the word 'cuckold' and it struck him more severely than the slap she had delivered. She had made him a cuckold. Anger, shame, resentment and fury trembled through his body. He remembered long ago reading an article about the Russian author Pushkin. The writer had been so outraged at being welcomed to the Grand Order of Cuckoldry that his anger had led him to a fatal duel. At the time Edwin had been surprised by the extreme of Pushkin's reaction. Now he marvelled the man had been so contained as to go through the formalities of organising a duel.

'Listen to me, Eddie,' Desdemona demanded. Her stern voice made him glance at her. She swam in his vision, blurred by the threat of his tears. She was a lace-trimmed mirage of harlot-red and inviting pink flesh. 'Tell me the truth as it applies to you. That's what I want to hear now.'

'I don't know what you're talking about.'

Desdemona climbed out of her chair and sat on his leg. Wordlessly he allowed her to put an arm behind his back and rest her other hand on his lap. He didn't want her to touch him. Not in this way. Not now. She had just been with another man. He had watched her sucking a stranger's cock. He wanted to defy her attempts at intimacy and let her suffer the same callous hurt and rejection that had brutally spiked him earlier. But, instead, he remained still as she made herself comfortable on his thigh. He couldn't recall the last time she had looked so desirable. He couldn't recall the last time they had sat in such an intimate position in their kitchen. The scent of her perfume and the sharper tang of another man's perspiration intertwined as he drew breath. Desdemona grabbed a fistful of hair at the back of his head. She held his face steady as she kissed him. Her lips were oily with lipstick and some other wetness he refused to contemplate. Her tongue stole into his mouth and chased intrusively over his teeth. When she pulled away he could see her eyes shone with a wet and sultry need.

'Could you taste Carl's come in my mouth?'

He groaned.

His erection thickened beneath her hand.

Desdemona's smile brightened into a gleam of hateful triumph.

'You could taste it, couldn't you?'

Edwin faltered on the verge of ejaculation. He tried to push her hand away but she continued to hold him firmly.

106

'This is what I mean when I say you're not being honest. You watched me suck another man's cock. You tasted the spunk in my mouth when I kissed you. And you won't admit the only truth that matters: *it makes your dick go hard.*'

He remembered Robin's words. *'If it don't make your dick hard, don't do it.'* He finally pushed her from his lap. Desdemona looked angry as she caught herself from falling to the floor but she resumed her seat with dignity and then sipped at her scalding coffee. The silence between them was oppressive and suffocating.

'Eddie,' she began. 'I love you and I respect you. But you're useless in bed. I've fucked other men because they give me something you can't. They give me satisfaction. Unless a miracle happens, and you're suddenly able to do something you haven't managed in the past three years, it will continue.'

He noticed her careful choice of words. They weren't lovers in her bedroom. She had 'fucked' other men. He understood she was telling him that she had no emotional commitment to any man other than him. But it was still a lot to take on board. And he couldn't marry what she was saying to a way forward in the conversation. Shouldn't she have been apologising for her disgusting behaviour and assuring him it would never happen again? Wasn't that what was supposed to happen when a husband caught his wife in bed with another man? Where was her remorse? Guilt? Contrition?

'I've chosen to let you know about this because I truly believe it's something we can share,' she sighed.

She reached across the table, as though she wanted to touch him as they spoke. He couldn't bring himself to suffer the contact, knowing that her hand had so recently been touching and stroking another man. Desdemona allowed the hand to linger between them, as though she was prepared to wait for him to respond.

'I get satisfaction from other men,' she continued. 'And I've always known you were aroused by the thought of me being unfaithful. If we can combine these two complementary attitudes, I think this will be the right way forward for us and our marriage.'

'You expect me to just tolerate the fact that you fuck other people?'

'No. I expect you to share the experience with me.' She drew a deep breath and offered him a conciliatory smile. 'I know this is a lot for you to accept, Eddie. And I'm aware that it's not conventional by anyone's standards.'

'That's a fucking understatement.'

She ignored his exclamation.

'But if this is what we both want, shouldn't we give it a try?'

He took a deep breath, ready to tell her that he couldn't live with a wife who fucked other men. He wasn't going to dress up the term with euphemisms like sleeping with others, or taking lovers or even the definitive description, cuckoldry: none of those were true. She was fucking other men. And he couldn't see how their relationship might continue as long as she was doing that. He had his pride and dignity, even if she possessed neither of those qualities, he was determined that she wouldn't make him into a laughing stock with her wayward habits and absence of morals. When he stared into her eyes and saw the naked devotion in her gaze he asked, 'How will it work?'

Ten

'We play this game by my rules,' Desdemona informed him. She had a hand in front of the bedroom door, preventing Edwin from walking in ahead of her. 'You're not allowed to speak. *You're no longer allowed to speak whenever we're in the bedroom.* Today I'm going to tie you to the bed. I'm going to tell you about my sex life. And everything stops the moment you ejaculate. If that's not acceptable say so now.'

She spoke with a crisp authority he had never heard before. Not from Desdemona. Heels made her taller, forcing him to look up to meet her eyes. The confident set of her shoulders gave her a breadth and presence he hadn't imagined. Her attitude and demeanour all suggested she was in absolute control. The challenge in her eyes bordered on daunting. He was in the presence of someone different to the woman he thought of as his wife. An unexpected spark of optimism brightened the gloom of his fears. He nurtured a moment's hope. He might enjoy getting to know this new facet of Desdemona's personality. This new Desdemona. Quickly, he tried to crush those thoughts before they swayed him with their hatefully bright outlook. How could anything possibly be all right after what he had seen today?

'OK,' Edwin agreed. His voice sounded meek. Hesitant. He cleared his throat before continuing. 'I'm no longer allowed to speak in the bedroom. And everything stops when I . . .' His voice trailed off. He didn't like to use the word ejaculate in front of Desdemona. On some level he considered it unseemly and vulgar. The other variations were even less acceptable. 'Everything stops when you say,' he concluded weakly.

Her smile was thin ice. She allowed him into the bedroom and demanded he lie down. As soon as he was in the centre of the bed she produced four sets of handcuffs and told him she was going to secure his wrists and ankles to the corners. The sheets were still rumpled. He could smell the pungent sweat of the man who had lain there before him. She had mentioned the name Carl but that meant nothing to him. He wanted to ask who Carl was but, even in these circumstances, he couldn't think of a way to voice the question. Also, she had forbidden him to speak. He didn't want to appear as though he wasn't heeding her rules. And there was the distraction of his arousal. His wife had transformed into the sultry temptress of his most lurid fantasies. She was securing him to the bed. And he had to physically battle the effects of his excitement.

She fastened his wrists with the cuffs. Edwin was still dressed but Desdemona didn't seem to think the clothes would present a handicap to what she had planned. He considered her in the dim light of the curtained room and marvelled at the sexuality she exuded. Black lace and red silk. Her lingerie was vulgar but that didn't stop it from being intrinsically exciting. She sashayed around the bedroom with a confidence he had never noticed. Numbly, Edwin realised this was now her domain. Her lips were fixed in a sultry pout. She moved as though she knew he was watching every roll of her hips. Savouring every shift of her glamorous body. When she glanced at him her expression was beguiling. Her eyes shone with a coquettish allure.

He cleared his throat. 'I think you look . . .'

'No!' Desdemona fixed him with a stern glare. She leaned over him, placed a finger over her lips, and shook her head. 'Don't speak, Eddie. I told you before. From this moment onward, you're not allowed to talk while we're in the bedroom. If you talk again whilst we're in here I'll make you spend the night in the spare room. I won't issue this warning again.'

He blinked in amazement and waited to see if she would smile to suggest she was only joking. Seeing the firm set of her mouth, he understood her threat was genuine. She was forbidding further attempts at conversation. A part of him recoiled from the idea of surrendering to such a subversive power game. Desdemona was acting like a dominatrix and using him as her submissive. The thought of participating was humiliating and degrading. But his erection grew harder under the influence of that idea. The stiffness between his legs was enough to convince him that he wasn't wholly repulsed by the prospect of being Desdemona's plaything. He forced himself to relax and endure whatever lay ahead.

'This is my bedroom.' Desdemona secured his ankles to the corners of the bed. 'I might allow you to sleep in here on nights when I'm not entertaining other men. But you can no longer come in here without my consent. You can't speak in here unless you have my express permission. Nod if you understand.'

Edwin paused for a moment. After a moment's thought he nodded.

She smiled and climbed onto the bed. Her heels punched hard into the rumpled sheets beneath him. The bed dipped with the weight of each footstep. Desdemona looked impossibly tall as she towered over him. The gusset of her panties remained dark and moist. From his viewpoint beneath her Edwin could see the shape of her sex moulded by the fabric. Remembering she had kissed him with the taste of Carl's come still in her mouth, he knew the moistness was caused only by her arousal. That understanding, and the implication that someone else's cock had pounded between her legs before she sucked it to climax, made his erection strain to the point of agony. He marvelled at the sight of her damp crotch and couldn't honestly remember seeing a more erotic sight.

'Do you want to smell my cunt?' Desdemona breathed.

He didn't know how to reply. She had forbidden him to speak but did that apply to direct questions? He could shake or nod his head, he guessed. But his mind whirled from the shock of hearing Desdemona say the forbidden C-word.

His hesitation proved unimportant because, without waiting for a reply, Desdemona squatted over his face. His world was engulfed by the sopping red crotch of her panties and the crimson side view of her stocking-clad legs. When he inhaled he could taste the chemical scent that always came with condoms. He drank the richer tang of his wife's wet sex. Her musk was a maddeningly sweet fragrance but he had never caught it so strong before. Today, *because she'd been with another man*, the perfume of her sex was overpowering.

'Do you know what you're smelling down there, Eddie?' Her voice was husky but tinged with patience. 'It's something you've never encountered before, darling. That's the smell of a satisfied cunt.'

He groaned. He could have come in that moment. He had to wipe every conscious thought from his mind as he struggled not to spoil the day and embarrass them both with his over-excitement. Desdemona lowered herself until the crotch of her panties pressed against his face. The wetness shifted over his brow, rubbed against his nose and then touched his lips and chin. A cool residue adhered to his skin. He didn't know if Desdemona expected him to kiss or lick her. But he figured she would tell him if she required any involvement other than his silent and servile adoration.

'Breathe the smell, Eddie,' she insisted. Desdemona wriggled her pelvis lower as she hissed her demand. 'Drink the smell of my cunt and understand you didn't cause this: you could never cause this.'

He gasped for air but made no attempt to pull away. He couldn't recall the last time he had been so aroused. The fact that he was sharing the experience with Desdemona only made it more satisfying. Again he realised he was close to spurting with an early climax but he resisted the urge. Concentrating on the feral fragrance of the wet crotch over his face, he breathed deeply and reminded himself he was tasting the perfume of the woman he loved.

'Don't come yet, Eddie,' she insisted. Her hands went to his belt. Although he couldn't see, he realised she was unfastening his pants. She pulled them open and released his erection with brisk and clinical efficiency. Her icy hand brushed against the fevered heat of his shaft. She worked on him with the detached air of a competent physician performing a medical examination. 'Don't you dare come yet,' Desdemona warned. 'I've got a lot to tell you but I'm not carrying on once you've come. That's the arrangement for today and you've agreed to abide by that condition.'

He said nothing, holding back his orgasm with a monumental effort of will. Her panties pressed heavily against his nose. He couldn't inhale without revelling in the rich fragrance of her wetness. It would only take the subtlest stimulation and the ejaculation was bound to explode from his shaft. Regardless of how much effort he put into holding himself back, he feared that moment of release would be on him before he had a chance to quash the impetus.

'I've been fucking Carl for the past year,' Desdemona began. 'He was the first extramarital cock I enjoyed. And, while he's not the biggest or the best, he brightens up my Mondays.'

Edwin trembled. She wasn't touching his erection but her words pushed him frighteningly close to orgasm. He suspected that she knew how strongly she was affecting him and wondered when she had grown so knowledge-able about his responses and reactions. It was hard to believe this was the same woman as the one who lay motionless beneath him each Friday night. The same woman who suffered his caresses with the absence of passion most women reserved for a smear test.

'Your cock really is pathetic,' Desdemona marvelled. 'The damned thing is so tiny and ineffectual. I bet you'd come now if I just touched it a little bit, wouldn't you?'

He wanted to tell her that she was right. And beg her not to touch him. And apologise for all his numerous inadequacies. Remembering she had forbidden him to speak in the bedroom, he simply clenched his teeth and resisted the urge to climax. His thoughts were so centred on holding back his ejaculation that it came close to being a personal vocation.

Desdemona stroked a single finger along his length. A light and sensitive caress. The threat of an eruption built in his sac and he knew he was on the verge of climaxing. She teased her finger up to his fraenum, tickling lightly beneath the rim of his glans, maddening him with the delicate whisper of her fingertip. Then she tore her hand away.

He shuddered.

Desdemona giggled.

She wriggled the crotch of her panties more firmly against his nose. 'Do you want to properly taste my pussy, Eddie? Do you want to see what my cunt looks like after I've had a proper fucking? It's another one of those things you've never seen before. I think it might be a revelation for you.'

He snatched tiny breaths into his lungs as he nodded. He suspected, regardless of how he answered, she was going to show him. There was no doubt in his mind that Desdemona now controlled the bedroom. And everything and everyone within. For some reason that thought brought an exhilaration and relief as powerful as any sexual climax he had ever endured. He was happy to submit to her authority. He was sure she had a much better idea of how to achieve satisfaction while he was

114

in the bedroom. It was the release of a burden that had always been more than he could handle.

Desdemona slowly peeled the panties from her hips. He watched the underwear being slipped away. Because she remained above him the perspective was skewed. First she exposed the glossy mocha ring of her anus. Then she showed him the glorious split of her sex. The labia were a dark and meaty purple. The wetness that glistened against her flesh shone in the muted light of the shaded bedroom. He could see the dark entrance into her vagina and realised he had never previously seen his wife's pussy looking so open, used or enticing. But it was the raw scent of her that struck him hardest. Her perfume was now so intense that it choked and intoxicated.

'You're close to coming, aren't you?' Desdemona laughed.

Even though there was a cruel edge to her amusement, he still thought this was the most intimate they had ever been in the bedroom. He didn't understand how they could be so spiritually close when she was tormenting him for his inadequacies and confessing her adulteries. But he believed they had made a connection far stronger than any of those they had previously shared.

A sliver of jealousy still spiked his thoughts. But its power was negated by the arousal it inspired. It was true Desdemona had taken her pleasure with another man. No, Edwin corrected, that was too coy a way of describing what had really happened: Desdemona had fucked Carl – whoever Carl might be.

The thought brought more excitement than anger.

'Do you want to taste my wet cunt?' She wriggled her hips. The slippery lips of her labia brushed lightly back and forth over his nose. 'My cunt's never been wet before when you've been near it. Do you want to taste it now that my juices are flowing?'

Edwin pushed his tongue against her.

He clenched the muscles of his buttocks in an attempt to stave the inevitable climax. Her flesh was warm and soft and sweet. The lips of her sex moulded to his mouth and dripped with a film of the most succulent musk. When he plunged his tongue deep inside he could feel the tiniest tremors tingle through the inner muscles of her sex. His neck ached from raising his head to meet her. His jaw soon grew weary from the awkward position he had assumed. But he was determined not to move his mouth away until Desdemona gave permission.

'Carl's only one of the men I fuck,' Desdemona explained. 'Like I said, he's not the biggest or the best. But he certainly brightens my Mondays. Do you want me to tell you about the other cocks that have been inside the hole you're now licking? Do you want me to tell you who else I've been fucking while you've been spending every hour of the day at work?'

He couldn't hold back the climax. The ejaculation was torn from him with a strength that was sensational and agonising. The eruption was hot enough to scald. Throughout his married life, *throughout his entire life*, Edwin had never tried to stave his climax with so much effort. And still, he reflected bitterly, it had only taken a few choice words from Desdemona and the pathetic puddle of spunk was shooting from the end of his cock and soiling his shirt.

He groaned: embarrassed and ashamed.

Desdemona pulled her sex away from his face and kissed him tenderly on the cheek. When she smiled down at him she was looking on him with genuine kindness. 'The rules are going to be fairly straightforward,' Desdemona explained. 'Things won't change from the way they have been for the past year, except for one important point. From now on I'll let you know what's happening.'

He knew she had forbidden him to speak. And there would undoubtedly be a penalty for disobedience. But

116

he had to satisfy his curiosity on one aspect of this new arrangement. 'Rules? What are the rules?'

'I can fuck whoever I want. I'll do whatever I please. With any man I choose. And you'll accept this without question.'

'What's in this for me?'

'You get the pleasure of hearing every detail. You get to see those men who don't mind you watching. You get to hear what I've done with those men who are too prudish to let you see their cock slipping into my cunt. You get to share my sex life in a way you've never been able to enjoy before.'

He considered the proposition. Her offer was tempting. Considering the way Desdemona had coaxed the climax from his shaft he supposed *tempting* was an understatement. She had discovered the secrets that truly excited him. Her proposal made sense on a lot of levels. But the arrangement was so alien to anything he had ever imagined for himself and his wife, he couldn't simply agree. 'What if this isn't what I want?'

'An alternative choice is always there for you,' Desdemona allowed. 'I love you, Eddie. I don't want us to go separate ways. But I can't stay trapped in a marriage where my husband doesn't satisfy me sexually.' With quiet determination she said, '*I won't* stay trapped in that relationship.' She began to unsnap the handcuffs as she added, 'Why don't you give it a couple of weeks? Maybe see how you feel after we've lived with this arrangement for a while? If you're still unhappy we can either go back to you pretending you know nothing, or we can start the messy process of getting a divorce.'

Hearing her say the D-word was harsh. It struck him worse than when she had said the C-word: and with none of the exciting connotations that the vulgarity had evoked. Trying not to show his upset, he said, 'You're expecting a lot from me, Des.'

She shook her head. 'I expected to marry a husband who was adequate in bed. I didn't expect to marry a

117

man who couldn't keep it up for longer than a minute and had all the sexual skills of a used teabag.'

He flinched from her volatile turn of phrase. His arousal returned as she berated him for his inadequacies. Even though he had only just climaxed, his shaft began to thicken with anticipation. It was instinctive to despise that response. It was the same loathsome knee-jerk hard-on that struck him whenever he thought of his wife with other men.

Desdemona drew a deep breath and smiled down on him. The warmth of her expression softened her harsh turn of phrase. 'Get yourself showered. Change out of those clothes. I'll make up the spare room so you can sleep there tonight. Perhaps we can talk more once you're cleaned up?'

She hadn't been joking, he realised. The threat for him to sleep in the spare room had been genuine. He digested and accepted this development with a simplicity that was frightening. 'What more is there to talk about? Are you going to tell me about the other men you've had?'

'Perhaps.' She grinned. 'But before we talk about anything like that, we need to decide where we're going on holiday.'

With that simple phrase, indicating a return to the humdrum normality of their everyday existence, Edwin realised his status as a cuckold had already become an established part of their lives.

Eleven

'*Either tell the bitch to fuck off, or learn to live with it.*'

Edwin waited to hear what else Desdemona had to say before heeding his brother's advice. His hands shook and the air that came from his lungs was released in small, measured sighs. The holiday brochures were spread before them on the coffee table but, rather than looking at their glossy pages, he could only stare at his wife. 'You said it had been a hard year,' he reminded her. She had spoken those words less than an hour ago. It seemed as if a lifetime had passed since then. The afternoon wasn't yet over, and he had only spent a morning in the office, yet so much had happened it was like trying to remember events from a previous century. With the lounge curtains open, and early evening light dwindling from the room, it felt as though at least twenty-four hours had passed since their time in the dusky twilight of Desdemona's bedroom. Edwin placed his hand over hers. 'You said it had been a hard year. Tell me about it?'

She nodded. In the silence that nestled between them he understood she was composing her thoughts. When she spoke her voice was calm and even. 'I spent the first year of our marriage hoping the sex would get better. I spent the second year berating myself for being so stupid during that first year. I invested in a lot of toys and tried to keep myself satisfied with dildos, vibrators and other paraphernalia. But doing it alone gets boring eventually, so I made up my mind to have another man.'

Edwin shivered.

They sat close to each other on the lounge settee. The coffee table before them was hidden beneath the array of glossy brochures but that was the closest the room had ever come to looking untidy. The Dresden china on the mantelpiece stood in uniform rows: each piece polished and proud. There were two framed oils on the walls and they were both Desdemona's originals. The flattering portrait of Edwin's face squared his jaw more than genetics had ever managed and gave his gaze a glint of steel that he had never assumed in real life. The facing image of Desdemona showed her nude but with her arms and legs wrapped around herself so that her modesty was kept firmly intact. Desdemona's self portrait had always confused Edwin because it showed a naked woman who looked like she was bound by invisible restraints. He wondered if, after today, the painting would continue to confuse him. The remainder of the room was a relaxing collection of beige and fawn. He always thought it epitomised their marriage. Every opulent fixture and furnishing had been funded from his income. But it had all been selected and creatively put together with Desdemona's artistic flair. The result was a room that was relaxing and comfortable but still stylish enough to impress. Now he wondered if that did reflect their marriage. Or only what he expected they should have. It was too profound a question. Rather than brooding on it he snatched a drink from the glass of wine in his hand.

Desdemona followed his lead and sipped from her tumbler of scotch and ice. 'I never wanted to be unfaithful to you,' she said simply. 'I only wanted the sexual satisfaction that I believed I deserved. If I'd thought there was a way you and I could resolve our differences in the bedroom – counselling, Viagra or French Maid outfits – I would have tried those options first. But you've always expressed distaste for artifice.

And I just saw your nose crinkle when I mentioned counselling. So that proves I was right to make the decision I made.'

He breathed through his nose and wondered if he should make a joke about her trying the French Maid's outfit. Somehow humour didn't seem appropriate for this conversation. He continued to sit in silence, listened to her words, and quietly admired her beauty.

Desdemona looked resplendent in the sultry lingerie. The glass of scotch was all but forgotten in her hand. One leg was curled under her backside: the stockinged heel a crimson kiss against her buttock. The other leg was idly draped over the arm of the settee, as though she had deliberately selected this pose to show herself in the lewdest possible position.

'I spent a long time making sure I found the right man. That was important to me. And it wasn't easy. I briefly considered placing a personal ad but writing down my requirements seemed tacky. Carl, the window cleaner, was my first option but I had to sound him out and make sure he was going to be discreet and trustworthy. I also needed to know if he was competent in bed. There would have been no point in my fucking another man who was useless between the sheets. I thought up various ways of trying to find out how suitable he might be but the easiest one was to use my art studio. I painted him nude.'

Edwin's spent length sprang immediately hard. His wife had propositioned another man. Lured him into her studio. Cajoled him to strip. And all so she could assess him as a potential lover. Her actions were so calculated it was chilling. Her thoroughness was impressive enough to engender fresh respect.

'Carl was a little shy at first but, once I'd coaxed him out of his clothes, he wasn't a disappointment. He has a nice, large cock – well, you saw that much when I was sucking him earlier – and he had difficulty keeping it soft. I pretended that was a problem at the time, although I privately thought I'd found nirvana. We shared a bottle of red to help him relax and to get me past my nervousness. I really didn't want to be unfaithful to you, Eddie. But I needed to do something.'

He nodded understanding, trying not to let her see that he was squirming in his seat and anxious to hear the rest of her story.

'Once I'd learnt enough about Carl to feel sure he was trustworthy, I made up my mind and decided to go for it. I told him I was trying to do something along the lines of a Renaissance painting, complete with a male nude sporting a small flaccid cock. I made sure I pressed close to Carl while I told him this.' She giggled softly and said, 'I was so close to him there was no danger of his cock being small.'

Her wicked smile was the most exciting thing he had ever seen. It reminded him of his adoration and devotion. It reinforced his belief that no woman in the world could thrill him with the arousal that Desdemona inspired. Edwin sat motionless in his chair frightened that one more small detail could prove too much for his powers of restraint. He sipped his wine and silently hoped the alcohol would wither the hardness in his lap. He didn't hold out much hope. But he figured the wine stood as good a chance of belaying his impending climax as he would ever have.

'I told Carl his erection was a problem. As I said the words I slipped my hand around his shaft. It felt really strange to be holding a real cock. After being married to you for so long I'd forgotten they could be warm, thick and exciting. Carl's was so large I could barely circle him with my fingers. More exciting, when I held him in my hand, he didn't try to shy away from me and tell me he was on the verge of coming. I'm not saying it for effect, Eddie. I'm not saying it to stress that you're an incompetent lover, or make you feel small, inadequate or awkward. But I came close to orgasm just from having Carl's cock in my fingers.'

He trembled in his seat. It was too easy to imagine his wife's small hand wrapped around Carl's thick, throbbing erection. He had already seen her sucking the man. The conversation effortlessly conjured up the idea of her stroking her fingers along his length. He put the wine glass onto the table suddenly fearful his grip would tighten and he might either snap the delicate stem or crush the bowl of the glass base.

Desdemona didn't seem to notice his movement. Her gaze had a dreamy quality that suggested she wasn't just reciting a memory: she was back in the past and reliving the experience. 'It was a life-changing moment,' she explained. 'I had two options and I could only pick one. I could either apologise to Carl for touching him, and then forget about the idea of having other men in my life. Or I could become an adulteress and finally get some of the satisfaction you'd never given me.'

He cringed from the easy way Desdemona belittled him and wondered if she knew that her scathing words were adding a lustre of twisted pleasure to his arousal. She glanced in his direction each time she delivered a scathing comment. He suspected she was checking to make sure her barb had hit its mark.

'I chose the latter option,' she said, grinning. 'I squeezed my hand hard around his cock and asked if I could help to soften it a little. He didn't need much more encouragement than that. Bending me over the desk in my studio, he took me from behind. He was so hard and vigorous I came in seconds.'

With his eyes closed Edwin could see Carl pounding between his wife's legs. He could hear her sex squelching with each thrust. Then the sound was lost beneath the shrieks of her orgasm. Her face was contorted in a grimace of ecstasy. Her body trembled violently. The details in his imagination showed the unglamorous surface of the desk in her studio. He could picture the spare brushes vibrating with echoes of Carl's vigorous tempo and see the half-squeezed tubes of oil paint rocking from side to side as their union neared its passionate climax. He snatched his glass from the table and drained the contents in one swift gulp.

'We fucked on almost every Monday after that,' Desdemona said simply. 'Carl's married, so there have been a few bank holidays when it wasn't convenient for him. And there have been rarer occasions when you happened to be here, which has also made things difficult.'

Edwin absorbed every word. She had said *difficult*, but she hadn't said *impossible*. Was she confessing to having fucked Carl on those bank holidays when he had been at home and she had been locked away in the sanctuary of her studio? The concept was maddeningly exciting. It was as though she had been flaunting her adultery under his nose. 'What about when it's . . .' He blushed. Coughed. Cleared his throat. 'What about those times of the month when . . .' He left the sentence hanging there, his arousal heightening beneath Desdemona's growing frown. Discreetly he pointed a finger that roved generally in the direction of her uterus.

'My period?' she snapped. Her reflective mood vanished as though it had never been there. In its place came contempt and impatience. 'For fuck's sake, Eddie. You shouldn't even be married to a woman if you can't say the word period.'

'I was being discreet.'

'You were being fucking irritating. That's what you were being. It's menstruation. It's not a crime.'

'I never said it was.'

'I don't do it to piss you off. I come on. I ovulate. It's a natural bodily function. Jesus Christ! You're such an old fart at times it really does annoy me.' She pulled herself from her chair and took her empty scotch glass to the kitchen as he called apologies after her. He heard the sound of a cap being spun from a bottle followed by the glug of the whisky being poured and the clatter of ice cubes dropping heavily into her drink. When she returned he apologised again.

'I don't mind Carl fucking me while I'm bleeding,' she said as she settled herself in the chair facing his. 'Being honest, I get so horny at *that time of the month* there's even a danger I could get pleasure from our *Friday night intimacy.*' As well as sounding angry she was also mimicking his euphemistic approach to delicate subjects. 'But Carl isn't the only man I fuck. He was the one who first suggested I should fuck his nephew, Dave. The lad's just turned eighteen and helps Carl out on the window round. Usually Dave does the entire street while Carl is servicing me in our bedroom. But, a couple of months ago, Carl asked if I fancied getting my hole filled by this adolescent stud.' Her voice had dropped down to a hoarse whisper. The antagonism had ebbed from her tone. She flexed a tight smile for Edwin and asked, 'I'm not upsetting you with too much information, am I?'

There was a challenge in her eyes that he couldn't resist. Every word she had spoken so far made him squirm in a discomfort of jealous embarrassment. He hated her and wanted her in equal measures. Each time she talked about extramarital sex his arousal soared. Every time she reminded him that it was his inadequacies that had pushed her into the arms of other men Edwin trembled from fresh excitement. He wasn't sure whether he was more angry or more aroused but he felt certain the combination was proving to be the headiest experience of his life. 'You're not upsetting me,' he said honestly. He examined his empty wineglass and stood to get himself another drink. He saw Desdemona studying the ineffectual bulge at the front of his pants and couldn't miss her sneer of derision. Humiliated again, and sweating with the effort of containing his explosion, Edwin hurried to replenish his drink from the kitchen and then returned to his chair in the lounge.

'Dave wasn't as good as Carl to begin with,' Desdemona resumed. 'But I trained him. And I trained him well. Unlike you, he's been more than willing to learn how to properly pleasure a woman. He does have a decent-sized cock and, after all the lessons Carl had given me, I knew what he needed to learn. He always comes to fuck me on those mornings when Carl can't brighten my Monday. Some Mondays, I'll ask Carl to send him over once he's finished fucking me. There's nothing quite like having a second cock slide inside you before noon on Monday. It's especially good if Dave can get to me quickly because that means Carl has left my cunt used and wet and open. Under those circumstances Dave can ride me for hours. His cock just slips into me so easily and he fucks and fucks and fucks.' Her smile was devilish. 'I have demanding appetites, Eddie, don't I?'

He didn't know how to respond. The urge to climax had moved from being irresistible to unavoidable. Sitting tense in his chair, not letting himself think of his wife's gaping sex lips, moist from one man's cock and filled by another, he trembled his way through a regiment of breathing that felt pitifully inadequate. 'Are those the only two men you see?'

'I don't *see* them, Eddie.' She sniffed impatiently. 'I fuck them.'

He considered using the word and then decided it was too strong to say in front of his wife. 'Are Carl and David the only two men?'

'Fuck! No!' she laughed.

The sound of her mirth was a taunt. But he respected that she needed to be this harsh. She was setting the ground rules for the future of their relationship. If he didn't like them he always had the option to decline. If she sugar-coated the situation there would be reprisals in the future.

'Carl and Dave are my Monday morning treats,' she chuckled. 'But they have friends. With you working such long hours I'm not averse to entertaining during the long days while you're busy in the office. My needs went unattended for a long while. Two whole years. I'm making up for lost time.' She paused and flashed him a concerned smile. 'Does that make me sound selfish? I don't suppose it matters if it does. I suppose I have been selfish for this last year. But if I don't do something about my sexual satisfaction, I'm certain no one else will.' She fixed him with a scathing expression that took him close to the point of climax. 'I know for certain you won't do anything about it because you're incapable.'

Edwin winced. He allowed the silence to linger between them for a while longer, sipping his wine and trying to regain a little of the composure that her revelations had scrubbed away. There were so many questions he had wanted to ask her but he couldn't remember any of them now. Those that did come to his mind seemed like ones she had already answered. 'Who else have you been with?' He tried to make the words sound conversational but his voice was strained with the effort of containing his arousal. 'Have you had anybody I know?'

Her laughter was simultaneously beautiful and chilling. He didn't know how the two sounds could sit together so perfectly. Draining her scotch, sliding over to him as though she were imitating a panther, Desdemona shook her head. 'I've told you more than enough for one night, Eddie,' she whispered. Her hand fell to the front of his pants and she clutched him tight. 'This next couple of weeks will be a journey of discovery for you, just like the last year has been a journey of discovery for me. There will be some parts you don't like. There will be some parts that you love. But all of it will be new and we don't want to rush one glorious moment, do we?'

He shook his head. It was the only part of his body he dared to move. Her warm hand encased his entire erection through his pants. 'I only asked . . .'

She shushed him until he fell silent.

'We can talk about this more once you realise that I'm now in charge of this relationship. Until then you

127

will have to be patient and just put up with those answers that I offer of my own free will. Do you understand?'

He nodded.

'I've fucked men that you know,' she whispered. 'I've fucked quite a few men who've shook your hand afterwards while my cunt was still dripping from having their cocks inside me.'

How he withstood the urge to climax was a miracle Edwin never understood. He desperately wanted to ejaculate but he feared that explosion would precede the end to this humiliating and illuminating experience.

'But I'll tell you all about them some other night,' she decided. Sighing heavily, clutching his groin tighter, she said, 'Why don't you go and take a shower? Once you've done that we can go through those brochures and work out where we're going on holiday.'

He shivered and stared at her uncertainly. 'Why should I need to shower? I only just finished showering an hour ago.'

She squeezed him tight. 'You need to shower because you've just come in your pants,' she explained.

It was only when she released her fingers, and he felt the ineffectual pulse of his second climax that day, that Edwin realised she was correct.

Twelve

Cuckolds Lights sits on a pair of treacherous ledges at the entrance to Boothbay Harbour, Southport, Maine. The etymology relates back to Cuckold's Point on the Thames, London. Cuckold's Point is the largest bend in London's river. Histories relate that King John gave various concessions and land around that area to compensate a miller whose wife he had seduced after a hunting trip. Horns, the traditional sign of a cuckolded husband (a reference dating back to the days of the Roman Empire) once marked the spot to commemorate this incident. Similarities in the shape of the coastline at Boothbay Harbour, and the learned input of a transplanted Londoner, resulted in the naming of Cuckolds Lights.

Edwin knew the history well enough. His cheeks burnt crimson each time he recalled those stories. The word cuckold usually blackened his thoughts every time he stumbled on it. Its derivative – the old story of the cuckoo leaving its eggs in another bird's nest – invariably fluttered through his thoughts until they were darkened by its dusty grey wings. But this Tuesday, staring at Desdemona's painting, and reflecting on all that had happened the previous day, he found he could consider the history with none of his usual reflexive antagonism. His mood was calm, relaxed and serene. A dozen or more jobs waited for him in his desk diary but he was happy to let them continue waiting.

Boothbay Harbour did not look particularly treacherous but the capacity for cruelty was there. Desdemona had captured the waters so that they appeared as dangerous as a sleeping tiger. Vicious white teeth lined the sharp edges of those waves nipping at the promontory. The tranquil sky suggested an idyllic location too far from civilisation for its own good. The neatly contained building – squat, yet made unique by its lighthouse tower – marked it as something worthy of her artist's brush.

'I've been asking the wrong question,' Edwin marvelled.

It was a revelation.

It didn't matter if there had been an empty condom wrapper in the waste bin: he no longer cared. It didn't matter if a stranger had completed the crossword, using the puzzle as an opportunity to make coarse demands on his wife: that was irrelevant. Her secrecy about the reason she had travelled into town was unimportant. Her relationships with Carl and Dave and all her other men were immaterial. Her fidelity, or lack of fidelity, was not the issue. The important question was: did it trouble him that she fucked other men?

He sat back down at his desk. Through the grim veil of the polarised windows the promise of a bright and glorious day loomed over the horizon. He watched the car park slowly gaining numbers. Jake's TVR roared into a space reserved for board members only. The top was down to show two occupants this morning: Jake and Sally. For the first time since he had met Jake, Edwin realised he didn't begrudge the man his hedonistic lifestyle. If not for the fact that he thought Jake was a puerile tit he could even have smiled at him as the young director waited for Sally to vacate the TVR so he could set the car's alarm.

Edwin picked up the telephone from his desk and called his brother. The phone was answered on the fifth ring. A weary voice demanded, 'Know what fucking time it is?'

'Morning, Robin,' he laughed.

The sound of his own good humour amazed him. He couldn't recall the last time he had genuinely sounded happy. It had been a long while since he remembered grinning, let alone laughing out loud. The day's revelations continued to strike him with poignant force. He hadn't laughed for a long time because he hadn't been happy for a long time. Yesterday he had discovered so many of Desdemona's treacherous secrets: and yet today he was laughing. The association of those two thoughts was a revelation in itself.

'Ed? You fucker. This how you get your chuckles these days? Waking up night owls?'

'I'm sorry,' he said honestly. 'I forget you work late. Curse of the office classes. We think everyone's life is nine-to-five.'

Robin grunted dour acceptance of this excuse. 'Don't worry yourself,' he growled. 'If not for you I wouldn't have any conversation today.'

Edwin puzzled over the remark until he remembered what his brother had said during their Monday telephone conversation. 'Alice still giving you the silent treatment?'

'Wants to know who put lipstick on my cock.'

Edwin did not think Alice was being unreasonable. But he also thought Robin wouldn't want to hear that from him. 'Have you told her?'

'No.'

'Who was it?' He held his breath as he voiced the question, sure he already knew the answer. 'Who gave you the blowjob, Robin?'

'You're beginning to sound like Alice,' Robin growled. In a transparent attempt to change the topic he asked, 'What were you calling for? You didn't just phone to find out about Alice and her silent treatment, did you?'

He pursed his lips, frustrated that Robin wasn't going to answer that one question. Remembering his reason for waking his brother, he said, 'I called to say thanks for the advice you gave last week. My friend appreciated your words of wisdom.'

'Great. Tell him to call into the bar and tell Alice I dispense words of wisdom. It might get the stupid bitch talking to me again. Either that or he can just talk to me. This silent treatment is really beginning to grind me down.'

Edwin's office door opened and Desdemona stepped inside.

He was struck by the incongruity of seeing his wife in the surroundings of his office environment. She was dressed in a charcoal business suit with the short skirt revealing black stockings over perfectly proportioned legs. The tailored cut accentuated her fine figure of full breasts, narrow waist and shapely hips. She grinned easily and blew a kiss across her open palm. Her lips were cherry-red and glossy.

Edwin winked for her.

'I'd best go now, Robin,' he said quickly. 'I just wanted to pass on the message.'

'Fair enough, Ed. Maybe you'll be at the pub tonight?'

'Unlikely. But I'll spare you a thought.' He put the phone down and grinned at Desdemona. 'That was Robin. Alice still isn't speaking to him.'

'They've got a problem?'

'Robin's been cheating,' Edwin said slowly. 'Alice is suspicious.'

Desdemona shook her head. If there was anything happening between her and Robin, Edwin realised she was doing a very effective job of concealing the relationship. It was difficult to know whether he should admire her for her acting abilities, despise her for her deceit, or curse the tangled web of his own suspicions. 'Tsk-tsk,' Desdemona sniffed blithely. With an innocent smile she added, 'Other people's marriages: they're a mystery, aren't they?'

He considered the glib question before responding. 'It's not just other people's marriages that are a mystery to me.' He appraised her again, smiling as he caught the scent of a Dior perfume. 'How come you're paying me a visit? Checking up on me?'

Desdemona grinned. 'Not exactly. I'm here to see Jay. I wanted to discuss the itinerary. He wants us to spend an entire week on the road visiting the company's regionals. I figure we can manage it in three days if we attack them on a different route. Because he's anxious to get these paintings as soon as possible I thought I should make an early start on them.'

'Twelve offices in three days?'

'Nine,' she countered. 'There's no need to include this one. I can trawl the local area for an appropriate landscape at my leisure. I've already got a couple of places that could be possibilities. The same applies to the registered office. That's only a few miles down the road from here. The office you've got in the States was never on the list.'

Edwin nodded. He was about to ask if nine offices in three days was still feasible – it sounded like a lot of travelling to him – but Jake chose that moment to walk through the door. As soon as he arrived Edwin realised he was no longer able to contribute to the conversation. Jake and Desdemona had no interest in him.

'Dezzie.' Jake grinned and embraced her, one arm around Desdemona's waist, the other falling to her backside. He pulled her into a brief but surprisingly intimate kiss. Edwin thought the pair of them looked as though they belonged together. The realisation turned the contents of his stomach sour with jealousy. 'This is a pleasant surprise,' Jake told her. 'If you've come to challenge me to a rematch at Pennies, I'm going to have to tell you it's too early in the day for me to start hitting the brandy.'

'Chicken,' she laughed. She allowed him to keep his arms around her, seeming comfortable to suffer his embrace. More than comfortable. 'I mainly came to propose a revised itinerary for our tour of your empire.' She eased herself away from him and reached inside her jacket pocket for a slender envelope.

Jake placed his hand inside the jacket. 'Have you got anything else in there that might interest me?' The question was delivered with good-natured lewdness.

Edwin stopped himself from gasping in surprise. Even after Desdemona's confessions of the previous day it was still a shock to watch her flirt so boldly with another man. Jake looked as though he was shamelessly fondling Desdemona's breast. The sight was more than Edwin could tolerate. He pushed his chair further into the kneehole, hoping the desk would conceal his excitement.

The idea of Desdemona with another man made him hard. It inflamed his senses. His mouth turned dry. His stomach hurt and sweat dripped from his body. Whenever his thoughts turned down that avenue the prospect of concentrating on anything else became impossible. But this was more than Edwin quietly contemplating his wife's infidelity. This was Jake Mathers openly groping Desdemona's breast while her husband sat in the same room. Desdemona allowed Jake's hand to linger inside her jacket. From Edwin's position it looked like the fingers were kneading and squeezing. Edwin forced himself to stare at the computer screen and pretend he was absorbed in his work.

They laughed easily together.

The sounds flowed over him like a suffocating tide.

'That feels remarkably perky this morning,' Jake mumbled.

'It's not the only thing around here that's stiffening up,' she replied.

He could cope with her being unfaithful. Now he knew what she was doing Edwin couldn't even see it as infidelity. Desdemona had sex with other men but she was openly telling him about the liaisons. It was hard to consider such an arrangement as being less than honest. But he didn't think he could deal with other people knowing he was a cuckold. While she had been keeping her relationships secret there had been no reason to worry about the opinions of anyone outside their marriage. But being in the same room with Desdemona and Jake, while both of them went through a brazen parody of foreplay: he sweated from the humiliation.

'Are you feeling OK today, Eddie?' Jake asked.

Edwin frowned at the question, and then remembered he had left the office the previous day under the guise of ill health. He released a trembling sigh and said honestly, 'Better than I was yesterday.'

'You look a little flushed.'

'I'm all right,' Edwin insisted. His voice rose as he spoke and he realised his tone was close to cracking from the stress of maintaining a façade of normality. The irony of the situation did not escape him. A moment earlier he had been distressed by the notion they were ignoring him. Now he was growing more upset as he suffered their consideration and concern. 'Really. I'm all right.'

Jake nodded and turned back to Desdemona. For the first time he seemed to notice her business suit and the powerful sexuality she exuded. His eyes glittered with avaricious excitement. 'I'm so glad you've turned up here this morning. There's something I'd love you to look at in my office.'

Desdemona's response was a lascivious chuckle. 'You couldn't make that sound more like a *double entendre*, could you?'

Jake shrugged and took her into his embrace again. He urged his pelvis against her and Edwin felt certain he could see the thrust of the man's hidden erection press against his wife's stomach. 'It's something you could start working on this morning, if you wanted,' Jake confided. 'Although it might be harder than you were expecting this early in the day.'

Desdemona's merry giggle made her sound impossibly young. Edwin watched his wife respond to Jake's embrace and place her arms lightly around him. His own erection sat painfully hard in his pants. His scrotum throbbed with an agonising need for relief. He held his breath for fear of releasing a sigh or a groan. Desperate to continue with the pretence that nothing untoward was happening, he locked his gaze on the computer screen and tried to make his fingers hit the correct letters on the keyboard.

'I'm proposing we tour your empire in three days instead of seven.' Desdemona spoke in a voice of businesslike efficiency. 'If that's OK with you we can leave Eddie to make the appropriate motel bookings for Thursday, Friday and Saturday while you *take me in your office.*'

Edwin held his breath.

He gripped tight at the edge of his desk.

Jake's suggestive comments resounded through his thoughts and muffled every other noise.

'There's something I'd love you to look at in my office.'

'You could start working on it this morning.'

'It might be harder than you were expecting.'

The crass intimation of each line was exciting. But more arousing had been his wife's response.

'. . . *take me in your office.*'

Edwin felt sure it wasn't his imagination. He was certain Desdemona had put an emphasis on those final five words.

'. . . *take me in your office.*'

Had the pair fucked on Saturday? Was Jake so good Desdemona wanted to use him again? Was her libido so demanding she already needed more satisfaction? Perspiration dripped from Edwin's body, as anxiety, jealousy and a furious excitement all blended to make him shiver.

'Eddie?'

He glanced up to see Desdemona thrusting an envelope towards him. Both she and Jake studied him with expressions of bemused concern.

'Earth to Eddie? Are you receiving us?'

'A little distracted,' he mumbled by way of apology. Nodding at the computer screen in front of him he said, 'I was busy working on this.' He took the offered envelope from his wife and flexed an embarrassed grin.

'Can you book accommodation according to this itinerary?' She glanced at Jake and asked, 'Should we be booking two single rooms or would it make it easier if we shared a double?'

Edwin sat as rigid as stone. If he had moved a millimetre he felt certain the ejaculation would have been wrenched from his body. Of course he had strongly suspected there might be something between them but this comment banished all doubt. His wife was not just flaunting her relationship with Jake: she was now using it as a tool for humiliation. The thrill was devastating.

'Two singles or a double?' Jake mused. He stroked his chin and pantomimed serious contemplation. 'I think we should leave that decision in Eddie's capable hands. I'm sure he'll know what will best satisfy his wife.'

Desdemona's voice was caustic with derision. 'It would be the first time he'd known how to satisfy his wife since the day we got married.'

Edwin said nothing. He remained absolutely motionless as Jake and Desdemona guffawed together. The pair had fucked on Friday night. He could see that now as clearly as though he was there and watching both naked bodies slam together with the urgent thrusts of drunken passion. Above the scent of Desdemona's Dior perfume and Jake's CK cologne he caught the fragrance of their intermingled arousal. The air in the office was thick and unbreathable but he couldn't decide if that was symptomatic of his own inability to move or a reaction caused by the mutual lust between Jake and Desdemona.

'Are you OK to make that decision, Eddie?' Jake asked.

Edwin nodded. He felt sick and excited. He could see Jake was again holding Desdemona's backside with one hand, his fingers lingering against the thin fabric of her skirt. From the breadth of his wife's approving grin it was clear she didn't mind the intimate caress.

'Eddie?' Jake prompted.

His sharp tone of voice snapped Edwin from his reverie. He glanced at his employer and nodded quick consent. 'I'll arrange bookings,' he said, taking the envelope from his wife.

'Cool,' Jake said. He started to usher Desdemona from the room and then paused to glance back in Edwin's direction. 'While you're playing the role of my secretary, call Sally on the switchboard and tell her I won't be needing my eleven o'clock this morning.'

Edwin almost choked on the lump that rose in his throat. He remembered what Jake had said a day earlier. '*I've pencilled Sally in to give me a blowjob each weekday at eleven o'clock*.' Did that mean he wouldn't have time to indulge his carnal appetites with Sally this morning? Or was Jake trying to tell him he expected Desdemona to satisfy all his carnal urges? Would he simply explain he expected to have his cock sucked at eleven o'clock each morning? And would Desdemona simply shrug, get down on her knees, and then suck his length with her glossy, cherry lips?

'Are you sure you're OK this morning?' Jake asked. 'You look a little flushed. Out of it. You're acting as though your mind's somewhere else.'

'I'm OK,' Edwin said firmly.

'Good.' Jake flashed a smile that appeared merciless. 'If you're sure you'll be here for the remainder of the day, I'll patch my calls through to you while Dezzie and I thrash this out.'

They had almost left the room when Desdemona stopped and hurried back to Edwin's side. He wondered if she was suddenly going to say that things had gone too far and she no longer wanted to be seen as someone so cheap and easy and willing to do all those treacherous things she had just intimated. The hope that she might have reservations about her actions made him stare at her with mute reverence.

Leaning close to his ear, whispering so Jake couldn't hear what she was saying, Desdemona said, 'I'll send you a picture of Jake's cock sliding into my pussy.'

Edwin came in his pants.

Thirteen

Tuesday dragged on forever. He visited the office's lavatories and tried to clean himself up but he couldn't remove the stench of his own ejaculate from his clothes. The persistent smell lingered like a continual reminder of his own inadequacies and impotence.

He placed a call to Sally and told her that Jake had cancelled their eleven o'clock appointment. She might have sounded disappointed or suspicious but he didn't know her well enough to recognise whether or not he was listening to a variation in her usual tone of voice. As he talked to her, Edwin's thoughts repeatedly placed Sally naked, gobbling Jake's erection and having her pussy fingered by the once-glimpsed Maisy. Although he barely knew the three people involved he could easily conjure a mental picture of the trio undressed and joined with mouths, cock and pussies. Sally called him Mr Miller. She thanked him and ended their terse conversation with a perfunctory goodbye.

He kept the phone in his hand and dialled the first of the motels in order to book accommodation for Desdemona and Jake as they enjoyed their three-day tour of the regional offices. The locations were easy enough to work out. Mathers & Wise maintained accounts at hotels local to their regional offices. Desdemona's itinerary was simple enough to follow and the chore should not have been a demanding one. But as he made the first call Edwin's stomach churned with familiar dread. His bowels convulsed as he realised the enormity of the decision he had been asked to make.

A faraway receptionist asked, 'Is this reservation for two singles or a double room?'

If he booked two singles it would look like an act of pathetic defiance. If he booked a double, Jake would know that Desdemona had her husband's open consent to fuck each night while they travelled together. The option of booking the singles held little appeal. Just because they were booked into single rooms didn't mean either of them would sleep where they were supposed. But it was unthinkable to book a double room for his wife and another man. It was almost as though he was spreading the lips of her pussy apart and inviting Jake to slide inside. It was almost as though he was holding Jake's cock and guiding it between Desdemona's labia. Both images left him quaking and on the verge of another climax.

'Hello? Sir?' The faraway receptionist sounded either impatient or concerned. He couldn't tell which and didn't really care. 'Are you still there?'

'I'm trying to book rooms for two people on Thursday night.' He had said those words before and they had been difficult enough. The ones he was now expected to say threatened to choke him. 'I don't think they'll mind sharing.' He didn't think he had ever voiced such a massive understatement. Drawing a deep breath, deciding he knew what he had to do and could later decide if he approved, Edwin said thickly, 'A double room will be fine.'

'Very good, sir. We have a double room free on Thursday.'

He acknowledged the receptionist's responses and gave her appropriate details for the booking and invoice arrangements. But all the time he was picturing Jake and Desdemona naked together on top of a double bed in a faraway motel bedroom. His erection had stirred back into life. His penis felt hatefully sore after his earlier ejaculation. But he couldn't stop his body from responding to the thought of his wife and his boss fucking together.

The hardness grew more uncomfortable as he booked rooms at different hotels for Friday and Saturday. His head pounded with the onset of a humungous ache. The stench of his earlier climax became a sickening reek. He felt dirty and uncomfortable and, while he tried to turn his mind back to the work before him, he couldn't stop himself from dwelling on the thought that Desdemona was still in Jake's office.

When the clock on his PC announced it was eleven o'clock he wondered if Jake was now forcing Desdemona to suck his cock. The same way he would have otherwise commanded Sally. It was difficult to imagine any man forcing Desdemona to do anything she didn't want. But after seeing her with Carl the previous day, Edwin suspected his wife would be eager to swallow Jake's length and then gulp down his semen. He wondered if the smell would still be on her breath the next time she kissed him.

Hurriedly he absorbed himself in his work and refused to let his thoughts go back to such senseless speculation. The chores were frustratingly simple. He dealt with each task without effort, and then double-checked his own work because he was sure he had completed it too easily. Lunchtime was marked only by the appearance of Sally, politely enquiring if he wanted anything while she was doing her one o'clock sandwich run.

He had never before looked at her as a sexual creature. Now that image was the only one he could think of. In his imagination her clothes had fallen away and she was licking her lips as she lapped up the last remnants of an ejaculation that had been shot into her mouth. Briskly, he shook the thought from his mind. His erection was already painfully hard and he didn't want to add to the embarrassment that came with the fetid stench hovering around him.

'I'd best not order a sandwich,' Edwin decided. He spoke brightly and with forced cheer, determined Sally wouldn't see he was tormented by an all-consuming angst. 'My wife's in a meeting with Mr Mathers. She might be expecting me to take her to lunch once they've finished.'

'I don't think that will be happening, Mr Miller,' Sally said quietly. 'Mr Mathers and your wife left the office around twelve. Jay said they'd be out for the rest of the day.'

Edwin squirmed in his seat.

It occurred to him that they could be doing something as innocent as driving around those local areas that Desdemona had thought appropriate for the landscapes. But he couldn't convince himself that was all they were doing. Had they grown tired of fucking in the office? Was the sterile environment too stifling for their carnal creativity? Or had they simply wanted to go somewhere where no one would mind her screaming in orgiastic ecstasy?

Edwin asked Sally to grab him a Big Mac.

When she returned, an hour later, he ate the burger without tasting it. The meal sat heavy in his stomach as his thoughts perpetually returned to the speculation of what Jake and Desdemona might be doing together. He was almost certain they were having sex. But now he wanted to know what sort of sex; how much pleasure Desdemona was enjoying; and where they were doing it. Had she taken him back to their home, so she could fuck Jake in her marital bed? Or was she busy screwing Jake at his apartment? Because there was a likelihood they could have travelled out to view local scenery, Edwin wondered if they might be parked in a lay-by, fucking in the back of Jake's convertible. Or across the bonnet.

He got himself a coffee that did little to help the burger settle. Then he did some more of the work that had been waiting for his attention. It was annoyingly easy to catch up on everything he had missed from the previous day. He was even able to push himself ahead again so he was in a position to assist less able colleagues with their workloads.

Around three o'clock he fished the new mobile phone from his pocket and checked to see if any messages had come in while he was mentally zoned out and involved with the mundane chores of his work.

The exterior screen told him no messages had been received.

He returned to his desk and made a call to the travel agents. Confirming the details he and Desdemona had discussed the previous evening he booked his first holiday in three years. Ordinarily he would have taken some pleasure from the experience of organising the vacation but, on this occasion, his thoughts were elsewhere and he was speculating what his wife might currently be doing with Jake. His chest was tight. Every breath was a laboured gasp for oxygen that was never quite sufficient. The pounding in his temples inspired a headache that threatened to crush his skull. After talking with the travel agents he sent an email to the head of personnel at HR and told them the dates when he wanted to book his holiday time. Throughout every conversation and exchange he was quietly amazed at himself for managing to continue with the minutiae of his day-to-day existence while his thoughts luridly returned to images of Desdemona and Jake.

'Mr Miller?'

Edwin glanced up from his desk to see Sally standing in the doorway. A shapeless coat concealed her figure. Her head was lowered and she raised her eyes as though shy of addressing him. Because she wore her coat he guessed it was close to five o'clock. He was surprised by the way the day had slipped past him even though every second had been an exercise in torture.

'Sally?'

'Mr Mathers put a call through an hour ago. He said him and Mrs Miller had been delayed. Mrs Miller said you should make your own arrangements for tea this evening because she won't be back home until very late.' She blushed, as though she was embarrassed by the message or some unrevealed aspect of its content. Hurriedly, she turned to the door as though anxious to make an escape.

'Was that everything they said?'

Sally's cheeks were an unbecoming pink. She inched herself closer to the door as though ready to flee if his questions became more than she could answer.

'Was that the entire message?' Edwin pressed.

Sally shot him a venomous glare. 'Mrs Miller asked if you would get some brochures from a cosmetic surgery clinic.' She looked as though she had said the words to spite him for forcing the issue.

Edwin didn't understand the reference. 'A cosmetic surgery clinic?' he repeated doubtfully. 'Are you sure that's what she said?'

Sally nodded.

'One of those places where they do nose jobs and liposuction and . . .' He couldn't let himself continue with the sentence. The only other surgeries he could recall they performed in such clinics involved genitalia and he wasn't going to indulge in such an embarrassing conversation with Sally. It had been difficult enough saying the word liposuction. 'Did she say why she wanted me to get brochures from a cosmetic surgery clinic?'

Sally's pink cheeks turned scarlet. She lowered her face and spoke to the floor as she inched towards the door. Edwin could see her fingers were already on the handle and she was going to bolt as soon as the opportunity presented itself. 'Mrs Miller suggested they might offer you some practical advice on increasing your penis size.'

Edwin was too stunned to reply.

Sally waited for a full three seconds before rushing through the door and slamming it closed behind herself. He could hear her manic giggles as she staggered down the corridor. His cheeks burnt a furious red and he couldn't recall a humiliation that had ever felt so complete. The shame made his erection hurt with the need for release and he tried to guess whether his wife's remark about the cosmetic surgery brochures had been a cruel way of adding to his embarrassment or a genuine request for him to better himself. Not sure he dared disobey any of Desdemona's instructions, he made a quick internet search for a local clinic, and then called for a brochure.

Simply admitting that he was calling for information on penis enhancement made him cringe. Giving out his name and address was enough of an ordeal to make his erection swell and bring him close to the point of ejaculation. There was no doubt in his mind that Sally would repeat Desdemona's message to everyone in the office the following day, compounding his shame and making his humiliation public and complete.

The band of muscles surrounding his chest drew tight.

Perspiring heavily, he prayed that the office grapevine might not operate as efficiently as it usually did. He supposed the prayer was a facile one – technology had yet to come up with any means of communication that could transmit information faster than the network of office gossips – but it was his only hope of saving face.

He waited until eight o'clock before leaving for home. The workload had been completed by seven but he refused to give up the sanctuary of his office for fear of meeting anyone who might have heard Sally's gossip. He picked up his mobile phone, closed down his PC, and checked the corridor outside his office twice before daring to leave the room. Mercifully he passed no one as he left. Admittedly, when he climbed into his car, he felt sure he was under the watchful eye of the Mathers & Wise building. It was easy to believe there were a score of gossip-fuelled workaholics staring through their windows and smirking down at him; trying to catch a glimpse of the man whose wife believed he needed surgery to make his penis effective. But Edwin knew those thoughts were only borne by his paranoia. He refused to give his inner doubts the satisfaction they would get from looking up at the blank eyes of the building's windows.

In the car he checked his mobile before turning on the engine. Desdemona's promise had haunted his thoughts throughout the day. '*I'll send you a picture of Jake's cock sliding into my pussy.*' He had climaxed when she whispered those words and they repeatedly brought him to the brink of another orgasm. Seeing there was still no message from Desdemona, he gunned the car's engine and tore out of the car park.

The thirty-minute drive sped past easily.

As soon as he was home Edwin went to the shower and stepped out of his soiled pants. He scrubbed himself for an hour, never sure that he had removed the smell of his ejaculate, and growing increasingly repulsed by the scent as it continued to offend his nostrils. After changing into jeans and a sweatshirt he doused himself with enough deodorant and antiperspirant to mask any remaining trace of the pungent odour.

He checked his mobile phone and was disappointed to see that there was still no message from Desdemona. Going into the kitchen he wondered if she expected him to have a meal ready for when she returned, or if it would be acceptable to prepare himself something now. He didn't feel particularly hungry but because he had only had a burger throughout the day he thought it would be wise to eat something. He found a ready meal in the freezer and pushed it in the microwave before calling The Horn.

'The Horn. How can I help?'

'Alice? It's Ed.'

'Oh! Hi, Ed. I didn't embarrass you and Des the other night, did I?'

'I've suffered worse embarrassment.' His thoughts went to Sally's pink face as she told him Desdemona's

147

message. His cheeks blossomed with the memory. The skin at the nape of his neck prickled. 'I've suffered much worse embarrassment.'

'Are you wanting to speak to the cheating bastard?'

'Is that Robin's new nickname?'

'No. It's an old nickname that's been brought out of retirement *again*.'

'If I could, please.'

'Do you know who she is, Ed?'

'Do I know who who is?'

'Don't fuck about,' she snapped bitterly. 'You and Des were here on Saturday night. Did you see which tart Robin was sniffing around? Do you have any idea which bitch's eyes I should be gouging out?'

'I didn't see anything.'

'No. I figured you'd be blind. What about Des?'

'It wasn't Des!'

'No!' Alice snapped back. 'I wasn't suggesting it was her. I was asking if she'd seen anything.'

Edwin stopped himself from sighing with relief. Trying to keep his tone neutral he said, 'She's out at the minute. I'll ask her when she gets back. I'll get her to call you if she thinks she spotted Robin with anyone in particular.' As the silence on the phone drew into an uncomfortably long pause he added, 'May I speak to Robin now, please?'

There was the sound of the phone being put to one side. Edwin heard Alice say, 'Can you tell the cheating bastard that his brother's on the phone?' There was a pause before he heard her explain, 'Because I'm not talking to the cheating bastard. That's why I'm asking you to do it.'

Edwin bit his lower lip and wondered if he had caused his brother unnecessary trouble by making this call. Deciding it was now too late for him to back out of the conversation, he waited until Robin picked up the phone.

'Ed?'

'I'd called to see if you and Alice had sorted things out,' he admitted. 'But I guess Alice has already answered that question.'

'Pious cow,' Robin grunted. 'If she'd been sucking it more often there would have been less chance of the fucking thing falling into someone else's mouth.'

Edwin recoiled from the anger in his brother's tone. 'I hope you phrased it more delicately when you explained that point to Alice.'

'She's no fucking innocent,' Robin growled.

He sounded truculent and volatile. Edwin wondered if part of his brother's anger was so obvious because Alice was in a position to overhear their conversation, and he was simply saying things that were intended to needle her into a reaction. It was almost a relief when he heard his mobile ring and he realised he had a genuine excuse to end the call. 'I just wanted to check that you were all right,' he explained. 'I guess I've called at the wrong time.'

'I'm OK,' Robin assured him. 'Thanks for taking the trouble to talk to me. The silence around here is getting pretty fucking intense.'

'Will it make things easier if you tell Alice who you were with?'

'It'd make things easier if Alice just grew up and moved on,' Robin barked. 'She's screwing the brewery's delivery driver, only she thinks I don't know about it.'

'Shit!' Edwin gasped. He marvelled that his innocent conversation had caused such a massive stir. He could hear a muffled exchange going on away from the phone and realised Robin was arguing with Alice.

'I've seen the way you look at the fucker.'

Alice's voice, faraway but angry enough to be heard: 'He's never left lipstick round my cock!'

'No. But he's had his fingers up your cunt, hasn't he?'

There was the unmistakable sound of a hand slapping a cheek. Edwin flinched from the noise, remembering his own feelings of humiliation when Desdemona had

149

silenced him with a similar blow. He held his breath. Strained his ears. Listened for how the argument would develop.

'Talk later, bruv,' Robin said quietly. 'Things are moving to a head.'

'It sounds bad,' Edwin said solemnly.

'There's a plus side,' Robin said slowly. 'Seems like Alice has decided to talk to me again. Later.' The phone went dead in Edwin's hand. He felt a moment's brief unhappiness for his brother, saddened Robin and Alice were fighting and still uneasy at the idea that Desdemona might be a contributory factor in their problems. Not allowing himself to think like that, he went to retrieve his mobile.

The icon on the LCD display told him he had received a photograph and a text message. His hands shook as he flipped the cover open and stared at the picture inside.

Desdemona had delivered on her promise.

Edwin stared at the picture of an erection sliding into his wife's pussy.

It struck him with small wonder that he could recognise his wife from a picture of her sex impaled on a stranger's cock. But he supposed it was easy to regard her from such an angle because it was a part of her anatomy he had always revered. The dainty lips were spread wide. They looked flushed, swollen and purple: as though they were sore from overuse. He didn't know whether to pity her or enjoy the swell of special pride that made his erection pulse with the threat of an impending climax. He contemplated the picture for an age, a tear trailing from the corner of his eye as he examined the broad length filling his wife.

When he wiped the wetness from his face he realised it was a tear of happiness. Knowing he could go back to consider the small picture at any time, Edwin fumbled with the buttons on the phone and opened the text message.

J&I contempl8ing l&scapes 2nite. C U 2morro. Dez. PS: sleep in spare room.

Fourteen

Edwin arrived for work on Wednesday early but groggy. The spare room had not been comfortable. His sleep had been broken with three separate ejaculations as he dreamt of the single photograph showing Desdemona's pussy astride Jake's cock. He didn't know where the time had gone but he felt sure the hours had flitted past in a malaise of fitful arousal. His wife was out of the house. Fucking his employer. And she had sent him a picture of what was happening with a message that he had to spend the night in the spare bedroom. Perversely, he thought, it was the closest he had felt to Desdemona since the day they got married.

The worries of the previous day were no longer a consideration. He laughed at that thought and amended that the worries of the previous three years were no longer a consideration. Despite feeling drained and weary, he threw himself into his work with cheerful abandon. The oppressive burden of his worries and fears no longer sloped his shoulders. The image of Cuckolds Lights was a pleasure to behold this morning. He quietly reflected that there had been many days when he couldn't bring himself to admire the beauty of the painting his wife had given him. Now his gaze was constantly drawn to its prepossessing charms. Forcing himself not to lose his day staring at the painting, he opened up a pair of spreadsheets and began to go through the checking and confirming required. He had been working for two hours before he realised he was no longer alone in the room.

'Good morning, Mr Miller.'

He glanced up to see Sally standing in the door of his office. His cheeks flushed with automatic embarrassment as he remembered the last time they had spoken. She had been passing on the message from Desdemona that he needed to consult a clinic to organise modifications for his inadequate penis. He blushed. When he glanced at Sally he wondered if she was remembering the same conversation.

'Hi, Sally,' he said with forced cheer. 'Is there a problem?'

She stared at the carpet rather than looking at him. As she had been when he last saw her, Sally was dressed in a large and shapeless coat. It was probably *haute couture* amongst her fashion-victim peers. Her bare, coltish legs protruded from beneath the coat, ending in a pair of ungainly looking platforms. She swayed her right foot in an arc before her left, looking as though she was hesitant about entering the room and reminding him of naughty schoolgirls waiting for punishment. That thought added to the fluster of his embarrassment. He quickly chastised himself for thinking something that was so kinky and inappropriate.

'Sally?' He said her name louder. 'Is something wrong?'

'I saw your wife last night.'

She said the words so quietly he wasn't sure he had heard correctly. When he realised what she had said he almost spluttered with surprise. 'You saw Des?'

'Mrs Miller. Dezzie. Yes.' When Sally raised her face her smile was twisted into a wicked grin. 'Dezzie kissed me.'

He was instantly hard. His stomach folded as though he had been punched. The arousal struck him so swiftly he had to sit rigid for fear of ejaculating again. The three eruptions that had spoilt his sleep had been strong enough to make him believe he would never climax again – although another erection had reluctantly appeared while he was soaping himself in the shower that morning. His breathing came in shallow gasps as he considered Sally's words. 'Mrs Miller ... Des ... she kissed you?'

'I kissed her back.' Sally grinned.

'That sounds ...' Edwin began. He swallowed thickly and shook his head sure he was beginning his response in an incorrect way. His mouth was as dry as cotton wool. 'That sounds like it must have been enjoyable.'

'Oh! It was very enjoyable.' She continued to swing her foot, the movement growing in speed as though she was building to a point. 'Do you want me to show you where she kissed me? It was a very special kiss. Would you like to see?'

'I ...' He shook his head. The room was suddenly too warm and the prospect of ejaculation frightened him. His tongue was too large to properly fit in his mouth. He stroked it over arid lips as dry as parchment. 'I ... er ... that is ...'

She stepped fully into the room with a grace he would never have expected from meek Sally in her ungainly shoes. Shrugging the shapeless coat from her shoulders with one athletic flex, she was suddenly by the side of his desk. He had never previously noticed her skirt was so short, or that the tight blouse she wore was so see-through. His face was close to her chest. He could easily detect the shape of her pert nipples and firm young breasts. Light from his window fell against her. He could make out the dark circles of the areolae beneath the stiff ridges that punched against her blouse.

'Do you want to see where she kissed me?' Sally asked again.

Her fingers fell to the hem of her skirt. She flexed her wrists inward, suggesting she was about to lift the garment. Edwin stared at the lower edge of the skirt and the chewed fingernails that held it. He was mesmerised by the sight of her slender legs and incredulous that he had slipped into a world where meek Sally from the switchboard was about to raise her skirt and reveal herself to him. His chest was tight with claustrophobic agony. The deodorant he had used that morning evaporated as his body became glossed by perspiration.

'You saw Desdemona last night? I thought she was with Mr Mathers?'

'She was. We all were. Me. Maisy. And Jay. Dezzie is great.' She made the final declaration as though arguing against his opinion. 'She's not what I expected from someone married to a guy like you. No offence.'

He hadn't heard enough of the words to properly take offence. His gaze remained fixed on the hem of her skirt and his eyes widened as she began to draw it upward. Her thighs were the colour of freshly poured cream. A musk came from her that he knew was the scent of arousal but he wouldn't allow his mind to acknowledge that fact. If he let himself accept that he was viewing the tops of Sally's thighs and catching her most intimate scent he knew he would not be able to hold back the eruption that threatened to burst from his loins.

'Do you want to see where she kissed me?'

She didn't wait for his reply. Instead she simply pulled her skirt high and exposed the triangle of white panties at the top of her legs.

Edwin clutched his desk. He wanted to drag his gaze away but he was mesmerised by the display. Momentarily he managed to raise his eyes to meet her face. He saw the glimmer of wicked pleasure she was getting from this torment. Her lips had curled into a sneer of triumph and he understood she was enjoying her twisted control over him.

'This is where Dezzie kissed me,' she breathed.

Her hands moved.

His gaze immediately shot back down to her panties. She hooked her thumbs beneath the waistband. Lowered them. Showed him the slight swell of a modest stomach. Then revealed a hip that was branded with the crudely drawn tattoo of a dark-blue butterfly.

Edwin had stopped breathing.

She eased the panties down further.

Past the smoothest expanse of skin he had ever seen.

Making the moment last for an eternity.

Sally moved the waistband over a mulberry blemish on her otherwise flawless flesh. Edwin quietly wondered how she could continue pulling the panties down and still not reveal a single pubic hair. It was only when she had exposed the neat split of her sex lips that he realised her labia was shaved and smooth and completely hairless.

'This is where Dezzie kissed me.'

The image slapped him with its vivid intensity. Sally was sprawled naked across a bed. Her thighs were parted and the only thing she wore was an encouraging smile and her butterfly tattoo. The clean expanse of her pussy lips gaped open as Desdemona's pretty, perfect face inched closer. His wife wore her bloodiest lipstick, transforming her mouth into something succulent and nearly vampiric. She drew a darkly purple tongue across her lips as she moved closer to the inviting slice of Sally's pussy. Her first kisses were gentle applications of her lips. Her teeth were the vibrant white of a Hollywood starlet. Pushing her tongue out, looming slowly closer, Desdemona stroked the tip of her tongue against the sweat-salted flesh of Sally's sex.

Edwin snatched a breath and tried to sit back. It was impossible to wrench his gaze from the sight of Sally's neatly shaved labia. Since marrying Desdemona he had never even thought of looking at another woman sexually. Yet Sally had simply sauntered into his office and was showing herself to him as though this was the most natural thing in the world.

'I can prove that she kissed me because that's her lipstick,' Sally confided. She pointed to the mulberry blemish on her mons pubis.

Edwin considered the mark and reflected that it did look like a kiss that could have been left by his wife's lips. It proved nothing. But the thought brought him to the brink of orgasm. He was staring at a young woman's pussy and being told this was a landscape his wife had already explored. The struggle to control his ejaculation was severe enough to make him shake.

'She got her tongue so deep inside me,' Sally breathed.

Her fingers teased the slit of her sex lips. She eased them apart to reveal flesh that was flushed with dark and exciting pinks and purples. The fragrance of her musk became stronger. Edwin's heart pounded so loud he could feel it shaking the table in his grip.

'Dezzie tasted me good and proper,' Sally told him. Lowering her voice to a husky whisper she asked, 'Would you like to taste what Dezzie tasted?'

If he had been able to reply Edwin didn't know what he would have said. The power of speech had been robbed from his abilities. All he could do was stare at the young exhibitionist temptress in his office and nod. His eyes were wide as he contemplated her vagina and he knew he would nod agreement to her every suggestion.

'Do you want to taste me, Mr Miller?'

He nodded again.

His head bobbed up and down like a toy dog on the rear ledge of a car window: a car with worn shocks, driving over cobbles or a cattle grid. The image of the nodding dog sat like an icon in his mind. It wasn't difficult to believe his eyes were equally glassy and devoid of intelligence. He could even imagine his tongue lolling comically from his mouth in a cartoon leer. The world stood still and he now only existed to see and taste Sally's pussy.

She stroked a finger against herself. He watched the digit press clumsily against her hole. For an instant he thought she was pressing too hard, and there was a danger she would hurt the delicate discovery of flesh she had shown to him. And then the finger had slipped inside. The hairless lips sprang back into place, quietly suckling around the digit.

Sally gasped.

Edwin didn't dare draw his own breath. His thoughts were equally divided between watching Sally and staving his ejaculation. If he allowed himself any distraction – even for oxygen – he knew he would either miss one glorious moment of this vision or explode in his pants.

She pulled the finger away. It glistened with wetness. As she pushed it close to his face, his focus shifted from the perfection of her pussy lips and fixed on the clear liquid that coated her chewed nails. The scent was now strong enough to fill his world. He could see she was pushing the digit towards his mouth. Unable to believe this was happening he extended a tongue as though preparing to accept her gift.

With malicious glee Sally wiped the back of her finger across his forehead.

Edwin remained motionless.

Sally daubed the finger down his left cheek and then his right, completing the gesture by drawing a wet moustache beneath his nose. He couldn't breathe anything except the fetid scent of her pussy. The smell was intoxicating and he simply remained in his seat as she giggled.

'That's what your wife was kissing last night.'

'What the hell are you doing, Sally?'

Jake's voice thundered from the door.

Edwin stared at him and tried to blink his thoughts back to the room.

Sally pulled her hand away from Edwin's face. She briskly tugged her pants back up, removing his view of her sex and the crude butterfly, and then pushed her skirt back down over her hips. She hurried to the floor, no longer looking graceful or inspiring, as she tried to retrieve her coat.

Jake stamped on the coat, effectively forcing Sally to grovel at his feet.

'What the hell did you think you were doing, Sally?'

'I'm sorry, Jay.' She sounded genuinely humbled and apologetic. 'I was just trying to have a little fun.'

'Fun?' Jake kept his foot on her coat as he glowered down at her. He acted as though Edwin wasn't in the room. His attention was fixed on Sally and he spoke to her as though they were alone. Edwin savoured the same rush of humiliation that he had only previously received from Desdemona. 'You call it fun to come in here, flashing your cunt at my employees?'

Sally cowered. She shook her head and stammered to provide a response but Jake spoke over her.

'How much fun do you think it will be when I spank your arse?'

Her smile brightened.

'How much fun do you think it will be when I tell Dezzie what you were doing?'

The bright smile evaporated.

'What do you think Dezzie will do to you?'

'Please don't tell,' Sally gasped. 'I was only trying to have a little fun.'

The words came out sounding pathetic and meek. Edwin felt a pang of sympathy for Sally, even when he realised his humiliation had been the source of her fun. He glanced at Jake, trying to guess what the man would do. Having never been in a similar situation – having never imagined such situations existed – he realised it was impossible to try to predict the man's actions.

'Christ but you're an annoying little slut,' Jake grunted. With obvious anger he kicked Sally's coat to the furthest corner of the room.

She sobbed as though he had lashed out at her instead of the bulky clothing. Seeming already to have acknowledged that she was in the wrong, Sally remained on her knees before him.

'Is this your way of getting revenge because Maisy wouldn't piss in your mouth last night?'

Sally's cheeks turned crimson. She turned to glare at Edwin, clearly mortified that he had heard this statement. Then she fixed her pleading gaze directly on Jake. 'Please don't tell Dezzie,' she wailed. 'I'm sorry, Jay. I really am.'

'It's Mr Mathers when we're in the office.'

'I'm sorry, Mr Mathers,' she said hurriedly. 'I'll do whatever you say if you promise me you won't tell her.' She grabbed at the hem of his jacket and stroked a hand over the bulge at the front of his pants. 'I'll do anything, Mr Mathers. Honest I will.'

He pulled himself from her reach. 'You're a fucking slut, Sally,' he growled. 'You'd do anything regardless of whether I had a hold over you. Stop fucking grovelling before I get really pissed off. Just get used to the fact that I will be telling Dezzie about your nasty little game of show and tell.'

When she began to sob, Jake grabbed a fistful of Sally's hair and dragged her from the floor. Her tears transformed into a brief howl of pain and then they lowered into something that suggested sexual arousal. As Jake dragged her to the side of Edwin's desk, pushing Sally face down across the surface, the girl's protests developed a lack of sincerity that was almost comical.

Jake kept one hand in the centre of her back and used the other to raise Sally's skirt. He pulled her panties swiftly down, exposing the bare cheeks of her backside.

Edwin held himself still as he stared at the girl, sure his climax would come if he studied her bare bottom for too long. The curves were delightful to behold. The cheeks made her rear look model-perfect. She was no longer showing anything as indiscreet as her pussy lips. The pose was almost modest. But it was still enough to make his scrotum tingle with the threat of release. His heart pounded and he again marvelled that his life had been transformed into such a gratuitous peepshow.

159

Jake's hand slapped hard against Sally's rear.

She cried out.

Edwin feared her exclamation would be overheard. He figured, with Jake administering the punishment, it would be the young director's obligation to explain the noise if anyone questioned its source. But that thought didn't stop him from glancing apprehensively in the direction of the office door.

'Stop acting like such a brat, Sally,' Jake grunted. He slapped his palm hard against her rear for a second time. This blow left a glowing red handprint on the pale flesh of her right buttock. The smack landed with enough force to tremble through the surface of the desk.

She began to sob.

'Don't think you can play games with me,' Jake hissed.

He slapped again.

The retort echoed from the walls.

'And don't think Dezzie will be any easier on you when I tell her what you were doing with her husband.'

'We hadn't done anything. Mr Miller will tell you. We hadn't done anything. I'd only shown him my pussy.'

'I'm sure Dezzie will think that's acceptable,' Jake snapped sarcastically. He slapped her again. The clap of flesh smacking flesh was loud enough to hurt Edwin's ears. Jake moved his hand away and left Sally lying across the desk. Her panties were around her knees, the elasticated waistband cutting into her skin. Her buttocks glowed red with handprints. The tremors of an orgasm shuddered through her body.

Edwin watched, aware his own climax was on the verge of shooting with the same cataclysmic force. He glanced at Jake, wondering if this interruption to his day was now concluded and if he was simply supposed to carry on with his routine as though nothing had happened.

'If Sally's arse wasn't so perfect I think I'd fire the simpering little slut,' Jake told him.

Edwin glanced at Sally's perfect buttocks. He was painfully conscious of his erection and the torment of his predicament became unbearable. He longed to touch the woman sprawled across his desk even though he knew there was no hope of sexually enjoying her. Pushing that thought from his mind, he glanced at Jake. 'There was no need to punish her like that. I'm sure she was sorry enough without you slapping her bottom so hard.'

Indifferent, Jake shrugged. He flicked the back of his hand against Sally's rear and told her to get back to the switchboard.

Humbled. Broken. Defeated. Sally wriggled from the desk, pulled her panties up, and then retrieved her coat from the corner of the room. Her shoulders drooped. She glanced in Jake's direction. Her eyes shone with adoration while her lips alternated between a smile and a scowl. Because he wasn't looking at her, she skulked quietly from the office and closed the door carefully behind herself.

Jake looked genuinely pained. 'I'm sorry, Eddie,' he began. 'But I'm going to have to tell Dezzie about everything that was happening when I arrived in here. I'm going to have to tell her about that silly little slut. And I'm going to have to tell her about you.'

Edwin frowned, wondering why Jake should have to apologise for that. It was only when he realised his wife would be livid that he understood there were going to be repercussions.

Fifteen

Jake's apartment was palatial. Edwin hadn't known what to expect but he hadn't thought the décor would be so stylish. The penthouse suite of a large building, it occupied an entire floor. To Edwin's socialist attitudes the place shrieked of inherited wealth and privilege. In the tired suit he wore for the office, Edwin felt small and out of place amongst the grandeur.

'Perhaps I should go back home and talk this through with Des there?'

'She wanted to deal with this here,' Jake told him. 'I've got no problems with that. Come on in.'

Jake's TVR was parked in the underground garage. He had brought Sally with him and Edwin met the pair in the complex's lobby. Jake led the way to a majestic lift and they rode in silence to the upper floor.

'You told Desdemona about this morning?' Edwin asked nervously.

Sally glared at him.

Jake said, 'Once I told her she asked if she could use this place to deal with the matter. Dezzie has a delicious sense of fun so I figured it would be cool. I think Maisy will be here too, so you'll get a chance to meet her.'

Three days earlier Edwin knew he wouldn't have cared about meeting Jake's university girlfriend. Now, uneasy at the prospect of how Desdemona was going to react when she saw him, he realised he was looking forward to encountering Maisy more than seeing his own wife. He tried to swallow the lump that had risen in his throat but he knew it was not going to go away. Following Jake's lead into an ostentatious hall, Edwin and Sally took his directions towards a spare bedroom.

'I'm just going to fix myself a drink,' he explained. 'Dezzie said she wanted you both to wait in there. She'll be along shortly.'

A wave of apprehension washed over Edwin. He had been scared when Desdemona said she wanted to talk to him on Sunday night. Serious fears that they were about to have a conversation that could portend the end of their marriage loomed large in his imagination. But, while that nervousness had been unsettling, he had at least understood the potential outcomes. This ordeal was a genuine step into the unknown and he had no idea what to expect when he encountered his wife this evening. He couldn't even speculate about the way things were going to progress.

'What's Dezzie going to do to us?' Sally asked.

He shrugged. Being honest, he had thought Sally would have a better idea of the night's potential outcome but he wasn't going to admit that much. Edwin had suffered enough shame and humiliation without having to confess that she probably understood how his wife would react better then he did. He led the way into a large and luxuriant bedroom, surprised the room was spacious enough to house a four-poster as well as a settee on one wall and a pair of armchairs on another. An unobtrusive door to their side led to what he assumed was an en suite bathroom. The predominant colour in the room was red with gold trimmings and he wouldn't allow himself to be surprised that one of the bedrooms in Jake's apartment was furnished like something from an eighteenth-century bordello.

'Sit down. Both of you. Dezzie will be along shortly.'

He turned and discovered a dark-haired woman in a business suit had followed them into the room. He recognised her as Maisy: Jake's girlfriend with the salacious and depraved appetite. Her face was austere, and not particularly pretty, but he couldn't help thinking she held herself as though she knew she was a sexual creature. He didn't know if it was the thrust of her breasts that made him identify her in such a way, or the shapeliness of her bare legs beneath her short skirt. Edwin supposed it could simply be that he was currently noticing the sexuality of everything that surrounded him. He was in the domain of a man who had blatantly enjoyed sex with Desdemona and Edwin wondered if that had happened in this same ostentatious bedroom. He was in the company of a young woman who had shown him her pussy and told him that Desdemona had gone down on her. And he knew that Maisy was bisexual and actively involved in some sort of *ménage à trois* with Jake and Sally. Any or all of those reasons could have turned his thoughts to sex and sexuality.

But Edwin felt sure it was more than that.

He believed there was an air of anticipation in the way that Maisy held herself. She was clearly privy to Desdemona's plans and would know how his wife expected the evening to progress. The lilt of her smile suggested she already knew too many of his secrets and would privately enjoy whatever it was that lay ahead. Edwin tore his gaze away from hers, uneasy with the predatory way she examined him.

He supposed a part of his excitement could have been caused by apprehension. He would soon be faced with the fury of Desdemona's humiliating anger and that had already proved to be an obscenely powerful aphrodisiac. Whatever the reason, he was aware that his erection was twitching back into pained life.

'Sit down there,' Maisy said, pointing at the armchairs.

Sally went first this time, hurrying to obey Maisy's orders. Edwin followed her slowly. Not sure what to expect. Not yet sure he was comfortable accepting instructions from strangers. He took the remaining seat and settled himself uneasily in the chair. It wasn't yet six o'clock. He kept checking his wristwatch as the seconds ticked slowly past. Maisy settled herself in the centre of the settee, crossing her legs as though deliberately trying to entice his view with a glimpse of her sleek bare thigh. She had a clipboard by her side and busied herself studying its contents.

With an effort of willpower, Edwin kept his gaze away from the woman's legs. He continually glanced at his wristwatch, blinking in surprise as six o'clock passed. Responding with more shock when the hands moved to quarter past the hour.

'Is my wife likely to be much longer?'

'I think she's just sucking off Jay at the moment,' Maisy replied evenly. 'Should I go and interrupt them? Tell her you're anxious to see her?'

The air rushed from his lungs on a breath of raw arousal. His entire body was suddenly alive with the familiar sensations of impending climax. From the corner of his eye he saw Sally smirk at his discomfort. Edwin briefly despised her. It was only when he remembered how pitiful she had looked being spanked to a climax that he was able to recognise her as a fellow spirit who revelled in submission.

'No,' he told Maisy. He was blushing but he forced himself not to stammer. 'If she's busy, there's no need to disturb her.' The words sounded pathetic and inappropriate. When he saw Maisy cover a grin with her clipboard he realised his embarrassment was close to being complete.

A further fifteen minutes passed before the bedroom door opened again. Jake entered first, looking relaxed in a sweatshirt and jeans. He held a frost-sweated bottle of beer in his hand. Desdemona followed him into the room, dressed in a business suit that matched Maisy's. Her smile was broad as she shared a joked with Jake. She settled herself on the settee – Jake to Maisy's right and Desdemona to Maisy's left – and the three of them glared across the room at Sally and Edwin.

His wife's smile had disappeared.

'They're still dressed,' Desdemona scowled. 'I wanted them naked.'

Maisy frowned. 'You never said.'

'I'm sure I did.'

Maisy shrugged lightly. 'No harm no foul.' She grinned. Standing up, clapping her hands and pointing first at Sally and then at Edwin she said, 'You two. Undress now. We want you naked.'

Edwin shook his head. He had been prepared to tolerate some silliness this evening. He supposed he deserved to face a modicum of his wife's upset for what had happened in his office that morning. But he didn't think his culpability stretched to this degree of humiliation. Getting out of his chair, plucking his briefcase from the side and marching over to the door, he glanced at Desdemona and said, 'We will talk about this back at home.'

Desdemona didn't bother looking at him. 'If you don't do as you've just been told we'll never talk about this, Eddie. I'll simply divorce you. Walk out of that door and our marriage ends now.'

The words were spoken with a finality that brooked no argument.

He hesitated, aware it wasn't a bluff.

Trying to catch her eye, wishing he could talk about this with her away from the distraction of Jake and Sally and Maisy, he silently willed her to look at him.

Maisy glanced at him sympathetically. She nodded her head in the direction of the empty chair and said, 'If you'll just undress and resume your seat, Mr Miller, we can begin.'

Edwin glanced at the door leading from the bedroom. And then he turned to look at the seat he had just vacated. It was a huge decision and he was unfairly being allowed no opportunity to decide if this was what he really wanted. Growling with bitter frustration, he went back to the seat and started to tear off his tie.

Sally was already naked.

She seemed untroubled by her nudity but Edwin knew Jake, Maisy and Desdemona had all seen her unclothed body before. He thought she looked more petite than the girl he was used to seeing, although he figured part of that was attributable to the bulky shapeless coat she liked to wear and the ridiculously clunky platform shoes. Her breasts were small and uninspiring. The smooth flesh over her sex had been poignantly arousing that morning. Now he stared at her as though she was nothing more than an unattired mannequin in a shop-window display. Her moment of being a sultry temptress had been spectacularly short lived.

'Take a picture. It'll last longer,' Sally snapped.

Edwin blushed and wrenched his gaze away. He heard Maisy titter on the seat behind him. Ignoring them all, not allowing himself to remember that he was in a room full of comparative strangers, Edwin went through the shameful process of removing his clothes. His suit felt grubby and drab in the splendour of Jake's apartment. He was ashamed to acknowledge it was probably the best item he was wearing. His shirt was marked with sweat stains from the perspiration he suffered after seeing Sally's private show that morning. The vest beneath his shirt was equally unflattering. He was happy to remove it even if it did reveal his scrawny chest and the threat of a middle-age spread that pressed at the waistband of his trousers. He was acutely aware of the coarse hair on his arms and back and the bald expanse down the centre of his chest.

'He's teasing us, isn't he?' Maisy giggled. 'Did he learn these tricks when he worked as a professional stripper? One of the Chippendales, maybe?'

Desdemona shrieked with laughter. Jake spluttered on his beer. Sally smirked. Edwin's blushes deepened. His cheeks were so hot he could almost smell the flesh as it sizzled and charred. He fumbled with the belt at his waist before his fingers finally developed the motility to unfasten the simple clasp. Stepping out of the trousers, leaving his shoes behind and realising his dark socks were probably making him look ridiculous, *more ridiculous*, he hurriedly pulled them from his feet and revealed himself in only a pair of wash-grey Y-fronts. His heart pounded, his face was the colour of a ripe beetroot and he silently besought Desdemona to allow him pity, dignity or forgiveness.

'Hurry it along, Mr Miller,' Maisy said sternly. 'We want you naked and sitting in the chair. You're taking much longer than we expected.'

Acting as though he was trying to defy her; acting as though he was working under his own free will rather than obeying her callous instruction; Edwin pulled the Y-fronts down to his ankles. The blood pounded noisily in his temples. His heart raced so fast he knew it would eventually stop. Seize. Explode. He was naked and standing in front of his wife and her friends and he had never known a deeper and more shameful humiliation. Dragging a deep breath into his lungs, despising the pathetic threat of tears that blurred his vision, he turned to make sure the chair was where he expected and then sat down.

'Fucking hell,' Sally murmured. 'It is tiny, isn't it?'

Desdemona smiled.

Jake was grinning but looking in a different direction.

Maisy made no attempt to disguise her obvious amusement.

Edwin desperately wanted to close his eyes. Instead he glared at Desdemona as she sat quietly beside Jake. Even when Maisy stood up and walked to the centre of the room he kept his gaze fixed on his wife.

'The reason you two have been summoned here this evening is because you've behaved inappropriately. Sally had no right to show herself to Mr Miller the way she did this morning. And Mr Miller should have reacted more responsibly when Sally's behaviour became so inappropriate. How do you respond, Sally? Guilty or not guilty?'

She spoke with the cocky authority of an arrogant graduate applying for a position with the Law Society.

Edwin had not been able to decide whether he liked or disliked Maisy. Now he knew that he positively abhorred the woman.

Sally was clearly intimidated but struggling to appear cool and collected. 'Whatever,' she grunted. She shifted in her seat, trying to assume a pose that showed she was unimpressed by Maisy's learned tone. The movement only served to make her look shiftless and uncomfortable. Crushed by the claustrophobic weight of his embarrassment, Edwin barely noticed.

'Answer properly, please, Sally,' Maisy insisted. 'Guilty or not guilty?'

Sally glared at her. 'You've made up your minds already. So it doesn't matter what I say.'

'Guilty or not guilty?'

'Guilty,' Sally spat.

Maisy turned to face Edwin. When her gaze lowered to his lap his cheeks flushed with fresh shame. She smirked quietly to herself and in a flash of pure psychic intuition Edwin knew she was thinking of the words 'small' and 'inadequate'. Maisy cleared her throat as though removing any sound of laughter. 'Sally came into your office this morning and exposed herself to you, Mr Miller,' she began pompously. 'You made no attempt to discourage her or eject her from your office. How do you plead? Guilty or not guilty?'

He told himself he didn't have to go through with this facile charade. If Desdemona and her new friends wanted to play stupid games of nudity and kangaroo courtroom scenes they could do whatever the hell they wanted. But those games didn't have to include him and he should not have to suffer the torture of sitting naked in front of an arrogant young stranger who was demanding he justify his actions. His mouth fell open as he prepared to bawl his defiance at her.

Across the room he saw Desdemona studying him. He remembered the last words she had spoken to him: the words that had kept him in the room and made him strip naked. '*If you don't do as you've just been told we'll never talk about this, Eddie. I'll simply divorce you. Walk out of that door and our marriage ends now.*'

'Guilty,' he replied.

Maisy turned to face Jake and Desdemona. 'The accused admit their guilt. I can see no reason to prolong this ordeal. I move we should commence with sentencing and punishment.'

Edwin barely heard the words. The blood flowed through his temples with a deafening roar. He was trying to meet his wife's eyes but Desdemona was looking everywhere except in his direction. She had a hand resting easily on Jake's thigh and occasionally shared his bottle of beer. The only times she glanced across the room it was to glare at Sally and fix the younger woman with a sneer of cool disdain.

'All in favour of moving on to the verdict?' Maisy asked.

Jake and Desdemona shouted, 'Aye!'

Maisy's grin was disconcerting as she rounded on him. Again her gaze dropped to his lap and her smirk flourished into something hateful. She was trying to suppress laughter. Before he had a chance to complain she spoke swiftly and with a commanding authority. 'Mr Miller. You weren't to blame for Sally's behaviour this morning. But you could have responded to the situation more appropriately. Your wife has already agreed the terms of your punishment. If you would simply lie on the bed your instructions are that you must not touch anyone else in this room. Your punishment will commence shortly. Do you understand?'

Edwin nodded. Still blushing. Despising the ordeal of being naked with strangers. Loathing their smirks and superiority. He climbed onto the bed and lay on his back. His gaze fixed on the canopy atop the four-poster and he tried to pretend he was anywhere else except in the centre of this humiliating and embarrassing ordeal. Maisy's crisp voice effortlessly cut through all his attempts at believing he was somewhere else.

'Sally. You're a stupid little tart.'

'What?'

'Dezzie told you that her husband wasn't a part of this. She said he wasn't fair game. Yet you still went into his office this morning, flashing your nasty pussy and acting like the little whore that you are.'

'That's not fucking fair!' Sally exploded.

'Because of your behaviour, you're tonight's bitch,' Maisy said sharply. 'Jay, Dezzie and me will spank your stupid little arse. And then you'll spend the rest of the night on clean-up duty. Do you understand?'

'I was last night's bitch,' Sally argued.

'Then you'll have no problems remembering what's expected of you.'

Edwin heard the heated exchange, only understanding a few words, and wondering what level of hell he had fallen to. He was lying naked on expensive sheets, listening to a ball-breaking bitch berate an unclothed slattern. His wife was nearby, intimately touching the director of the company for which he worked. He could have believed it was the most hateful and deplorable situation imaginable if his erection hadn't throbbed with the need for release. His scrotum was a tight sac that ached to be emptied.

'How do you want to play this, Dezzie?' Maisy asked.

Desdemona loomed into the range of Edwin's vision near the bottom of the bed. She looked more beautiful than he remembered. He watched her from such a peculiar angle it reminded him of the stylistic shots that were the signature of Hitchcock movies.

'If Sally is so eager for Eddie to see her pussy I want it over his face for the rest of the evening.' She held up a long, elegant finger. 'I don't want your pussy touching him, Sally. I just want it over his face so he can see every tiny detail.'

'You heard the lady,' Maisy barked.

Edwin briefly wondered why Sally was so eager to obey the humiliating instructions. He knew that he was

171

only there because his wife had threatened to divorce him if he left the room. But Sally was enduring the abuse of the others and he couldn't conceive of her motivation. Was she doing it because she adored Jake? Maisy? Or did she simply relish the humiliation? It was impossible to guess an answer and, when she positioned her naked body over his, remaining on her hands and knees and deliberately keeping her pussy out of his reach, he knew he wouldn't be able to ask the question.

'Jay, sweetheart?' Desdemona called cheerfully. 'Could you give Sally the fucking she deserves? I think she needs it good and hard. And you're the only man here who can supply that.'

Edwin felt sick.

Jake called enthusiastic agreement. A moment later the naked man was behind Sally, forcing a sheathed erection against the smooth lips of her sex. His knees were close to the sides of Edwin's head. The bed bobbed and swayed like a stormy ocean. Edwin's nausea rose as though he was succumbing to seasickness. Because Sally's pussy was held over Edwin's face, he could see every detail of the penetration. He could see all nine inches of Jake's huge erection, and the short scrub of dark hairs covering the man's balls. The scents of sweat, male arousal and feminine musk combined to bring him close to gagging.

'Are you ready for a hard one, Sally?'

'I shouldn't be the bitch tonight,' Sally complained. Despite her words she made no attempt to extricate herself. Edwin could see she was forcefully wriggling her pussy onto the end of Jake's cock. The lips dimpled inward and then began to engulf him. 'I was the bitch last night,' she mumbled. 'This is totally unfair.'

Jake slapped a hand against Sally's buttock. The retort was loud enough to make Edwin flinch. 'Stop your whining, Sally,' he said. 'It's unbecoming.' It was as much as he said before he plunged into her.

The wetness of her sex squelched as Jake's length was driven home. Edwin was amazed to see so much of it disappear inside the petite woman above his face. The sight had already made his inadequate erection hard and he wondered how long he would be able to resist his own climax as he was treated to such an intimate display. The bed rolled and yawed beneath him as Jake rocked his hips back and forth. Droplets of Sally's musk splashed occasionally on Edwin's face. He conceded that he could close his eyes and not have to watch the penetration that was happening inches above his nose but he worried that such an open act of defiance would result in further punishment and humiliation.

'We all know you like being the bitch,' Jake laughed. 'I don't know why you pretend otherwise.' His voice was even and unbroken by exertion. If Edwin had heard him without knowing the circumstances he would never have believed he was listening to a man forcing his cock in and out of a nubile young girl.

'I don't like being the bitch, Jay. Tell Maisy and Dezzie to stop making me their bitch. They'll listen to you.'

'You don't just like being the bitch. *You love it*.'

'That's not true.'

More movement on the bed dragged Edwin's attention from the monotony of the conversation and the hypnotising view of Jake's length pushing in and out of Sally's pussy. He could see the ridge of a condom's edge binding around the base of Jake's shaft. It dimpled the flesh so severely Edwin thought the discomfort looked unbearable. He could also see the man's scrotum tightening, as though Jake was getting ready to ejaculate. The thought was exciting enough to make him feel ill.

'You're a cock-monster,' Jake told Sally. His laughter was derisory.

'I'm not a cock-monster.'

'You were trying to give Eddie the horn so you could fuck him.'

'No way.'

'You'd deep throat him now if you thought Dezzie would let you.'

'I couldn't deep throat that tiny cock of his,' Sally sneered. There were traces of exertion in her voice, as though the pounding was taking a toll. 'It wouldn't reach the back of my throat. More likely it would get stuck between my teeth.'

Edwin shrivelled from the insults but they only served to make his erection swell. Sensing that someone was very close to his side, he started to turn. The familiar fragrance, and something intimately recognisable in her warmth and movement, told him it was Desdemona. It had been more than twenty-four hours since they had been this close. He didn't think they had spent such a long time apart in their entire marriage. The unreal circumstances of the reunion did not stop him from feeling the familiar rush of satisfaction that her nearness always inspired.

'Don't turn around, Eddie,' Desdemona whispered. 'Carry on staring upward. Keep your eyes fixed on Sally's tight little cunt.'

His wife's words were whispered into his ear. She squeezed close. Sheltering with him beneath the canopy of Sally and Jake. Her body touched his and he knew she was now naked. The silken sensation of her breasts against his arm and her thigh brushing over his leg reinforced the idea that she was nude against him. He released a quivering sigh.

'Did you enjoy looking at her pussy this morning? Did this pathetic cock of yours get hard?' A cool finger brushed the base of his shaft. He realised it was probably chilly because she had held Jake's bottle of lager.

'I didn't ask Sally to show me anything,' he spluttered. 'I didn't invite her into my office and demand she should strip. You know I would never do that, don't you?'

'Answer the question, Eddie. Did you enjoy looking at her pussy?'

She squeezed her hand around him and yanked hard on his cock. The sensations of pleasure and pain were perfectly balanced. He couldn't decide whether he should scream from agony or explode through ecstasy.

'Did your little dick go hard?'

'Yes!' he gasped. 'Yes it did.'

She tugged viciously on him. This time the pleasure had gone and there was only pain. 'You won't do it again, will you? This worthless little dick is my property, isn't it? You'll never *ever* think of putting it anywhere except where I tell you. Do you understand?'

He could have argued and said she was being unfair. He could have pointed out she was living a carefree lifestyle where she had whichever lover she chose regardless of her marriage or her husband's opinion. He could have said the arrangement was inequitable. If she had free reign to fuck others the same conditions should apply to him. But he knew their arrangement was not balanced in that fashion. Would never be balanced in such a way. And he had never had any interest in the prospect of doing anything with Sally. Desdemona was taking her pleasure from fucking other people: he was taking his pleasure from Desdemona fucking other people.

'Do you understand?' she demanded.

The condescension in her voice was humiliating. The pain she ignited with her vicious grip was severe. 'Yes,' he gasped. She pulled so hard on his length he feared the skin would tear away in her hand. His foreskin felt as though it had been shredded. His scrotum was stretched beyond its capacity. Bee-stings of agony stabbed between his legs as her grip caught pubic hairs and wrenched them free from their follicles. 'Yes,' he hissed. 'Yes. I understand.'

She released her hold.

He was instantly enveloped by a glory of relief. The sensation was almost strong enough to make him climax.

Ignoring him, Desdemona reached up to Sally's pussy.

He watched her fingers encircle Jake's length and become smeared with the wetness from Sally's sex. Lowering her hand, pushing her fingers into Edwin's mouth, she said, 'These are the only circumstances when you're allowed to taste another woman's pussy. Do you understand me, Eddie?'

He couldn't reply. Her fingers filled his mouth and the noxious flavours of condom, Jake's sweat and Sally's juices were cloying enough to make him want to vomit. His erection continued to sit painfully hard. His balls were a punitively tight sac. And he feared he was ready to burst. The arousal flowed through him in a barrage of brutal spikes.

'Do you understand me, Eddie?' Desdemona hissed. 'The only circumstances when you're allowed to taste another pussy are when I've given you explicit permission.'

'I understand,' he mumbled meekly. Her fingers made it hard to speak. Worse still, the flavour of sex filled his mouth. He could taste Sally's pussy and Jake's condom with every word he uttered.

She laughed. It was a callous sound. Sliding her fingers from his lips, she breathed a soft and sultry sigh. 'Do you know that Maisy's licking my cunt while we speak?'

He hadn't known. But as soon as she said the words he could feel Desdemona had shifted position and he was aware that there was the weight of another body further down the bed. He clenched his hands into fists and closed his eyes tight. Every effort was invested in not embarrassing himself by ejaculating at the sight and sensation of all that was happening around him. Sally's shaven labia hovered above his face. Jake's erection plunged rapidly in and out of her. His naked wife lay next to him, taunting him with obscenities and humiliations. And now he had learnt there was another woman between Desdemona's thighs, burying her tongue deep into his wife's most intimate cleft.

'Maisy's great at licking my cunt,' Desdemona purred. 'You could never manage to be that good if you practised for a million years.'

Her words cut deep.

His arousal throbbed with more insistence.

'Jay's going to fuck me once he's finished riding Sally. Do you want to watch and see how a real man fucks me, Eddie?'

He almost wailed. He knew he wasn't going to be able to hold back the climax for long. He also knew, when it did come, it would be violent in its power. The environment was too charged with sexual excitement. Her words were unbearably inspiring. And he knew he was the most sexually incompetent person on the bed. His inadequacies and the subsequent shame compounded with his arousal. He was so close to the brink of ejaculation he thought the orgasm must already have been wrenched from his shaft.

'Do you want to see that, Eddie?'

She snaked a hand down his stomach. Her fingers weren't touching his erection but they were dangerously close. If she put too much pressure on the wrong erogenous zone Edwin was certain he would not be able to contain the explosion.

'Do you want to see Jay slipping his big cock in and out of my tight, wet hole? Would it give you a lot of pleasure to watch that?'

His features were a grimace of anguish. It should have been the last thing that any husband wanted to watch but he was suddenly desperate to see Jake's erection buried in his wife's sex. Admitting as much in the silence of his own thoughts hurled him to the point of climax. Confessing it to his wife would almost certainly push him beyond the point of restraint. The best he could manage was to grit his teeth and offer a terse, desperate nod.

'And my hole really is wet now,' Desdemona whispered. She released a throaty chuckle and added, 'Maisy's got her tongue all the way up there. She is such a good little cunt-slut.'

'Thanks, Dezzie,' Maisy called. Her voice was muffled. She slurred her sibilants as though her mouth was too wet to pronounce them properly. 'It's a pleasure to be your cunt-slut.'

Edwin dragged air into his lungs.

His wife was naked and laid next to him. Strangers surrounded him: fucking gratuitously and unmindful that he was watching. A woman licked his wife's pussy and Desdemona had just referred to her as a cunt-slut. It seemed a miracle that he had resisted the urge to orgasm but he didn't know how long that marvel was likely to continue.

'I want to see him fucking you,' Edwin whispered.

She placed a kiss against his cheek and grinned. 'You really are a sick little fucker, aren't you?'

He nodded agreement. Perhaps she was sexually involved with several strangers, and didn't care whether her orgasms came from men or women or a combination. But she wasn't the one who needed to see their partner fucking someone else in order to reach the height of sexual satisfaction. If either of them could be properly labelled as a sick little fucker, Edwin knew he was the one who fell under that description.

'I'll fuck Jay until you come,' Desdemona breathed. 'I'm not saying I'll stop once your pathetic little cock has shot its load. But you won't be allowed to watch me after that. I'll send you home after you've spurted and I'll inform you of the rest of your punishment later. Do you understand what I'm telling you, Eddie?'

He nodded acceptance of her terms. He didn't fully understand what she was saying. The effort of fighting off his ejaculation was taking up most of his concentration. But he had followed her main condition: once he climaxed he would be forced to leave.

Desdemona pulled herself from his side. He got his first chance to see properly that she was naked, her glorious body looking so splendid that Sally seemed bland and uninteresting in comparison.

Desdemona pushed Sally away from Jake. The younger woman looked set to protest her rude treatment but Edwin wasn't watching her. His gaze was fixed upward on the sight of Jake's wet length nuzzling against Desdemona's pussy lips. His wife's fingers gently gripped Jake's cock and placed it against the centre of her sex.

The condom on his erection glistened with Sally's wetness. In the bright lights of the bedroom Edwin could see every glossy detail of the slick shaft that was about to plunge into his wife. Desdemona's sex lips were an open split of purple flesh, flushed from the teasing of Maisy's tongue. The blonde curls that covered her sex were darkened to an oily black. Her pale-pink fingers, shaft, labia and thighs were only illuminated by the glint of gold from Desdemona's wedding ring.

She moved her hand as soon as Jake's glans was inside.

And then Jake pushed completely into her.

Edwin felt the orgasm pulse through his body.

He groaned with frustration, shamed by the scathing giggles of Maisy, Sally and Desdemona. His wife pulled herself from Jake's cock with a promise that he could finish her later. She dragged Edwin from the bed, not allowing him the opportunity to begin wiping the semen from his chest.

'You've been a good boy, Eddie.' Desdemona smiled.

The patronising praise genuinely warmed him.

'You were a naughty boy not resisting Sally,' she added sternly. 'But you've taken your punishment like a man.' She laughed, shook her head and said, 'Well, you've taken it like I knew you would.'

The insult made him despise her and love her with equal force. He wanted to kiss her and embrace her but

179

knew she would not allow such shows of affection in front of Jake, Maisy and Sally. A part of him wondered if she would ever allow such intimacy again.

'I'll reward you for accepting your punishment,' Desdemona whispered. Placing her lips close to his ear, cupping her hand against his cheek so that the words were only shared between them, she said, 'You may go home now. Pack my suitcase for my three days away with Jake. Sleep in the spare room again tonight. Goodnight, darling. I'll see you again on Sunday.'

He blinked. Bewildered. 'Is that it?'

Desdemona shook her head. 'No. I've got one other punishment planned for you and Sally. But that's all you have to suffer this evening. Now go home and do as I've told you.'

As soon as she had said the words, Edwin knew he was dismissed from Jake's apartment. He retrieved his clothes from the chair and left without being acknowledged. From the corner of his eye he saw that Jake was now straddling Maisy while Desdemona kissed her mouth. Sally's face was buried between Desdemona's thighs. The sore length in his pants began to ache. And Edwin realised he was already at the stage of arousal where he was ready to come again.

Sixteen

Edwin's Thursday at the office fled past with a barrage of apologetic conversations.

Sally: 'I'm sorry about yesterday morning, Mr Miller.'

Jake: 'Sorry I didn't get a chance to say goodnight when you left.'

Desdemona: 'I'm sorry I didn't get home last night.'

Robin: 'Sorry to do this to you, Ed. But I need digs for a day or two.'

He was so involved with his work, concentrating his focus on the mundane chores of the office, that he didn't realise the final apology coincided with the end of the day. It was almost seven o'clock. Desdemona and Jake had departed on their tour of the regionals and he couldn't let himself think about what they would be doing together. The distraction would be more arousing than he could bear. He glanced out of the window as he accepted Robin's call and realised the day was slipping towards twilight. The car park was as deserted as when he had arrived that morning.

'Digs?' Edwin repeated. 'What's happened?'

'Alice and me have still got our differences. She decided it would be easier to work out our problems if I fucked off out of her face.' He grunted mirthless laughter and added, 'That wasn't her first choice. But since I'm not going to drop dead . . .'

'You want to stay at ours?'

'You've got a spare room haven't you? I wouldn't normally ask but . . .'

He left the sentence open. Edwin was trying to remember if there was still a spare room at his house or if that had now become the place where he was expected to spend his nights. 'Sure,' he said quickly. 'Are you coming over tonight?'

'Just for two or three nights,' Robin promised. 'A week at the most.' His voice was tinged with obvious relief and Edwin realised his brother had been on the verge of being homeless. He felt momentarily proud of himself for being able to offer assistance in a time of crisis. That sensation was quashed by a weight of self-doubt. He didn't think Desdemona would mind him inviting Robin to stay, but she had expressly told Edwin to sleep in the spare room. He wondered how he was going to obey that instruction without his brother noticing something suspicious. His thoughts were dragged back to the conversation as he heard Robin say the stay would be as brief as possible. Until he had either resolved his differences with Alice or found himself a permanent alternative.

'However long it takes,' Edwin said generously. 'I'm still at the office but I'll be back home around eight.'

'I think you work a little too hard,' Robin grunted.

The words made Edwin pause. He was sure someone else had said the same thing to him. And recently. He dismissed the memory as irrelevant and ended his call with his brother. Hurrying from the office he almost bumped into Sally as she waited outside his door.

'What the hell are you doing here?'

The exclamation came out harsh with his surprise.

Sally was defensive. 'I work here.'

'Not at this time of night, you don't.'

She scowled. Handing him a white envelope she said, 'This is your wife's idea. She didn't think either of us got sufficiently punished last night. Dezzie, Jay and Maisy spent most of the night trying to come up with the best

182

punishment. Maisy came up with the broad outline for this one. Jay and Dezzie added the refinements.'

She continued to hold out the envelope while Edwin vacillated. He hadn't allowed himself to think about the ordeal of the previous night. Every time his mind started to drift back to the image of Jake's cock sliding into Desdemona's wet pussy he had deliberately pushed the thought away and urged himself to concentrate on something (*anything*) else. But now, faced with Sally and her reminders of all that had occurred, Edwin couldn't stop the rush of arousal sweeping over him.

Sally regarded him in silence, still holding out the envelope.

'What is this?'

'It's from Dezzie for you, Mr Miller. These are the instructions for how she wants us to be punished. That's all I was told. I don't know what else it contains.'

Gingerly accepting the sealed envelope, Edwin tore it open.

The corridor around them was deserted. His bowels churned as he realised he was with a woman he knew intimately. He had watched Sally having sex. He had tasted her most intimate secretions. She silently shamed him with her knowledge of his naked and inadequate body. The sounds around them echoed with the emptiness of the building and reinforced his feeling that they were alone.

'What does it say?' Sally asked.

Edwin glanced at the sheet of paper. 'Haven't you been told?'

'Dezzie gave this to me last night with instructions to hand it to you on your way home this evening.' With obvious petulance she added, 'Dezzie said it was the second half of our punishment.'

He read the letter and then encouraged her to walk by his side as they vacated the offices. Although the building seemed empty he couldn't risk reading its contents aloud while there was a danger of them being

183

overheard. Sally complained at first but there was no genuine rancour in her voice. As soon as she was in the passenger seat of his car he started the engine and then read the contents of the letter aloud.

'*To Eddie and Sally . . .*'

With some bitterness he realised she hadn't started the letter with 'Dear' or 'Darling'. It read like an open communication from a business acquaintance. If his name had fallen later than Sally's in the alphabet he suspected Desdemona would have put her name first. The distant tone of the correspondence stirred a twisted blend of disgust and desire in his stomach.

'*I shall be away for the next three nights with Jay and Maisy.*'

Edwin glanced at Sally. He wondered if she had known that Maisy was going to accompany Jake and Desdemona. The expression on her face said she wasn't particularly interested in that aspect and he realised he would be the only one who spent the remaining three days considering all the potential intimacies the trio could be enjoying. As soon as that thought crossed his mind he was crippled by the nuisance of an erection. A wave of lightheadedness swept over him.

'Go on,' Sally encouraged. 'What else does it say?'

'*Sally: you will spend the next three nights naked in bed with Eddie. Eddie: you will spend the next three nights naked in bed with Sally. Neither of you is allowed to have sexual contact with the other. Eddie is not allowed to masturbate. Sally can frig herself senseless like the nymphomaniac cock-monster that she is.*'

'I'm not a cock-monster,' Sally complained. 'I'll bet it was Jay who told her to put that bit in the letter. He always calls me that.'

Edwin said nothing. He motioned for Sally to put on her seat belt and pointed the car towards his home. He stopped briefly at McDonald's, picking up burgers for the pair of them. They continued the journey in silence. Desdemona's letter had said little more than that which he had read aloud. She repeated that she would be away for three days. She mentioned that she intended fucking Jay and Maisy at every available opportunity. And she told Edwin she would see him on Sunday.

Again he was crushed by the lack of affection in the letter. But somehow, that total absence of sensitivity for his feelings only served to make his arousal more pressing. She wasn't just thinking about other men: she was actively fucking them. More exciting was the knowledge that she wasn't just fucking other people: she was sharing a part of her life with them that she would never share with him.

He quivered on the verge of climax.

'Have you got any alcohol in this house?' Sally asked, walking through to the kitchen. She held her boxed burger in one hand and sat at the kitchen table to eat her meal.

'I've got alcohol,' Eddie admitted. 'But do you think it would be wise?'

She frowned. 'What's wrong with having a beer, Mr Miller?'

'You don't think we might get drunk and accidentally do something?'

Sally laughed in his face. 'I'd have to be pretty drunk to fuck you.'

He blushed and realised she was quite right. Not bothering to argue his point he simply went to the fridge and retrieved two tins of beer. The conversation between them was stilted, although not as bad as he had feared. Sally spoke easily about Jake and Maisy, describing herself as a sexual submissive and explaining how her involvement with the other two satisfied something she couldn't get from a regular relationship. She was surprisingly articulate and a lot of what she said about her pleasure – the way it seemed to come from knowing her partner was satisfied, rather than from her own climaxes – made him think of his own reaction to Desdemona's adultery.

Edwin listened patiently as they went through a further three beers. He couldn't decide if it was because of the alcohol or his loneliness that he was beginning to find Sally's company enjoyable.

'Shit! But you can talk!' Sally giggled eventually.

Edwin could have pointed out that he had said approximately three words while she had monopolised the evening's conversation. But he guessed it was prudent to merely allow her to keep her opinion.

'You've kept me here, nattering away for the last hour, and I'm bursting for a piss.'

The alcohol had made her company more convivial but it had also eased the restraint she normally used on her vocabulary. Edwin figured he could endure the embarrassment of coarse language. He was almost certain he could put up with that more easily than the punishment Desdemona had elected he should suffer. And so he said nothing about Sally's expletives. He gave her directions for the lavatory and, when she had gone, he stared at the telephone and wondered why Desdemona hadn't called him. It was close to nine-thirty at night. He hadn't seen her since they had been at Jake's apartment. And he knew she was having sex with another man and another woman. It was clear she was enjoying herself too much to bother talking to him.

His arousal soared to the point of ejaculation.

Upstairs he heard the flush of the lavatory. The noise was unexpectedly loud, making him sure Sally had used the bathroom without closing the door. He briefly wondered what madness had made his wife think it was a good idea to burden him with the girl for those days she was away. It was only as an afterthought that he realised Desdemona probably hadn't seen it as a good idea: she had only viewed it as a punishment.

He was about to get himself another beer from the fridge when the doorbell rang. The lateness of the hour, and the sudden knowledge of who he would find there made him wonder how he could have overlooked something so important. He opened the door to greet Robin, his mind wishing it would work faster so he could invent a plausible excuse to explain the pretty young blonde sharing his house in Desdemona's absence.

'Good of you, Ed,' Robin said, lumbering into the hallway and dragging a fat suitcase with him. He also carried a case of lagers, grunting obviously with the weight. 'Owe you big time for this one, bruv. Des don't mind I'm crashing here, does she?'

'Des doesn't know yet,' Edwin admitted. 'She's away for the next few days.'

Robin's smile of understanding looked briefly like a knowing leer. Edwin told himself he was being stupid for imposing such an attitude on his brother's innocent reaction. And, when Sally appeared at the top of the stairs and started to walk cheerfully down them, his thoughts were less occupied with his brother's response and more frantically involved in trying to excuse her presence.

'Didn't know you had company,' Robin was smirking. This time Edwin didn't think there was any danger of mistaking his brother's intimation. Robin pronounced the word 'company' as though it was something deliciously vulgar.

Edwin performed introductions. 'Robin. Sally works with me. She's staying over while Des is away. Sally, this is my brother, Robin. He's staying here for a couple of days.'

Sally nodded at Robin, assessing him with a cockiness that was probably fuelled more by alcohol than genuine arrogance. 'Do you need a hand with those beers, Rob?' she asked, nodding at the case he held.

'Cheers, Doll,' he said, handing them to her. 'When you're old enough I'll let you taste one.'

'Cheeky bastard!' She grinned but struggled slightly with the weight of the beer. 'I'll go and put these in the fridge. You want a cold one, Rob?' she called as she carried the case through to the kitchen.

'Yeah. Thanks, Doll.' He stared at Edwin with an uncertain grin twitching on his lips. 'Fuck! Ed!' he gasped. His voice was lowered to a conspirator's whisper. 'I never realised you and I had so much in common. Nice bit o' skirt.'

Edwin squinted in his effort to understand the comment. 'What the hell have we got in common?' When understanding came to him he almost recoiled in disgust. 'Christ, Robin. NO. It's not like that. Sally's just staying over here for a few nights while Des is away. That's all.'

'Sure.'

'Des knows that Sally's here.'

'Sure.'

'It was Des who asked Sally to stay over.'

Robin nodded. He dragged his bag the remainder of the way into the house and then closed the door. 'If you'd told me you had a houseguest I wouldn't have imposed.' He pronounced 'houseguest' with the same intonation he had used to emphasise 'company'.

'You're not imposing,' Edwin assured him. He wanted to say other things and stress that he and Sally were not involved in a relationship. Before he could begin to reiterate the truth a flash of inspiration struck him and he realised there was a way to get around one of the earlier problems he had envisaged. 'With Sally being here you'll have to sleep on the couch tonight. Sally's in the spare room and I'm in Desdemona's bedroom.' He flinched from those final two words, wondering if he had said more with that slip of the tongue than he intended.

If the statement had been glaringly obvious Robin either missed it or chose to make no comment. He pushed his way past Edwin, heading towards the kitchen. 'You got that cold one, Doll? I'm gasping here.'

Edwin expected the remainder of the evening to be fraught with stilted silences and the sort of tense atmosphere that usually made him avoid serious drama

188

on the TV. There was no way he could explain the real reason for Sally's presence. And there was no opportunity to subtly tell Sally that she wasn't to say anything about their punishment to his brother. Not that he thought there was any danger of Sally explaining that to Robin. Edwin couldn't rationalise it in his own mind so he doubted Sally would be able to put the situation into words. Squirming with embarrassment, trying heartily to act as though Sally was a platonic friend of the family who had just never been introduced or mentioned to his brother, he was almost relieved when his mobile phone signalled an incoming message.

He left the room to attend to the call.

It wasn't, as he had hoped, Desdemona phoning so they could each hear the sounds of the other's voice. Instead it was a single photograph of his wife's face. At first he thought it looked like she was sweating. It was only after he had studied the image for a few moments that he realised the beads of perspiration on her brow, cheeks and jaw were all pearly white. She was grinning in the picture. Her expression of satisfaction was so obvious it radiated from the small LCD screen.

Edwin's erection sprouted instantaneously.

He was bathed in a sudden and glorious sweat.

His heartbeat pounded as adrenaline soared through his body and left him struggling to resist a climax. The glorious picture had him trembling so badly he realised he would have to wait for a moment before rejoining Robin and Sally in the kitchen. Trying not to leave the pair alone for too long, he measured every breath and focused his thoughts on anything except the picture he had just received.

After Desdemona had told him he was a cuckold, Edwin had believed it would only mean a small change to their lifestyles. She would get sexual satisfaction from other men and he would get his sexual satisfaction from either witnessing her pleasure or listening to her graphic details of what she had done. The one thing he had thought was implicit was that no one else would know about their special arrangement. Friends and family would have no reason to discover she was adulterous. None of their acquaintances would find out that Edwin sanctioned her behaviour. But, clearly, Desdemona thought the rules could be bent as they suited her own needs. Edwin marvelled at his own naïveté.

Less than a week into the arrangement and already he was struggling to navigate interaction between his brother and one of Desdemona's lovers. Worse still, instead of remaining with the pair, and trying to direct the conversation so that it didn't touch on any subject likely to require an embarrassing explanation, Edwin was hiding away from them so they couldn't see his arousal at having received a picture of his wife dripping in another man's spunk.

He drew a deep breath and forced himself to return to the kitchen. His heart continued to pound and his grin felt stretched and blatantly false. The mobile phone was stuffed in his trouser pocket and he wouldn't let himself think that the picture of his wife with her creamy facial was so close to the ineffectual length of his cock.

'I'm just about ready to get off to bed,' Sally said when he returned. She glanced quickly at Robin and said, 'No offence to you, Rob. I'm just knackered and I've got an early start in the morning.'

'We both have,' Edwin agreed. He glanced at Robin and said, 'Are you all right making yourself comfortable on the couch while I get Sally settled in the spare room?' Blushing at the way that might be construed, he added hurriedly, 'Before I go to my own bed in Desdemona's room.'

He cringed from his own stupid words, wondering when the bedroom had become Desdemona's room. He didn't know if Robin had heard the hateful subtext that underscored his babbling this second time. But at that moment he didn't care. Taking Robin's acceptance of the situation as a given, Edwin said goodnight to him and ushered Sally up the stairs to the spare room. He pushed her inside, promised he would be back as soon as possible, and then hurried back down to make sure Robin was sorted for blankets, a pillow and other necessities.

Robin was still in the kitchen, chugging on a tin of lager, and holding a thick pen over that day's crossword. Without looking up he asked, 'The fuck's going on here, Ed?'

Revising his plans, Edwin grabbed a fresh tin of beer from the fridge.

'What's going on where?'

'Doll,' Robin growled. 'Who the fuck is she? Are you two fucking?'

Edwin's heart pounded. The sweat on his forehead was a branding iron of guilt. He drank too much of the lager too quickly and almost spluttered its contents down his shirtfront. 'You don't believe in beating round the bush, do you?'

'Des will have your balls if she finds you in bed with that one.'

Edwin opened his mouth to reply and then closed it quickly. He wanted to say that Des wouldn't catch him in bed with Sally, but that would only sound like he was arrogantly involved in an affair. It crossed his mind to say Des wouldn't care if she caught him in bed with Sally, but that implied something he didn't want to suggest to his brother. He toyed with the idea of explaining the situation as it was to Robin, and then realised his brother would ridicule him for placing himself in such a submissive position. Eventually, after another mouthful of beer, he said, 'The situation isn't what you think it is.'

'Does Des really know that Sally's staying here overnight?'

Edwin nodded. He considered pointing out that he had been honest when he said Desdemona had been the one to insist that Sally spend the three nights in the house while she was away. The only thing that stopped him was his fear of saying something inappropriate or incriminating. He hadn't yet managed to mention the house's main bedroom without implying that it belonged solely to his wife.

'Des does know.'

'And you're fucking her?'

'Sally? No! Jesus, Robin. We're not all as sex-obsessed as you.' He berated himself for the harsh words. His brother didn't deserve that kind of insult. Especially on his first night away from the family home during an argument that was clearly rocking the foundations of his relationship with Alice. 'I'm sorry,' Edwin said quickly. 'I'm just a little uncomfortable with that sort of talk. Sally's a friend of Des's. She works with me. She's staying here while Des is away. There's nothing more to it than that.'

Robin stood up and clapped him on the shoulder. 'I should apologise,' he said softly. 'You're good enough to let me kip down here for the night and I come into your house making judgements you don't deserve.' Drawing Edwin into a short and masculine embrace, Robin patted his back and said, 'Sorry, bruv. You're a saint for putting up with me.'

Edwin pulled himself free from the hug, told Robin where the spare sheets were and said he was to get whatever he needed to make his stay comfortable. Feigning more tiredness than he genuinely felt, he forced himself not to run up the stairs to escape the embarrassment of further conversation. On the landing he breathed a sigh of relief, thankful the trauma of the day was now ended and he would be able to forget about it for a short while as he slept.

He entered the spare room and found Sally naked on top of the bed.

192

Seventeen

Immediately, Edwin tore his gaze away from her. 'You're naked,' he hissed. Staring at the bland wall, deliberately keeping his eyes from returning to Sally's body, Edwin could still see her slender frame, her small, unassuming breasts, and the smooth cleft of her sex.

'Dezzie's letter said we both had to be naked,' Sally reminded him. He was grateful she kept her voice low, as though she intuited it would be uncomfortable for him if his brother thought they were involved in a relationship. 'I'm just obeying her instructions.' She shifted her gaze over Edwin and added, 'Shouldn't you be naked too?'

His erection had subsided. Talking with Robin, and fighting the panic that came from trying to keep his new lifestyle secret, had distracted him sufficiently so that his arousal could wane. But as soon as he heard Sally's whispered words, suggesting he undress and join her in bed, the stub of flesh turned again to iron.

'This is humiliating,' he murmured.

'It's a punishment, Mr Miller. Dezzie didn't mean this as a reward.'

'But we don't have to be naked, do we?' he pleaded.

She stared at him with unspoken pity. 'I think we're getting off light with this punishment. I also think, if Jay, Dezzie or Maisy find out we didn't follow their instructions to the letter, they won't be so lenient with the next punishment they make us suffer.'

He glared at her, concentrating his gaze on her face, and wondering why she couldn't see what he was trying to say. 'I'm only suggesting we wear pyjamas.'

Sally nodded and looked genuinely sympathetic. 'We can't,' she said gently. 'Pyjamas isn't naked. If Dezzie even suspects we didn't follow her instructions exactly as she'd written them, she'll think the worst, won't she?'

Her pragmatism both surprised and annoyed him. She was his junior in the office and less than half his age. Yet she was the one more easily able to face the reality of what they had to do. Against her sexual worldliness he felt old, stupid, ignorant and inferior. Turning the light off, then quickly removing his clothes, he climbed into the bed and pulled as much of the sheet over his body as he could make available. He lay facing away from her, trying to pretend he was alone in the bed. But he had always known it would never be that simple. His eyes soon adjusted to the grey illumination that filtered through from the lamppost outside. He could barely hear Sally's breath next to him. But he was constantly aware of her weight being so close. He could even detect the faint scent of deodorant that she must have applied that morning.

His erection remained hard.

The temptation to touch himself bordered on irresistible.

He was alone in bed with a naked and attractive young woman. Even though he didn't want to do anything with her, that didn't stop him from being aroused by her nearness.

Sally shifted clumsily beside him and he realised she was placing herself beneath the sheets. The narrow bed felt hatefully small as her bare buttocks brushed against his back.

'Are you asleep, Mr Miller?'

He almost climaxed. Catching his breath, tensing the muscles in his groin and praying it would be enough to stave the explosion he trembled against the mattress and gasped, 'Not yet. Why do you ask?'

'Dezzie's letter said I could . . .' she paused and then seemed to decide the point was not worth making. 'Never mind,' she concluded. 'I'll just go to sleep.'

He said nothing. He was hovering close to the embarrassment of a climax and knew the effort of continuing the conversation would tear his thoughts away from the necessary concentration. He stayed motionless for an age. Pretending he was alone in the bed. Trying to forget that she was lying next to him. Not allowing himself to think what she might have been about to suggest.

It would have been easier to distance himself from the reality if the bed had not started to tremble. He wasn't sure when the sensation began. At first he thought it was an echo of the tremors that tortured his body. The effort of containing his orgasm took a tremendous toll and he knew he was shivering from the exertion. But the subtle rocking caused enough movement so that he knew it wasn't generated by his own pathetic quivering.

'What are you doing, Sally?'

'I thought you were asleep.'

'How am I expected to sleep when you're fidgeting like that?'

'I wasn't fidgeting. I'm fingering my pussy.'

Edwin held his breath. As soon as she said the words he could taste the flavour of her arousal and knew that he was lying next to a woman with her hand pressed against the sodden folds of her sex. Her breathing had deepened to a pant of arousal. He swallowed to clear his mouth of the taste.

'Do you have to do that?'

'Yes. I'm horny. And it helps me sleep.'

'It's not helping me sleep.'

'Dezzie said I could. It was in her letter.'

He couldn't argue the point. They were being punished and they were following the instructions of the letter.

It was humiliating that he didn't have the courage to defy his wife but he could only see that sort of action ending their relationship. Closing his eyes, trying to force himself to sleep, he listened to the room's silence and then cringed when it was broken by the sly slurp of Sally pressing a finger inside her labia.

She caught her breath, clearly excited by the contact. He realised the body next to his was stiffening. The rocking of the bed grew slightly more vigorous and the scents and sounds of Sally's masturbation consumed his every thought. She writhed between the sheets. Her gasps came occasionally. Then with growing frequency. Her breath hitched in staccato gulps. He empathised with the nearness of her encroaching climax. When she shifted position, and her leg brushed against his, Edwin thought he was going to explode. When she finally arched her back from the bed, and muttered a soft and muffled groan, he realised she had finally satisfied herself.

She fell back against the bed, sighing with contentment.

Edwin knew he should have been able to relax then. Sally had sated her body's urges and that meant they could both lie still and sleep. But he remained involved in the act of staving his ejaculation. He quietly willed himself to focus on some mental image – any mental image – that didn't make his erection ache and throb.

'Are you still awake, Mr Miller?'

He could smell the sweet scent of her breath. The flavour of sexual musk lingered on the warm air. Immediately he knew she had licked her hand after fingering herself. He tried inching towards the edge of the bed, wanting to distance himself from her. Although he didn't want to acknowledge that Sally was sexually attractive, she was exciting him in ways he hadn't imagined.

'Yes,' he grumbled. 'I'm still awake.'

'Can I ask a question?'

'If you must.'

'You get turned on when someone else fucks your wife, don't you?'

He shivered before replying. His teeth were gritted and he no longer had the urge to be angry with Sally. He could only be honest. Since climbing into bed it felt as though he had spent his entire life trying to stop himself from ejaculating. 'Yes,' he grunted. 'I get turned on when someone else has sex with my wife. Was that your question?'

'No.' She shifted position and he realised she had turned to face him. Her knee brushed the back of his thigh. Soft flesh stroked his shoulder and he could feel her breast touching his spine. The intimacy was intolerable and more than anyone could expect him to withstand. He wanted to moan and beg her to stop tormenting him. He thought he might have sobbed and pleaded with her if he had believed Sally understood how much her nearness was affecting him.

When she spoke she sounded indifferent and ignorant to his arousal. 'My question is,' she began, 'which turns you on more? Seeing someone fuck your wife? Or imagining someone fucking your wife?'

It was hard to breathe. Alone in the dark. Naked with a woman who had just masturbated. A woman who talked about others fucking his wife. He couldn't conceive of a more arousing situation. If he had allowed himself to dwell on any aspect it would have pushed him past the point of restraint.

'Why do you need to know this, Sally?'

'Just curious.'

She placed a hand on his arm. Her fingers were warm and moist. He tried not to think why they would be moist. But, once the reason came to him, the image wouldn't leave his mind. He hadn't thought that Sally was a particularly tactile person but he supposed he didn't know her sufficiently well to make such a judgement. Nevertheless, he found himself wondering if she touched his arm to reassure herself of his presence in the darkness or simply to excite him with the prospect of her nearness.

'Which turns you on more, Mr Miller?' she asked again. 'Seeing someone fuck your wife? Or imagining it?'

'I don't know. I've never thought about it in those terms.'

She wriggled against him. Her entire body was pressed against his. He had never suspected his own skin could be so sensitive but it presented him with a perfect picture of the woman lying behind him. Her slender legs were bare and intertwined with his. Her smooth pussy pressed beneath his left buttock. Her flat stomach went up to the small of his back and then her small, pert breasts pushed beneath his shoulders. He could feel the rigid thrust of her nipples pressing against his flesh. Aware that there was no way to avoid conversation, and begrudging the communication as much he enjoyed it, Edwin asked, 'Which excites you more in your sex life? The fantasy or the reality?'

Sally momentarily tightened her embrace around him. 'That's a good way of asking the question. I suppose it means the same thing.' She paused and added, 'And I can see why you didn't have an answer. It's not an easy choice to make, is it?'

'No.'

They were silent for a moment when he feared he was growing too involved with the naked woman embracing his bare body. Minutes earlier he had shared her tremors as she frigged herself to a climax. Now he was sharing the anticipatory stillness as she racked her brains to supply an answer. Her concentration was so intense he could almost feel the waves of energy flowing from her like some form of pernicious radiation.

'It's really difficult to answer,' she said eventually. He was relieved to hear that her tone was beginning to sound drowsy. 'Until I met Jay I always thought fantasy sex was way better than anything that could really happen. I've always been turned on by the idea of being submissive but most guys my age have never known how to deal with that. Jay was the first man I've ever met who spanked my bum while we were fucking, and I do like that.'

Edwin said nothing. He tried to remain still. Blood pounded through his body hard enough to make the mattress vibrate.

'And Jay and Maisy were the first time I'd ever done things with a couple. Maisy is gorgeous, and she's got a wicked imagination. She licked my pussy while I sucked Jay's cock. Then she squatted over my face while he fucked me.'

Edwin wanted to roll onto his stomach but he knew he couldn't move. If he changed position it would mean Sally's body would stroke more firmly against his and that would prove too much. He had just about grown used to being in her embrace. Any surreptitious movement would eradicate all his defences.

'When Jay introduced us to Dezzie we did a whole lot more things,' Sally confided. 'Mrs Miller really knows how to enjoy herself.' There was a proud smile in her voice and Edwin was absurdly touched that Sally held his wife in such high regard. 'But, even though it's good with Jay, Maisy and Dezzie, I still don't think the reality is ever as good as the fantasy. I don't think it ever can be.'

'Why do you say that?'

Despite the fact her words were causing unnecessary excitement; despite the fact that she was half his age and shouldn't really have been able to teach him anything about life that he hadn't already learnt for himself: Edwin was anxious to understand the reasoning behind her remark. Her intelligence and insight surprised him and he was anxious to hear the basis for her opinion.

'Surely the reality is better than the fantasy because *it is reality*? Surely that has to make it better than the fantasy, even if the reality is disappointing?'

'But that's just it.' She pressed closer.

Now her breasts were crushed against his back. She shifted the position of her leg and he felt the smooth and hairless pussy lips stroke the rear of his thigh. The sensations thrust him to the brink of climax. He held his breath and remained as rigid as a statue.

He didn't think the effort would be enough.

'The fantasy is always better,' Sally told him. 'When I just closed my eyes while I was masturbating, everything was perfect. I was in a room with beautiful men and women. Jay, Maisy and Dezzie were there: but it was like they were being played by movie actors, or something. They all wanted to tease and humiliate me. They taunted me like no one could ever manage in real life. Your wife kissed my pussy. Jay threatened to pull on my nipples until I screamed. Maisy was going to piss into my mouth. It's never been that good in real life.'

Edwin shivered.

'In reality I'm only there as a submissive and everyone else is usually so wrapped up in each other they forget about me. When I'm on clean-up duty as the bitch, I'm expected to lick Jay's spunk from Maisy's pussy. Or they get me to suck him hard so he can fuck your wife again. I love being told to do those chores. But it's a reality that just gives fuel for my fantasies. Do you understand what I mean?'

He released his breath slowly, sure that doing it too fast would cause his erection to spurt semen onto the cotton sheets. He didn't dare move. 'You're surprisingly perceptive for someone so young.'

'Thank you, Mr Miller.' She wriggled against him.

He closed his eyes, knowing the climax was going to come regardless of how much effort he employed. The fear that Desdemona would be angry that he had climaxed while lying in bed with Sally was only a small part of his reluctance to ejaculate. On some ridiculous level of personal pride he thought it would be like an act of infidelity if he came while being in bed with another woman. Even though he had explicitly obeyed Desdemona's instructions and made no attempt to touch or taste Sally, he was still listening to her and growing more and more excited.

She pressed closer. This time he felt the determined force of her pussy lips as they slipped against the back of his thigh. The flesh was wet, warm and sticky. The contact was more exciting than he could fight.

'Do you find the fantasy better than the reality too?' Sally asked.

'I'm not sure. I must give it some thought.' He drew a deep breath and asked, 'May I ask you a question?'

'Sure.'

'Why are you pressed so close against me?'

Her body quivered with an apologetic laugh. 'I was trying to steal some of your side of the bed,' she explained. There was a tinge of guilt in her tone as she added, 'I came pretty hard before and there's a damp patch on this side.'

Edwin sighed softly.

'Yes,' he admitted. 'There's the same problem on this side too.'

Eighteen

Sally's question kept coming back to him during the days while Desdemona was away. '*Which do you prefer? The fantasy or the reality?*' It played on his mind throughout the Friday he spent in the office. '*Which do you prefer? The fantasy or the reality?*' The question kept returning to him throughout the Saturday. Sally had joined him for his weekend stint in the office, on the proviso that he wouldn't spend too long in the building. Ordinarily, she admitted, she spent her Saturdays either lounging around in bed or shopping in the town centre. She didn't fancy the idea of a day in Edwin's house with only Robin for company. And she couldn't face the barrage of questions she would receive from her girlfriends if she appeared for a few hours while Edwin worked before disappearing again to spend another night in his bed.

Edwin listened to these explanations, aware that even though they had shared a bed and their most intimate secrets he still knew very little about her. For some reason the thought made him feel guilty – as though he was abusing her. He stopped on the drive down to the office to pick up a handful of magazines for Sally to read while he went through his Saturday morning chores in the office. For the majority of the morning Sally sat in the corner of his office, listening to music through the headphones attached to her MP3 player and rustling pages as she leafed through one magazine and then another. By noon she was pacing around the room, glancing at her wristwatch and asking if he was going to drag the torture out for much longer.

'Fantasy or reality?' he mused.

She glanced at him. Her impatience dissolved and the smile she graced him with was genuine and likeable. 'Are you still trying to answer that one?'

He nodded. He could see her gaze was drawn to the bright day outside the office and realised he couldn't keep her trapped in there much longer. He was no longer sure what he was doing there himself. Ordinarily he found his work was a distraction that stopped him from brooding about Desdemona. But since she had been away for so long he found the most demanding tasks weren't enough to prevent him from thinking about his wife. The single photograph she had sent him on Thursday evening had been her only contact.

He knew her itinerary took her on a circuitous tour of the British Isles. The first day had taken her to two points in Scotland. The second had travelled through three areas in the north of England and an office in the Midlands. Today she would be making a single stop in Wales and then visiting two locations down south. Because she hadn't contacted him through the Friday he didn't expect to hear from her until she arrived back home at Sunday lunchtime.

And he didn't think a single second had passed when he hadn't been wondering what she was doing. He shook his head, quietly revising that opinion. He knew she had been in his thoughts during every single second but he hadn't been wondering what she was doing: he felt certain he knew.

Desdemona was touching Jay's cock. Desdemona was licking Maisy's pussy. Desdemona was naked and being fucked by the pair of them. Desdemona's bare body was sandwiched between Jay and Maisy as the three of them fucked and sucked and licked their way to blistering climaxes. The images were strong enough for him to see every detail. He could smell the scent of his wife's wet pussy and hear the liquid sound it made as Jay plunged into her. Her orgasms came with a noisy fury that made him hard and painfully aware of his inadequacies as a lover. Her guttural roar of satisfaction – a sound he had never inspired – perpetually rang in his ears.

'Mr Miller?'

He glanced up on hearing Sally's concerned voice and realised he had been lost in his own thoughts. 'Sorry,' he mumbled. 'Miles away.'

'Had you decided on your answer?' she asked. 'Fantasy or reality?'

He nodded. 'I think so. But I don't understand why it should be.'

She laughed. 'What made up your mind?'

He considered his answer before replying.

The memory of first seeing Desdemona with Carl's erection in her mouth was a phenomenal aphrodisiac. His wife's ripe lips around another man's cock was an image that brought him to instant erection. The humiliating ordeal at Jake's apartment – an evening where he had seen another man's cock pushing into his wife's pussy – had proved more exciting. As had the few photographs she had sent him via his new mobile. But they were only small additions to the true pleasure. The arousal that came from wondering what she might be doing; who she would be doing it with; and how much she would share with him on her return: those were the elements that truly stirred his excitement. From that perspective he reasoned the fantasy would always be better than the reality.

'Come on,' she pressed. 'Tell me. What made up your mind?'

'The last few days,' he admitted. He turned off his computer and glanced outside the window. 'Let's get out of here.'

Sally needed no further prompting.

They picked up a KFC on the return journey, phoning home to ask Robin if he was also hungry. Sally insisted on stopping to rent a couple of movies claiming that, if she had to spend another night sitting in with two boring old men, she at least wanted a little entertainment. Edwin realised the insult was made in a good-natured fashion and happily covered the cost of the DVD rentals. Robin had cold beers waiting for them when they got back and, although his mood was almost as cold as the tins he handed out, he was amenable to spend the remainder of the day eating chicken, drinking lager and watching low-budget horror movies.

Sally showered and changed while Edwin kept the chicken warm in the oven. The mail had arrived while he and Sally were at work. He glanced through the confirmation details of the holiday he and Desdemona had booked, and then blushed as he opened a plain brown envelope that contained details about penis enhancement surgery.

The brochure reminded him of his shame when Sally had given him the message from Desdemona. A sweltering flush burnt his cheeks and he was struck with an instant and unrelenting erection. Fearful Robin might catch him with the humiliating paperwork, he put the brochure discreetly aside and tried to turn his thoughts away from embarrassment by glancing at the newspaper and puzzling over the half-completed crossword. Robin had taken a shot at it while he and Sally were at work. His handwriting, blue-ink block capitals that had been written neatly but firmly, was large enough to spread outside each small box he had completed. Edwin tried to remember where he had seen similar writing and why it seemed important. He had almost put that consideration from his thoughts when Robin burst into the room with a frown on his tired and unshaven face.

'The fuck's going on here, Ed?'

He glanced up at the sound of his brother's impatient whisper.

Robin pointed towards the stairs where they could both hear Sally singing in the shower. 'Something's way off kilter here,' Robin insisted. 'Tell me what's happening.'

'I already told you,' Edwin began. 'Nothing's happening.'

'You told me bollocks,' Robin snapped angrily. 'You're fucking her, aren't you? You're fucking Sally while Des is away.'

'No. I'm not.'

'You're sleeping in the same room.'

Edwin blushed. He had thought Robin might find out about that anomaly. The three of them were sharing a small house. The spare room was close to the bathroom and it had been inevitable that Robin would see him going into the room where Sally was supposedly sleeping alone. Both he and Sally had tried to be discreet but he had always known there was a chance that the fact they were sharing a room might be noticed. Defensively he said, 'I sleep in the same room as a bedside lamp. That doesn't mean I have sex with it each night before I flip its switch.'

'You and Sally sleep in the same bed together. But nothing sexual happens between you? That's what you're telling me?'

'I'm not telling you anything,' Edwin said stiffly. 'I'm trying my damnedest to keep my private life private. You're the one who keeps saying things.' He didn't know where the argument was headed. Or why his brother felt the need to intervene. But he was almost relieved to hear the bathroom door open.

'I'll be down in two minutes,' Sally called. 'I'm just getting changed.' She spoke with a light shiver in her voice, as though her body was still wet. Edwin guessed, if either he or Robin had glanced up the stairs, they would have seen she was half naked and only wrapped in a skimpy towel, or completely undressed with her bare body bejewelled by droplets of shower water. The thought made Edwin aware of his erection. It was fiercely hard and ready to erupt.

Edwin and Robin regarded each other in stiff silence.

Edwin tried to rationalise his brother's anger and upset but he couldn't see a reason for it. Robin was a serial philanderer. He was the vociferous defender of any man accused of straying. Whenever he picked up a tabloid and saw salacious reports of errant husbands and boyfriends, Robin usually denounced the stories as intrusive and unnecessary. 'Everyone's fucking someone they shouldn't,' was one of his favourite sayings. He invariably followed the remark with, 'As long as no one finds out, everyone's happy.' But on this occasion he seemed to think Edwin had committed a mortal sin. His reaction was out of character. His anger was both surprising and disturbing. Edwin wondered if Robin's upset was caused through a selfish motive, in that he was worried about his brother and sister-in-law breaking up and leaving him without the convenience of temporary accommodation. Edwin had always assumed, if he ever did cheat on Desdemona, Robin would have applauded him for becoming a fellow adulterer. He had never thought his brother would adopt the pious attitude he currently espoused.

There was a possibility that Robin was transferring his own relationship problems onto Edwin's situation. Alice was reluctant to discuss their future until she knew what had happened in the past. At least, Edwin supposed this was what his brother meant when he said, 'She still wants to know who gave me the blowjob.' Their discussions had reached a frustrating impasse and Edwin figured there was a chance Robin could believe he was in a position to prevent the same mistake from happening to someone else.

Edwin even supposed Robin could be concerned for the potential upset facing Desdemona. His wife and brother shared a good friendship and Edwin wondered if that might be part of the reason why Robin was angered by the idea he was cheating with Sally behind Desdemona's back. But, whatever the reason, Edwin wished Robin would forget his concern because the arguments and explanations were now growing tiresome.

'Chicken. Beer. Movie,' Sally said as she entered the room. Her hair was still damp from the shower. She looked comfortably refreshed rather than being made-up and ready to spend the day impressing them with her delicate prettiness. She wore a plain skirt and zip-fronted jumper. There were no shoes on her feet and Edwin got the idea she had not bothered with bra or panties either. Ordinarily he assumed that thought would have inspired his arousal but this time he realised it was just another aspect of accepting Sally around the house. He had spent the previous night sleeping naked next to her and it had only been when she masturbated and repeatedly mentioned his wife's name that he had climaxed. He quickly shut that memory from his mind before it presented him with the discomfort of another erection.

'What movies d'you pick, Doll?'

'A couple of slasher flicks that I never got round to watching when they were first released.' She popped the tab on her beer and picked up the hot carton of chicken with a tea towel. 'You don't mind slashers do you, Rob?'

'Long as the special effects don't make me hurl my chicken.'

She laughed, a pleasant and almost musical sound. Edwin and Robin exchanged a glance as she led them from the kitchen and into the lounge. It was apparent Robin still believed they were sexually involved. And, while Edwin privately conceded that was partly true, the phrase 'sexually involved' didn't properly describe his relationship with Sally.

The men placed themselves in armchairs, facing the TV set while Sally was left with the expanse of the three-seater settee between them. She placed her chicken and beer on the floor before kneeling in front of the DVD player and loading the first disc.

Edwin saw that her short skirt was not long enough to cover her while she knelt and bent over. Her bare buttocks were shown to the room along with the smooth and hairless split of her sex. The lips looked incredibly soft and kissable. The full force of his arousal struck him hard. He placed the box of chicken over his lap to disguise the erection that pushed at the front of his pants. He glanced at his brother, hoping Robin hadn't noticed Sally's accidental exhibitionism and knowing it would provide ammunition for another confrontation.

Robin gaped.

Edwin turned away before he could meet his brother's gaze.

Sally took charge of the remote and, with the DVD loaded, she settled herself back on the settee. Her legs were crossed and the hem of her skirt fell mercifully over her thighs, concealing her shaved pussy.

Edwin silently prayed that Robin might forget what he had seen. Busying himself with the chore of negotiating beer, chicken and following the violent plot of the film, he hoped his brother would become engrossed in the movie and stop suggesting there was a relationship between himself and Sally. He supposed it was hoping too much and, when Sally later paused the movie (announcing that she needed to piss), he was not surprised that Robin leant forward in his chair.

'She's not wearing knickers,' he hissed.

'She's just been in the shower,' Edwin said. It had sounded like a reasonable explanation in his mind. Spoken aloud the sentence came out pathetic and defensive.

'She flashed her fucking pussy at you and that's all you can say?'

'She didn't flash her fucking pussy!' Edwin couldn't contain his exasperation. 'She's a guest, Robin. She's just had a shower. She didn't put knickers on. Then she forgot when she was bending over. I don't go checking whether or not you're wearing underwear.'

'You don't have to,' Robin snarled. 'There's no danger of me flashing my pussy at you.'

Edwin knew that if he laughed it would go a long way to dispersing the antagonism that had grown between Robin and himself. A moment of shared amusement would dispel the seriousness of their argument. They could possibly heal the rift that had developed over the past couple of days. Instead of being able to laugh, he could only stare at his brother with a glower of frustration. Robin's sanctimonious attitude was annoying. He was concealing the true cause of his upset – whatever that might be. And Edwin was tired of defending himself against imagined crimes. He called up the stairs, 'Can you fetch two more beers on your way back, Sally?'

'Sure.'

In the stillness of the house they could hear the sound of water trickling into the lavatory. The clarity of her voice, and the immediacy of her response all suggested she was peeing with the bathroom door open again. Edwin saw his brother work this out and realised it was more evidence for his case. Not wanting to suffer another row Edwin stood up, walked out of the room and called to Sally, 'Don't worry about the beers, I'm fetching them.'

'Grab one for me, Mr Miller.'

He only returned to the lounge when he had heard Sally descend the stairs. The afternoon stretched into the evening. Under other circumstances Edwin would have described it as a wasted day. Instead, because he was enjoying the mild buzz from the lager, and occasionally exciting himself with thoughts about what Desdemona might be doing, the time passed quickly and pleasantly. He watched Sally's gory choice in movies without any real interest, and tried not to notice his brother was repeatedly casting glances in Sally's direction. When it came time to change the DVD and watch the second film, Edwin tactfully volunteered to deal with the discs while Sally found fresh tins for them.

Robin remained ominously silent.

Throughout the second movie Edwin began to understand why Robin was constantly glancing in Sally's direction. During the more exciting parts of the film she nervously clutched at the hem of her skirt. Edwin didn't think Sally was aware she was doing it – the girl had so many nervous habits his own paranoia seemed like an occasional nervous tic in comparison – but each time another brutal murder was acted out on screen, Sally lifted her skirt in apprehension. Although Edwin wasn't in a position to see what she was showing, he suspected Robin had a very good view.

And he couldn't blame his brother for looking.

The first time he had seen the shaved split of Sally's sex, Edwin had been aroused and enchanted. When he had been forced to lie beneath her while Jake pushed his cock in and out of her pussy, Edwin had been pushed to the brink of ejaculation. The easy flow of her musk, and the way it had moistened his face like an autumn mist, were sufficiently poignant memories to make him squirm in his seat.

Robin's features were a caricature of disgust and excitement. His raised eyebrows and gaping mouth remained fixed until the end of the film. Edwin could see his brother held a tin of lager over his groin and instantly understood that the sight of Sally's sex had also excited him.

'Cheers for that, guys,' Sally said. 'They were fun.'

Edwin said, 'They were disturbing. Since when did evisceration become entertainment?'

'It's surprising what you can see when you're watching one of these horror movies,' Robin said calmly. He glared at Edwin when he spoke so that they both understood what he meant.

Edwin kept his features stoic and said nothing.

'I know this may sound rude,' Robin continued. 'But I'm pretty tired and ready to crash out for the night. Are you two OK to leave me alone in here while I sleep?'

'Sure thing,' Sally said quickly. She flexed a quick grin for him, said goodnight, and waited until he had said, 'G'night, Doll,' before disappearing from the room.

'There's something going on between you and her,' Robin mumbled.

'There's nothing between Sally and me.'

'Why won't you tell me?' Robin's voice was lowered to an urgent hiss. 'Why are you trying to keep this such a big secret?'

'Do I keep asking who left lipstick marks around your cock?'

Robin had the good grace to blush. 'That's nothing to do with you.'

Edwin believed he could have argued that point but he ignored it. 'This is just the same. Except the lipstick marks on your cock got there because you were straying outside your marriage. That's not something I'm doing.'

'I'm only being a pest about this cos I'm concerned for you, bruv,' Robin pleaded. 'I'm in the middle of a relationship breaking up right now and I've been through enough before to know it's not fun. Whatever Sally is giving you . . .'

'She's not giving me a damned thing.'

' . . . you've got to ask yourself if it's worth the cost of your marriage.'

They studied each other in a long silence.

'Des is back tomorrow,' Edwin said eventually. 'You'll be having Sunday dinner with us, won't you?'

Robin nodded.

'You can hear it from her then. You can tell Des that Sally stayed over each night. You can tell her about all of your suspicions. Des knows what's going on here and she knows it's not something that threatens our marriage.'

Robin considered him in silence for a moment. 'I'm glad Des knows what's going on,' he admitted. 'Because

I'm damned if I do.' He raised an eyebrow and asked, 'You'd really have no problems with me telling her everything I've seen?'

'As long as it doesn't bore her,' Edwin replied confidently. 'You can tell her what the hell you want.' He said no more and went upstairs to join a naked Sally in bed. As he undressed he discovered that the front of his underwear was sticky from his prolonged arousal during the evening.

Nineteen

Desdemona returned home shortly after noon. Jake remained outside in the TVR, leaving the engine running as he waited for Sally. Edwin hurried to retrieve his wife's suitcase from the car, explaining that Robin was staying until he had sorted things out with Alice and anxiously telling her how much he had missed her and how pleased he was that she was back. His delight at seeing her again was made embarrassing by the frantic way he rushed around like a zealous lapdog trying to impress her with new tricks.

'Did you get my picture?'

'You looked beautiful in it.'

She flicked the praise away with one hand. Glancing at Sally, standing in the doorway, Desdemona raised a questioning eyebrow. In an instant his wife was transformed into the domineering goddess who was now the master of their bedroom and sex life. She tilted her head and silently beckoned the younger woman to approach. Edwin marvelled at the way she was able to wield such effortless authority.

'Thank you for letting me stay with Mr Miller,' Sally said meekly. She paused for a moment and then said, 'I'm sorry for what I did on Wednesday morning at the office. I won't do it again. I promise.'

'Did you learn your lesson?'

'I think so. It was very boring here.' Sally glanced apologetically at Edwin and added, 'No offence, Mr Miller.'

Edwin shrugged. He supposed it must have been boring for her. She had been forced to endure early nights and little in the way of recreation. It had only been relentless torture for him as he was forced to lie celibate in the same bed next to her nubile frame while she fingered herself to climax after climax. In the grand scheme of things, he thought her punishment had been crueller and more severe.

'We found some beautifully remote scenery in the Highlands of Scotland,' Desdemona told Sally. She placed an arm around Sally's shoulder and lowered her voice to a confidential whisper. The pair looked like conspirators. 'Do you know what the three of us did while we were up there?'

Eyes wide with anticipation, Sally shook her head.

'Water sports,' Desdemona confided.

Sally's face crumpled with disappointment.

Desdemona acted as though she hadn't noticed. 'I'd thought you were a dirty little bitch for even suggesting such a thing,' she admitted nonchalantly. 'I'd thought you were a sick and twisted little slut with the most depraved appetites. But you were right about water sports.'

Edwin wasn't sure he was following the conversation but it was apparent Sally understood every word. It was also clear she felt cheated of a missed opportunity.

'Jay had been screwing me in the open air,' Desdemona continued. 'I'd been licking Maisy's pussy, and then she just pissed all over my face.'

Edwin immediately understood Sally's expression and sympathised with her plight. It was the same look he had found on his own face when he thought about his wife indulging in a pleasure he would never be able to enjoy. Sally looked torn between resentment, disbelief, envy and euphoria. He empathised with every one of those reactions.

'I'll have to tell you all about it the next time the three of us are together at Jay's,' Desdemona promised. In a

215

pious voice she added, 'You could have discovered the pleasures for yourself if you hadn't flashed your pussy at Mr Miller. I'm sure Jay would have brought you with us.'

Sally glared at Edwin with open hostility. As though he was responsible for her missing the opportunity to experience the pleasure of water sports. Edwin flexed an apologetic shrug but he could see that the gesture, like most of the things in his life, was hopelessly inadequate.

Desdemona and Sally kissed before she joined Maisy and Jay in the TVR, and then the three of them sped off with a noisy blast of the engine. Edwin dutifully carried his wife's bags into the house and led her through to the kitchen where Robin sat at the dining table.

'Enjoy your trip, Des?'

'It would have been better if you'd been there,' she replied. 'I could have shown you so many new sights.' She sat at the table and Edwin fumbled with the kitchen implements in his haste to present the meal he had painstakingly prepared. Desdemona explained to Robin that she had been appraising locations for landscape paintings. Robin gave her an update on what had happened to make him leave Alice and take up temporary residence at the Miller household. There had been no progress towards reconciliation. If anything, the couple looked as though they were going to separate.

'Stupid bitch told me to pack my bags and fuck off,' he grunted. 'Can't believe she's thrown me out like this, Des. It's fucking humiliating.'

'You know you can stay here as long as you need,' Desdemona told him. 'I trust Eddie's been making you comfortable?'

Robin hesitated before replying. He cast an accusing glance in Edwin's direction and then offered a grudging nod. 'Sure. Ed's been good enough to let me stay.'

'That's not exactly what I asked,' Desdemona told him. She glanced at Edwin and sighed. 'Why am I sensing discord between you two boys? What's been happening while I've been away? You haven't been arguing, have you?'

'Nothing,' Robin said quietly.

Edwin drew a deep breath and decided it would be easier to state the facts so that Desdemona had a better understanding of the situation. 'Robin was concerned I might be having an affair with Sally,' he said quickly. 'I tried telling him there was nothing between us. But he wouldn't believe me. I still don't think he believes me now.'

Robin glared at him.

Desdemona considered Edwin in silence for a moment. 'Did you tell Robin what was really going on?'

He considered the suggestion and then recoiled in horror at the implications. Blushing madly, despising his cheeks for burning such a bright and painful red, he shook his head. 'I was being discreet.' It sounded like a lie. It sounded as though he had said nothing because he was trying to avoid suffering further embarrassment. In truth his motive for not saying anything had been to avoid the humiliation: but wasn't that a good description of being discreet?

Desdemona shook her head and regarded him with a look of weary disappointment. 'Do you want me to tell Robbie what's really happening?' She turned to Robin and added, 'Just like with the way Eddie makes love, it won't take more than a minute.'

Edwin cringed.

Robin chuckled.

Edwin saw the tension that had held his brother loosen its grip on his shoulders.

'Edwin doesn't satisfy me in bed,' Desdemona told Robin. 'I might have mentioned that to you before?'

Edwin squirmed in his seat. The weight of a shame-induced erection sprouted from his loins. He went to the oven and tried fervently to find some food that either needed checking, stirring or serving.

'His cock is too small and he's never been able to keep it up for longer than a minute. Usually, the moment it pushes inside me, Edwin spurts and leaves me soiled and frustrated.'

Edwin said nothing. The searing weight of his brother's gaze pushed into his shoulder blades. But he wouldn't bring himself to turn around and meet the man's eyes. It was easier to pretend they were discussing someone else. And he wasn't involved in the conversation.

'I put up with this for two years of our marriage,' Desdemona went on. 'But, eventually, I thought enough was enough. I decided it was time I should get myself properly laid so I've been going through a succession of lovers since then.' She smiled, raised her glass and added, 'But you know most of this already, Robin. You've known it since the night you first fucked me.'

Edwin glared at his wife and then his brother. Jealousy, shame, anger and outrage all vied for his emotions. Arousal was the strongest one and it left him winded. He stood in silence for a moment, glaring at Robin and remembering his brother had written in exactly the same handwriting that had been used to put the word SUCKMEBITCH across the centre of that long ago crossword. Robin had been with Desdemona when she bought the mobile phones. Desdemona had been talking to him from The Horn when Edwin heard the sounds of the mechanical pot-washer in the background. Wearily, he joined the pair at the table.

Desdemona continued blithely. She seemed unaware of Robin's incredulity. Indifferent to her husband's reaction. 'I decided I didn't like the dishonesty of being unfaithful. And because Edwin has always been telling me I should take a lover, I thought he would enjoy being a cuckold.' Her sly smile was the most loathsome thing Edwin had ever seen. And the most beautiful.

'All of which led me into bed with Eddie's new boss, Jay. And his two girlfriends, Maisy and Sally.' Desdemona described the scene with an offhand elegance that was breathtaking. She could have been discussing something as commonplace as supermarkets, shoe styles, or her preferred hair salons. 'It was very exciting and exotic to be involved with three other people at the same time. And I can't tell you how exciting it was when I got my first taste of pussy.' She fixed Robin with a punitive expression and said, 'Women lick cunts far better than any man could ever manage. Even you've never managed to go down on me that well.'

Edwin trembled.

Robin blushed.

Edwin noticed that his brother was now avoiding his gaze.

'The four of us tried quite a few variations on a theme,' Desdemona continued. 'And while it was very exciting, it seemed Sally couldn't resist teasing poor Eddie here. As a consequence I punished Sally by making her spend the last three nights with Eddie. I also punished Eddie by making him spend the last three nights with Sally.' Her smile inched wider. 'They were instructed to sleep naked in the same bed but neither of them was allowed to touch the other. It was Maisy's idea and quite an inventive form of retribution.'

Robin finally glanced at Edwin. His upper lip was wrinkled into a sneer of contempt. 'You slept in the same bed as Sally and you didn't fuck her?'

'I've been telling you that since Thursday.'

Robin shook his head. He looked as though he was having difficulty accepting the concept. 'You were naked in bed with Sally, every night for three nights, and you didn't fuck her?'

'I'd been told not to.'

Robin shook his head. 'You fucking pussy.'

Desdemona chuckled.

Edwin squirmed on his chair. He crushed his thighs together as he tried to control his impending orgasm. Once again Desdemona had exacted a searing humiliation for him. He was now the object of his brother's scorn and the conversation about his inadequacies still

219

lingered in the kitchen like the aromas of the meal before them. He did not think it was possible for his shame to be more complete.

Reaching across the table to stroke Robin's cheek, Desdemona said, 'You wouldn't have shown any qualms about servicing her, would you?'

'Christ! No!'

'You never showed any qualms about servicing me, did you?'

He blushed again and glanced guiltily towards Edwin. Sneering with renewed contempt Robin tore his gaze away and stared fondly at Desdemona. 'You sound like you've been doing without for too long. Is there anything I can do to help you with that problem?'

She laughed and shook her head. 'This last week I've had too much cock,' she confessed. 'My pussy is sore from all the fucking.' She lowered her voice to a husky drawl and said, 'But you don't have to use my cunt, do you? You've never had any qualms about fucking my arsehole in the past, have you?'

Edwin bit his tongue to suppress a whimper.

Robin grinned. He reached for Desdemona's face and pulled her towards his mouth. They kissed as though Edwin wasn't there. Exploring each other in a gratuitous display.

The sight pushed Edwin close to orgasm. He watched Robin's hand fall to Desdemona's breast and squeeze her through the fabric of her blouse. His large fingers looked massive against the soft mounds of flesh. He squeezed until she gasped. Instead of sounding pained, Edwin realised Desdemona's cry was a murmur of pure pleasure.

Sally's question came back to him. *'Which turns you on more? Seeing someone fuck your wife? Or imagining someone fuck your wife?'* He remembered his eventual answer but now he wondered if it was true. He had said the fantasy was better than the reality but was it possible that any fantasy could be better than watching this?

Desdemona dragged her chair closer to Robin. She placed a hand on his lap and this time it was Robin who moaned. Her fingers slipped to the zip of his jeans and her hand disappeared inside. Edwin was amazed to realise he was watching his wife casually stroking his brother's penis. The rush of excitement was so strong there was an agonising moment when he thought he would simply faint. He willed himself not to blackout, certain the pair would continue regardless of whether he was conscious or not.

'I've missed this cock of yours, Robbie,' Desdemona mumbled. 'Should I put another lipstick line round the base: *just to prove it's mine?*'

Edwin shivered and understood that Desdemona was the mystery woman causing the break-up between Robin and Alice. He couldn't decide if it was right or wrong: immoral or immaterial. He supposed Robin would have put his cock somewhere else if Desdemona hadn't been there. But he wasn't sure that lessened her involvement in the relationship's break-up.

He quietly reflected that Robin supported some impressive double standards. His outrage at the thought of Edwin cheating on Desdemona seemed inappropriate for a man who had been screwing his brother's wife. But Edwin could see that Robin wasn't viewing the situation in such black and white terms. More likely he was concerned that Edwin's relationship with Sally was going to cause upset to Desdemona. His anger at the idea of Edwin's affair was probably fuelled by concern for the woman he was illicitly fucking. Edwin considered this in wonder, and then a misty haze of excitement shrouded his thoughts as he watched his wife expose his brother's length.

The cock was much larger than his own meagre erection and impressively thick. Robin wasn't as well endowed as Jake, but he was big enough to make Edwin feel small and impotent. The foreskin had peeled back from a bulbous purple glans. The swollen dome was slick with a veneer of pre-come. Staring at his brother's cock, Edwin watched in wonder as his wife moved her lips to the end and daintily kissed the glossy eye.

'You're ready to come, sweetheart, aren't you?' she whispered.

The softness of her tone and the intimacy of her actions made Edwin feel as though he had been shunned. He stared at his wife's mouth over Robin's erection and trembled on the verge of climax.

'Of course I'm ready to come,' Robin sighed. 'That little tart you had tormenting Ed has been flashing her shaved snatch all over the house. My balls have been bursting for the past three days.'

'These balls?' she enquired.

Her hand moved inside the zip again. From the way she moved her wrist Edwin guessed Desdemona was massaging Robin's scrotum. She kept one hand around his shaft and her lips remained close to the end of his cock.

'They feel ever so swollen and full. I'll bet you're going to come a bucketful when you finally let go.'

'You're teasing me, Des.'

'I am, aren't I?' she agreed.

But she made no hurry to stop what she was doing. Taking her time, continuing to massage him for a moment and extracting her own obvious glee from holding his impressive hardness, she slowly moved her mouth back to his cock. 'Let's see if I can leave the lipstick mark lower this time. Let's see if I can beat my personal best.'

Edwin could see her words were spoken directly to the end of Robin's shaft. He could imagine the weight of each syllable lightly caressing his brother's glans. He had never before envied Robin. But, in that moment, he truly wished he were in his brother's position and revelling in the sensation of Desdemona's lips whispering to his cock.

And then she placed her mouth over it.

He didn't know how her face was able to go so far down the length of Robin's erection. Later, when he had time to think about it, Edwin assumed his wife had opened the back of her throat and swallowed his glans and the first few inches of his shaft. At the time it simply looked as though she had devoured him. It was incredible to conceive that she had opened her mouth so wide for him and managed to accept so much of his erection between her lips.

Slowly, Desdemona pressed her mouth around the base of Robin's shaft. She pressed her lips tight, her eyes straining to look upward and meet the approval of Robin's gaze. Her cheeks dimpled as she sucked on him and Edwin watched his brother grimace with a mixture of pleasure and satisfaction. When he glanced back at Desdemona's face she was staring at him while her mouth was filled with his brother's shaft.

Edwin trembled.

Robin groaned.

Desdemona gasped.

The sound coming from her mouth was muffled and wet. But she didn't draw her face away. Her throat moved convulsively and Robin shivered in his chair. He slapped one hand against the table, rattling a plate and a spoon and causing a noisy clatter to emphasise the silence that had held the kitchen. And then Desdemona was slowly drawing her face away. A sliver of white cream dripped over her lower lip as she smiled at him.

'You really were desperate to come, weren't you?' she murmured.

He released a soft and breathless sigh. His head nodded up and down and a foolish grin broke across his features.

Desdemona finally turned to face Edwin. Her eyes shone with a devilish glint of excitement. 'I haven't given you a proper welcome since I got back,' she said with theatrical surprise. 'Isn't that remiss of me?'

He blinked, still trying to come to terms with the fact that he had watched his wife suck his brother's cock to climax. Desdemona's face was immediately in front of his before Eddie realised she had moved. Her breath stank of semen. Her lips dripped with remnants of unswallowed spunk. She tilted her head slightly as she moved to meet him, extending a tongue that was coated with a milky white veneer. 'Do you want to kiss me, Eddie?' she asked. 'Do you want to give me a kiss and welcome me back home?'

As soon as their lips met he climaxed.

Twenty

Edwin spent a lonely and restless night in the spare room. Without Sally there he was able to stretch out but that extra space brought little comfort. Desdemona had told him he was not allowed to ejaculate unless she gave him permission. He was determined to abide by that condition in his attempts to prove his love for her. But he felt certain it would not be easy. In truth, he thought it would be more difficult this evening than it had when a naked young woman slept by his side, masturbating and pressing her body against his.

The spare room was next to Desdemona's bedroom – the room that had formerly been their shared bedroom. The heads of both beds would have touched if not for the partition of a stud wall. For the first time he realised the barrier was a lot thinner than he had ever imagined.

He could hear the sound of the bedsprings creaking when Desdemona climbed onto the mattress. He could also hear her giving Robin instructions as she told him how to lick her and where to put his tongue. The words evoked perfect mental pictures that were luminescent in the darkness of the spare bedroom. The images were so bright and vivid he could even see them when his eyes were closed.

'Lift your head a little, Robbie. Rub your tongue over my clit. Now push it inside. Christ! Yes! That's just right. Only Maisy and Sally have ever done it better.'

Edwin shifted from side to side. It was impossible to get comfortable and he eventually became still, fearing any movement would eventually have an adverse effect. Desdemona had told him not to ejaculate until he received her permission. The pressure of the thin sheet against his erection was tantalising. He worried that it might prove more than he could battle against. Holding himself still, he listened as his wife urged Robin with further explicit instructions.

'Go on, sweetheart,' she coaxed. 'Make me wet. Get me ready for you.'

It was easy to picture her sex gaping open and ready for Robin. He could imagine the lips parted and the downy hairs darkened by moisture. The image was a sea of liquid pink flesh and glossy arousal. If he had been close to her, Edwin knew he would have caught that intoxicating taste of her excitement. A solitary tear fell from the corner of his eye as he quietly wished she would let him breathe that sweetest of sweet scents.

'Go on, Robbie,' Desdemona whispered. 'I'm wet enough. You can push it now. But push it hard. Yes! Force it up there.'

Edwin held his breath. He tried to imagine what was happening but something didn't quite work in his mind. Desdemona had painted a word picture of her labia sopping wet and gaping in readiness for Robin's erection. But the resistance and effort he could hear suggested she was either not ready for the penetration or not as aroused as she had expected. He vacillated for a moment, wondering if he should knock on the wall or rush into the bedroom and assure himself Desdemona was comfortable with what was happening. The thought of bursting in on her and Robin was enough to make his arousal evaporate, but his wife's enjoyment was more important than his own shame or discomfort.

'That's it,' Desdemona grunted.

Her voice was guttural and almost animal in its intensity. She was close to shrieking and he knew she was in the throes of a massive pleasure. But he still couldn't equate her satisfaction with the struggle she had endured to get Robin inside.

'Now finger my pussy while your cock's up my arse.'

Edwin bit his knuckles.

Her words explained his misunderstanding. They took him so close to the brink of orgasm he feared he had felt his erection pulse against the dry sheets.

Desdemona roared.

Her voice carried easily through the walls and he couldn't rid his mind of the image of Robin's thick length ploughing into her anus while his fingers fumbled at the wet split of her sex. The bedsprings creaked and groaned. The sounds illustrated every thrust. But those noises were almost lost beneath Desdemona's cries of passionate satisfaction.

'Christ! Yes!' she bellowed. Her voice was breathless and raw. 'Fuck my arse, Robbie. Fuck it hard. You know I need it that way. You know I have to feel you up there.'

Edwin squeezed his eyes closed and tried not to listen. He didn't know how he was resisting the urge to climax but he knew he had to maintain the effort. He was listening to his wife and brother fucking. That thought alone would have been enough to drive him into ecstasy. But knowing they were involved in such a forbidden act – an act he had never dared ask Desdemona to perform with him – Edwin struggled not to let the climax spill from his tiny shaft. He twisted his hands into fists and punched them impotently into the mattress beneath him. His entire body shivered with the effort of restraint. He held every muscle tense and rigid.

The tempo of the squeaking bedsprings grew urgent.

Desdemona's screams became louder. Her exclamations were forced with each vigorous thrust. Edwin imagined her lying on her back, raising her pelvis so Robin had access to her anus. He expected she had wrapped her heels around Robin's back. The mental image was so clear he could picture his brother's thick shaft plunging in and out of the tight ring of muscle. He could see it all in such vivid detail – including the way her rectum distended slightly each time Robin pulled his thrust back – that he believed he could also smell the stench of sex the two radiated.

He didn't know whether that last part was a figment of his imagination, the smell of his own excited perspiration, or a fault in the flimsy stud wall that separated them. He only knew the fragrance of sexual musk was almost enough to force his climax.

'Don't you dare come inside my arse,' Desdemona snapped.

The bedsprings fell momentarily silent.

'Not in your arse? Where the fuck am I meant to come?'

They both sounded breathless. They were involved with their own passions and as close to the point of orgasm as Edwin had been since they exiled him to the spare room. He strained his ears to hear what was happening, unwilling to miss a moment of their grunted conversations.

'I want you in my cunt. That's where I want you to come.'

'This is my last johnny,' Robin explained. An inflection of nuisance hardened the patience in his words. 'If you want my cock anywhere else tonight it's going there bareback.'

Edwin's hands were balled into fists. They could have crushed diamonds. His eyes were squeezed so tightly closed he saw explosions of white light erupting on his retina. He had never resisted the urge to ejaculate for so long. The effort made him vertiginous. His breath came in rapid snatches. Too fast to be of use to his lungs. Dizziness threatened to engulf him and he knew, if that came, his ejaculation would quickly follow.

'Bareback suits me fine,' Desdemona announced.

Her words were followed by a moan and Robin's grunt.

Edwin didn't know how he knew but he felt certain they were both exclaiming as Robin's cock was torn from Desdemona's anus. The hole would be left momentarily open, leaving her gaping and wide before the rosebud of her rectum closed itself again. The tiny muscle would look sore and wet. And, he imagined, tremors of sensation continued to tingle through her bowel.

The perspiration that now soaked him was sufficient to make the sheets stick to his skin. He hadn't breathed in an age, certain that so much movement would force his climax.

The bed began to creak again.

Desdemona's cries were louder this time and far more impassioned.

Robin had thrust easily inside her and Edwin wondered how wet his wife's pussy had been to allow such an easy entrance. Robin's cock was thick and it was incredible to think she could be so aroused that the broad girth simply slid into her warm and welcoming confines. Edwin listened. His second-hand enjoyment of her pleasure had moved beyond intolerable and shifted towards being unbearable.

She gasped. Sighed. Groaned. Called Robin's name. Edwin knew he was not included in her arousal but that didn't stop his enjoyment. He could hear her delight in each breath she released. It was a torment not to be allowed his own climax and share her pleasure. But refusing that indulgence was the one thing Desdemona had insisted before taking Robin into her bedroom.

'Go on,' Desdemona urged. 'Make me come. Fill me.'

'You've come twice, you greedy bitch.'

'Then make it three times.' She sang the words as her voice raised an octave. Her excitement sounded so intense Edwin could imagine her nails scratching Robin's back as Desdemona's desperate need made her claw at him.

'Three times,' Robin consented.

'Push it deep,' she demanded. The pitch of her voice quavered on the point of being a screech. 'I want to feel it all now you're bareback. I want to feel every fucking inch.'

They screamed together.

She called Robin's name at the height of her climax. Robin cried out with a wordless growl of satisfaction. Edwin wasn't sure he heard either of the exclamations. His fists were pressed over his ears and he steeled every muscle in his body for fear the ejaculation would now pulse from him in sympathy with their shared orgasm. Breathless, more aroused than he had ever thought possible, he pressed himself into the comfort of the mattress and fervently forbade himself from the release he craved.

'Which turns you on more?' Sally had asked. *'Seeing someone fuck your wife? Or imagining someone fuck your wife?'*

Her question came back to him and he knew he had been undecided about his ultimate answer. He still wanted to believe that being a witness to the event was of paramount importance. It had excited him watching Jake slide his cock into Desdemona's pussy and it had been glorious watching his wife swallow Robin's explosive ejaculation. But he didn't think either of those experiences could compare to the thrill of hearing Desdemona's orgasm while his mind painted fantasy pictures of her satisfaction and bliss. If Sally had asked him after this experience there would have been no hesitation in his response. And he now knew it was neither the fantasy nor the reality that he favoured. Ultimate satisfaction came when the fantasy had become the reality. The ordeal of discovery left him wasted. He was exhausted and more thrilled than he could believe possible. Every nerve ending in his body throbbed and hummed with a charge of excitement.

And he finally believed he had found contentment.

His erection remained hard. As proud as its meagre size would allow. But that was unimportant. He felt now he could close his eyes and sleep with a satisfaction that had eluded him for so many years of his marriage. Smiling happily, allowing himself to relax, Edwin almost choked with surprise when his bedroom door opened.

Desdemona stood there naked. She was illuminated by the hall light and looked like a vision from his most intense fantasies. Sweat plastered her hair to her scalp. Her chest rose and fell with the rapidity of a recently achieved orgasm. He could see a radiance emanating from her that he had never known in all the years of their lovemaking.

'Did you hear us?'

Her screams had been so loud he would have heard them if he had still been at the office. 'Yes. I heard you.'

'Did it excite you?'

'You know it did.'

'Did you come?'

He shook his head. It had taken every effort not to climax as he listened to his brother's carnal grunting and his wife's ecstatic responses. But Edwin had staved the orgasm exactly as she instructed. He felt absurdly proud of the achievement. His love for his wife heightened when he saw the glint of Desdemona's approving smile.

'I said I'd reward you if you didn't come.'

He nodded.

The power of speech was suddenly beyond him. His wife had looked beautiful on their wedding night. Every day since he had thought she was the most divine creature that ever walked the earth. But this evening she was transformed into a sultry and splendid goddess. Her beauty had been transcended by the strength of her orgasm. The disarray of her hair. The used and sweated state of her appearance. She was elevated to the woman of his wettest dreams. The heroine of his most fulfilling fantasies.

She stepped slowly into the room and climbed onto the bed.

He gazed up at her. Adoring her now she was drenched in shadows. Placing her feet by the sides of his face Desdemona lowered herself to her haunches. She pressed the wet and open split of her sex over his mouth. The rich scent of her musk struck him like a slap. Its flavour was made piquant by the strength of her arousal. But more than that, overpowering that beautiful and craved-for aroma, he inhaled the scent of the semen that dripped from her hole.

His heart stopped in his chest.

The sudden urge to ejaculate came on him so quickly it took every effort to staunch the flow before it could punch its way from him. A droplet of the white dew fell from her pussy and drizzled onto his chin.

'Lick me clean and I'll allow you to come,' Desdemona said quietly.

He didn't hesitate.

The knowledge he was tasting semen repulsed him.

But that didn't stop him from greedily lapping the white film from Desdemona's pussy lips and hungrily swallowing every drop. The slick feel of the spunk brought him close to gagging. But, beneath that repugnant flavour, he could taste the glorious musk of his wife's wetness.

'Lick me properly clean, Eddie,' she whispered. 'And then you're allowed to come.'

He didn't reply. His hands went to her buttocks, touching the slick warm flesh of the woman he loved as he buried his tongue into her hole. He didn't say another word. He only carried on licking and marvelled that so much happiness could be his.

Twenty-one

Ten o'clock was the latest Edwin had ever arrived in the office. He felt groggy after a night bereft of sleep but his mood was more ebullient than it had ever been. Nodding a cheerful greeting towards Sally. Breezing happily into his office. He removed the small gold plaque from his pocket and also produced a screwdriver, mini-drill and brass-headed screws. He placed them all on the neat surface of his desk before phoning Jake's telephone number.

'Is there any chance I could see you this morning, Mr Mathers?'

'Is it important?'

'It's important to me.'

'I'll be there shortly.'

Sally appeared as he ended the conversation, handing him a mug of coffee and explaining she had been concerned when he hadn't been there when she arrived. 'I thought you'd died in your sleep, Mr Miller,' she said.

Edwin could have told her that the previous night had been so blissful there were several times when he too had thought the same thing. He politely thanked her for her concern. Stopping her before she left, he asked, 'Do you still think the fantasy is better?'

'Have you decided you prefer the reality?'

He wondered if he should tell her that it was best when the fantasy became a reality. Then decided that

233

was a lesson Sally would probably learn for herself. 'I've found what I want,' he said eventually.

Her smile was broad. Suggestive. Knowing. She placed a hand over her mouth and rushed out of the office as he thanked her again for the coffee: and for so much more.

Alone he held the plaque briefly beneath the oil painting and then went back to his desk to find a tape measure and a spirit level. Removing his jacket, loosening his tie a little, he returned to the task of fixing it to the wall with the air of a professional workman determined to do the job properly. The mini-drill punctured the wall easily. As he was making the hole Edwin realised there were protocols he should have followed before doing something as bold as fixing the plaque. But he figured that with his exemplary work record he was overdue a little indulgence. Checking his measurements with the spirit level, closing one eye and squinting to make sure everything was as it was supposed to be, he began to screw the plaque into place.

Jake entered the office as Edwin tightened the final screw. He smiled approvingly when he read the black etching on the brass plate. *Cuckolds Lights by Desdemona Miller.*

'You've missed the apostrophe,' Jake noted critically.

'No,' Edwin corrected. 'Cuckolds Lights doesn't have an apostrophe.' He felt a burst of inner pride erupt as he realised he had said the name without blushing or embarrassment. He ushered Jake to take a seat and then resumed his usual position. The clutter of drill, screwdriver and spare screws on his desk made him feel as though he had changed at a fundamental level. He shook his head, not allowing himself to think about those small differences. Or how they might affect his future. Clearing his throat to show he was about to speak business, he contemplated Jake for a moment and then said, 'There's something I'd like you to do for me.'

Jake raised an eyebrow. 'Is this a professional favour or a personal one on account of the fact that I'm boinking your wife?'

Edwin digested the word 'boinking'. His disgust for the corporate nepotism programme returned. He reasoned that only a university graduate would ever come up with the term 'boinking' as a euphemism for sexual intercourse. Struggling to maintain a poker face, adamant he wouldn't allow his distaste for Jake to show through in this conversation, he said, 'I suppose it's a little of both.'

Jake silently encouraged him to continue.

'It's about the holiday you were forcing me to take,' Edwin began. Instead of sounding snippy his tone was professional and competent. 'I'd like you to reconsider your decision about my taking a mandatory fortnight's leave.' Not allowing Jake the opportunity to interrupt, he added coolly, 'And I'd like your assurance that my refusal to take mandatory leave won't adversely affect my forthcoming performance review.'

Jake laughed uncertainly. 'What the fuck is this about, Eddie? I thought you'd booked the holiday? Dezzie was telling me you're flying off to the States to enjoy the east coast. Maybe travel up to Maine and see Cuckolds Lights for yourself. I got the impression it's a done deal.'

'Everything's booked,' Edwin admitted. 'But there's still time for me to change the names. Send my brother in my place.'

Jake contemplated this for a moment, his grin slowly becoming more perplexed. 'Does Dezzie know you're planning to do this?'

Edwin shook his head. He could feel a blush colouring his cheeks but he didn't allow the reddening to alter his determination. 'No,' he said simply. 'Desdemona doesn't have any idea about this. It's going to be a surprise.'

This time Jake's laughter was laden with incredulity. 'I don't claim to know your wife better than you do,

235

Eddie. But I do know she doesn't like surprises. I can arrange the special dispensation if that's what you really want . . .'

'I really want that.'

' . . . and I can tell HR that the rules of mandatory leave don't apply to you,' he went on.

Edwin smiled. Satisfied.

'Shit!' Jake exclaimed. 'I can guarantee you the results of your performance review now, if you want me to.'

'No,' Edwin said simply. 'I'll do the performance review honestly, if that's all right by you.'

Jake shrugged the detail aside, as though it was unimportant. 'Those things can all be done,' he admitted. 'But Dezzie will be mightily pissed at you when she finds out what you've done.'

Edwin couldn't contain his smile. He had a brief mental image of a fortnight alone while his wife and his brother were intertwined on a variety of foreign hotel beds as they enjoyed their holiday together. The idea had warmed him as he drifted to sleep the previous night. It had continued to thrill him as he drove into town that morning and then waited for the brass plaque to be etched. But now he had the added bonus of Desdemona's anger to anticipate. If she was genuinely furious he thought the humiliation she would administer was likely to be fantastic. Edwin's grin grew broad as he realised he was beginning to like Jake Mathers.

nexus

The leading publisher of fetish and adult fiction

TELL US WHAT YOU THINK!

Readers' ideas and opinions matter to us so please take a few minutes to fill in the questionnaire below.

1. Sex: Are you male ☐　female ☐　a couple ☐?

2. Age: Under 21 ☐　21–30 ☐　31–40 ☐　41–50 ☐　51–60 ☐　over 60 ☐

3. Where do you buy your Nexus books from?

☐ A chain book shop. If so, which one(s)?

_____

☐ An independent book shop. If so, which one(s)?

_____

☐ A used book shop/charity shop
☐ Online book store. If so, which one(s)?

_____

4. How did you find out about Nexus books?

☐ Browsing in a book shop
☐ A review in a magazine
☐ Online
☐ Recommendation
☐ Other _____

5. In terms of settings, which do you prefer? (Tick as many as you like.)

☐ Down to earth and as realistic as possible
☐ Historical settings. If so, which period do you prefer?

_____

☐ Fantasy settings – barbarian worlds
☐ Completely escapist/surreal fantasy

☐ Institutional or secret academy
☐ Futuristic/sci fi
☐ Escapist but still believable
☐ Any settings you dislike?

_____

☐ Where would you like to see an adult novel set?

_____

6. In terms of storylines, would you prefer:

☐ Simple stories that concentrate on adult interests?
☐ More plot and character-driven stories with less explicit adult activity?
☐ We value your ideas, so give us your opinion of this book:

_____

_____

_____

7. In terms of your adult interests, what do you like to read about? (Tick as many as you like.)

☐ Traditional corporal punishment (CP)
☐ Modern corporal punishment
☐ Spanking
☐ Restraint/bondage
☐ Rope bondage
☐ Latex/rubber
☐ Leather
☐ Female domination and male submission
☐ Female domination and female submission
☐ Male domination and female submission
☐ Willing captivity
☐ Uniforms
☐ Lingerie/underwear/hosiery/footwear (boots and high heels)
☐ Sex rituals
☐ Vanilla sex
☐ Swinging
☐ Cross-dressing/TV

☐ Enforced feminisation
☐ Others – tell us what you don't see enough of in adult fiction:

_____

_____

_____

8. **Would you prefer books with a more specialised approach to your interests, i.e. a novel specifically about uniforms? If so, which subject(s) would you like to read a Nexus novel about?**

_____

_____

_____

9. **Would you like to read true stories in Nexus books? For instance, the true story of a submissive woman, or a male slave? Tell us which true revelations you would most like to read about:**

_____

_____

_____

10. **What do you like best about Nexus books?**

_____

_____

11. **What do you like least about Nexus books?**

_____

_____

12. **Which are your favourite titles?**

_____

_____

13. **Who are your favourite authors?**

_____

_____

14. **Which covers do you prefer? Those featuring:**
    (Tick as many as you like.)

☐ Fetish outfits
☐ More nudity
☐ Two models
☐ Unusual models or settings
☐ Classic erotic photography
☐ More contemporary images and poses
☐ A blank/non-erotic cover
☐ What would your ideal cover look like?

_____

15. **Describe your ideal Nexus novel in the space provided:**

_____
_____
_____
_____

16. **Which celebrity would feature in one of your Nexus-style fantasies?**
    We'll post the best suggestions on our website – anonymously!

_____

THANKS FOR YOUR TIME

Now simply write the title of this book in the space below and cut out the
questionnaire pages. Post to: Nexus, Marketing Dept., Thames Wharf Studios,
Rainville Rd, London W6 9HA

Book title: _____

NEXUS NEW BOOKS

To be published in November 2007

THE WICKED SEX
Lance Porter

Meet Bee, an athletic mail-order bride from the South Seas who soon has her middle-aged husband-to-be under more than just her thumb. Or Ms Valerie Sales, a sexually insatiable company executive who enjoys beating men at their own game, both in the boardroom and the bedroom. These are just two of the irresistible women who appear in this collection of erotic short stories about modern-day amazons, goddesses, giantesses, *femme fatales*, Salomes and matriarchs, women who use all their sexual allure and prowess to dominate the hapless males they encounter. If you think women are the weaker sex then get ready for a wicked awakening.

£6.99   ISBN 978 0 352

UNIFORM DOLLS
Aishling Morgan

This is a story straight from the heart of a lifelong uniform fetishist and conveys the sensual delight to be had from wearing uniforms and enjoying others in uniform. Whether it is the smartness and authority of military dress, the sassy temptation of a naughty schoolgirl, or the possibilities offered by an airhostess, policewoman or even a traffic warden, it is all described here in sumptuous and arousing detail, along with unabashed accounts of kinky sexual encounters.

£6.99   ISBN 978 0 352

If you would like more information about Nexus titles, please visit our website at www.nexus-books.com, or send a large stamped addressed envelope to:
  Nexus, Thames Wharf Studios,
  Rainville Road, London W6 9HA

NEXUS BOOKLIST

Information is correct at time of printing. To avoid disappointment, check availability before ordering. Go to www.nexus-books.com.

All books are priced at £6.99 unless another price is given.

NEXUS

☐ EMMA'S SECRET DOMINATION	Hilary James	ISBN 978 0 352 34000 9
☐ EMMA'S SUBMISSION	Hilary James	ISBN 978 0 352 33906 5
☐ FAIRGROUND ATTRACTION	Lisette Ashton	ISBN 978 0 352 33927 0
☐ IN FOR A PENNY	Penny Birch	ISBN 978 0 352 34083 2
☐ THE INSTITUTE	Maria Del Rey	ISBN 978 0 352 33352 0
☐ NEW EROTICA 5	Various	ISBN 978 0 352 33956 0
☐ THE NEXUS LETTERS	Various	ISBN 978 0 352 33955 3
☐ PLAYTHING	Penny Birch	ISBN 978 0 352 33967 6
☐ PLEASING THEM	William Doughty	ISBN 978 0 352 34015 3
☐ RITES OF OBEDIENCE	Lindsay Gordon	ISBN 978 0 352 34005 4
☐ SERVING TIME	Sarah Veitch	ISBN 978 0 352 33509 8
☐ THE SUBMISSION GALLERY	Lindsay Gordon	ISBN 978 0 352 34026 9
☐ TIE AND TEASE	Penny Birch	ISBN 978 0 352 33987 4

NEXUS CONFESSIONS

| ☐ NEXUS CONFESSIONS: VOLUME ONE | Ed. Lindsay Gordon | ISBN 978 0 352 34093 1 |

NEXUS ENTHUSIAST

☐ BUSTY	Tom King	ISBN 978 0 352 34032 0
☐ CUCKOLD	Amber Leigh	ISBN 978 0 352 34140 2
☐ DERRIÈRE	Julius Culdrose	ISBN 978 0 352 34024 5
☐ ENTHRALLED	Lance Porter	ISBN 978 0 352 34108 2
☐ LEG LOVER	L.G. Denier	ISBN 978 0 352 34016 0
☐ OVER THE KNEE	Fiona Locke	ISBN 978 0 352 34079 5
☐ RUBBER GIRL	William Doughty	ISBN 978 0 352 34087 0
☐ THE SECRET SELF	Christina Shelly	ISBN 978 0 352 34069 6
☐ UNDER MY MASTER'S WINGS	Lauren Wissot	ISBN 978 0 352 34042 9
☐ THE UPSKIRT EXHIBITIONIST	Ray Gordon	ISBN 978 0 352 34122 8
☐ WIFE SWAP	Amber Leigh	ISBN 978 0 352 34097 9

- - - - - - ✂ -

Please send me the books I have ticked above.

Name   ....

Address   ....

              ....

              ....

              .... Post code ....

Send to: **Virgin Books Cash Sales, Thames Wharf Studios, Rainville Road, London W6 9HA**

US customers: for prices and details of how to order books for delivery by mail, call 888-330-8477.

Please enclose a cheque or postal order, made payable to **Nexus Books Ltd**, to the value of the books you have ordered plus postage and packing costs as follows:

UK and BFPO – £1.00 for the first book, 50p for each subsequent book.

Overseas (including Republic of Ireland) – £2.00 for the first book, £1.00 for each subsequent book.

If you would prefer to pay by VISA, ACCESS/MASTERCARD, AMEX, DINERS CLUB or SWITCH, please write your card number and expiry date here:

....

Please allow up to 28 days for delivery.

Signature ....

Our privacy policy

We will not disclose information you supply us to any other parties. We will not disclose any information which identifies you personally to any person without your express consent.

From time to time we may send out information about Nexus books and special offers. Please tick here if you do *not* wish to receive Nexus information.   □

- - - - - - ✂ -